MOLLY BIT

a novel

DAN BEVACQUA

simon & schuster
new york london toronto sydney new delhi

Simon & Schuster
1230 Avenue of the Americas
New York, NY 10020

Copyright © 2020 by Daniel Bevacqua

First Simon & Schuster hardcover edition February 2020

SIMON & SCHUSTER and colophon are registered trademarks of Simon & Schuster, Inc.

For information about special discounts for bulk purchases, please contact Simon & Schuster Special Sales at 1-866-506-1949 or business@simonandschuster.com.

The Simon & Schuster Speakers Bureau can bring authors to your live event. For more information, or to book an event contact the Simon & Schuster Speakers Bureau at 1-866-248-3049 or visit our website at www.simonspeakers.com.

Interior design by Carly Loman

Manufactured in the United States of America

1   3   5   7   9   10   8   6   4   2

Library of Congress Cataloging-in-Publication Data

Names: Bevacqua, Dan, author.
Title: Molly Bit : a novel / Dan Bevacqua.
Description: First Simon & Schuster hardcover edition. |
New York : Simon & Schuster, 2020.
Identifiers: LCCN 2019002027 | ISBN 9781982104580 (hardcover) |
ISBN 9781982104566 (trade pbk.)
Classification: LCC PS3602.E833 M65 2020 | DDC 813/.6—dc23
LC record available at https://lccn.loc.gov/2019002027

ISBN 978-1-9821-0458-0
ISBN 978-1-9821-0457-3 (ebook)

For Hannah

You are in public because we are all here. It is solitude because you are divided from us by a small circle of attention.

—Konstantin Stanislavski, *An Actor Prepares*

LIFE

COLLEGE

1993

1

EVERYBODY WANTED TO BE FAMOUS. THE SCREENWRITERS, THE
directors, the musicians, the poets, the playwrights, the comedians:
they all wanted fame, but the actors wanted it most of all. They
wanted fame so bad it pained them in their hearts when they tried
to fall asleep at night. It was like the thought of not getting famous
killed them, or like the way they longed for it was a sort of murder,
but of themselves, and if they didn't get famous, they might die right
there in their beds.

It was that kind of school.

Molly took the elevator down to the dining hall. She'd only ten
minutes earlier broken up with her high school boyfriend, Luke,
over the phone. She felt bad about this, but not as bad as she had
been feeling. She'd slept with other people, but in no practical universe could you call this cheating. She was nineteen. It was a question of experience, of whether or not she would make good on a
promise to herself to chop off the old, dead parts and come out new,
to burn them off, if need be, like she was a house fire. Hers was a
deep sensation. Some afternoons, light would fall on her through a
window in the library, a single ray through a single pane that found
her as she lifted her head up from a book. The light was God or the
future. The same was true for certain odd or even numbers, or for
the experience of déjà vu: these were signs, messages designed to
inform her she was among the chosen. She could not help but feel
this way.

In the elevator, she glanced up at the numbers going 5, 4, 3, 2. Beside the read-out, up near the ceiling, someone had graffitied in black Magic Marker *Mmmmm . . . Molly Bit.*

"That's hot," Rosanna Archer said. "That's good advertising."

"Good advertising for what?" Molly asked.

"For you," Rosanna said. "For your sexy actress life."

They were seated across from each other at a booth in the dining hall. Rosanna was from LA. She was six feet tall with long, wavy hair the color of a crow. Out the window, snowy gusts of ice and fog screamed down Tremont Street. It hadn't snowed in four days. It was only the wind. It was psychotic in that part of the city. It plucked snow and trash and lost gloves and hats from off the tops of drifts and whipped the mess around. Molly watched a baby-less stroller cartwheel across the street and slam into the front door of O'Malley's.

"What the hell am I doing here?" Rosanna asked.

"Seriously," Molly said. "Why aren't we in California?"

"Everything is better in California," Rosanna said. "Waking up is better in California. Going to bed is better in California. The parties are better. The drugs. The weather. The people. It's all better. You have to come visit me over break. We'll get wasted on the beach. Do you realize how totally incredible that would be? How totally awesome?"

"I know," Molly said. But she didn't know. She'd never been to California. She'd been to two places: Vermont, where she was from, and now Boston. This was the sum total. There was no possible way she could afford a trip to California.

"It's gonna be the best," Rosanna said.

All of Molly's friends were rich. All of them. They were so rich they didn't even know. Rosanna's parents were in advertising, but not the marketing or the creative sides. They did something else. Something with the money. They lived in the Palisades, wherever that was, and kept another home in Malibu. Molly's father was a soil tester. He drove around Vermont and dug holes in the ground for a living. Her stepfather paid for her tuition. The rest, her living money, was student loans.

"Thanks for the swipe."

"No problem. I've got a ton of meals left on my card," Rosanna said. "We should give them out to the homeless later. I wanna feed that guy with the frog voice. '*Spare any change?*' Or that dude who rides his tricycle down Newbury Street. I think he's sort of cute. I like the way he rings his little bell."

Half the students had gone home for winter break already. The dining hall felt empty, but that was only in comparison to the usual mob scene. There were dorms on Arlington and Beacon, but everybody ate on Boylston, in Molly's building. She saw Greg Watson reading by himself at one of the long tables. She gave him a small wave, but he was the nervous type, and he pretended like he hadn't seen her.

"Why are you saying hi to that guy?" Rosanna asked. "He's bald."

"He's nice. He's my friend."

"Are you sleeping with him?"

"No. I'm not," Molly said. "We're in Short Story together. He's a writer. He's good."

Her own stories were terrible, Molly knew. All of her protagonists were small-town girls let loose in the big city. Nothing would happen to them for pages and pages, and then they'd cry. In workshop, Greg said her dialogue was good.

"Who would do that?" Rosanna asked. "Why would someone

write something they knew was never going to make any money? People are starving to death out there, and this guy's writing short stories. It makes me sick."

Rosanna wanted to be a producer. Or she was, Molly guessed. In Rosanna's life, and in the way she spoke of it, the present and the future had achieved a unified chronology. She was who she would be: powerful, demanding, impatient.

"Where is Eric?" Rosanna asked, forking a gelatinous wobble of scrambled egg into her mouth. "That's what I'd like to know."

"He called me at four in the morning," Molly said.

"How did he sound?"

"Stimulated," Molly said. "He kept referring to himself as a 'coke genius.' He said it like a hundred times."

Greg stood up from his table. Out of the corner of her eye, Molly saw him look in her direction. She didn't look back. A seriousness had overtaken her.

"He said he was close to being done with the edit."

"How close?"

"Close-close. Like done."

"I despise him," Rosanna said. "I'm finished with Eric. If it wasn't for the festival tonight I'd never talk to him again."

There were an endless number of short film festivals at the college. The New Voices, The Senior Showcase, The Gay and Lesbian, The Underground, The Experimental, The Comedy, The For Women Only, The African American, The East Asian, The Documentary, The Jewish Diaspora, The Left of Center. Eric and Rosanna's submission was for The New Horizons Short Film Festival. The NHSFF was considered to be the most prestigious film festival on campus by virtue of it having an actual "Best Of" category. Eric was the film's director, Rosanna its producer, and Molly its star.

"If he screws me on this, I'm gonna screw him back," Rosanna said. "And not the way you do."

This was a low blow. Molly and Eric had slept together numerous times, yes, but she felt gross about it, and because she felt gross about it, she didn't think Rosanna, or anyone, should mention it at all. Instead, her friends should pretend like it hadn't happened. That's what she did.

"I don't know what you're talking about."

"Yes, you do," Rosanna said. "He better get it down here by two, is all I'm saying. He thinks he's Soderbergh, but he's not Soderbergh. I know Soderbergh, and Eric Os isn't Soderbergh."

"We've got our Movement final in an hour," Molly said. "He'll be there."

"Why do you have a final in Movement?" Rosanna asked. "What could that final possibly be? What do you do? Have a seizure?"

We move, Molly wanted to explain. Her final was to perform the life cycle of a woman, from birth to death, in three minutes. She'd been rehearsing for weeks. The piece involved six other people and a rocking chair. It was complicated. Everyone at school liked to laugh at the way the actors prepared. They enjoyed the end results— the plays, the scenes, the movies—but all the work that went on be-forehand registered with them as silly. It wasn't hard to understand why. Most people were afraid of their bodies, Molly knew. They also weren't crazy about someone who openly spoke about feelings, es-pecially if those feelings belonged to other, imaginary people. Molly tried not to hold it against them, although she often failed.

"Don't be mad," Rosanna said.

"I'm not mad."

"Yes, you are. Your face is like a sign that says, 'I Am Going to Cut Your Head Off.' I'm sorry, okay?"

"Okay," Molly said. "What about you?"

"What about me?" Rosanna asked.

"What are you gonna do?"

"I'm gonna finish my eggs, smoke a cigarette with you, and then go get a massage," Rosanna said. "I need to be relaxed for this thing."

After the cigarette, Molly went to the bursar's office. There was something wrong with her account. She couldn't register for classes in the spring semester.

"You've got a hold," the clerk said. She tapped the keyboard and stared into the screen. "You've got a bunch of holds."

The clerk was Chinese, a junior. She was in one of the better comedy troupes, Apple Pie Town. Molly had seen her in a skit where she'd played the Bruce Willis character in a surreal episode of *Moonlighting*.

"For what?"

"Two obscure room fees that are blatantly cruel and unnecessary, an overdue library book about the Holocaust, and you never paid for your meningitis shot," the clerk said. "You owe five hundred and thirty-seven dollars and twelve cents. Or, you could bring the Hitler book back, and it'd be an even five-eighteen."

She had no idea where that book was.

"Bummer," the clerk said. "So the first number then. It would have to be the first."

Molly could sense the restless, impatient rage of those in line behind her.

"What does it all mean?" she asked.

"It means you can totally come back to school and everything next semester," the clerk said. "But you can't go to classes. And you can't eat or sleep. Not here. Not until the hold's gone."

Molly walked across the street to the bank. She asked the teller if she could see her checking account balance. The teller was youngish and cute, but then he eyed her in that too long way, and she felt creeped out. He wrote down her account balance on a white slip of paper and passed it to her. She flipped the paper over. It was the number 8.

Eric wasn't at the Movement final. She went into the bathroom and tried to clear her head, but it proved impossible. Desperation infected her. It was a feeling of bottoming out, a chalkiness to her face and hands. But wasn't that the whole thing? Wasn't it *onslaught, onslaught, onslaught, feeling, feeling, feeling*? Wasn't it either too much or not enough? Wasn't it a long, boring freak-out?

She passed through her mother onto the floor. A stranger wrapped her in a blanket. She slept and slept and cried for years. The world was out of reach. More than half of everything was dark. Her fingers grew, her arms, her legs. A man spoke at her, a woman. Gentleness turned away. There were too many people to account for and then a short spell of loneliness. She read a book. She walked into a room, sat, and stood up in another. She did this again, and again, and again. From out of nowhere, from off stage, a man ran into her. There was a certain amount of love. She screamed in pain and was confused by the child. The man disappeared. She pointed out an object, a person, a building. She saw these things as if for the first time. She kept on going down the line. A certain kind of loneliness no longer bothered her. Or it did, but she behaved as if it didn't. Work. Work. Work. She performed her suffering. The moon was the clock on the wall. She listened to the loud tick of it. The child returned. A swell of pure emotion overcame her, like a great and mysterious illness. More than half of everything was light. There was too much loneliness to account for, and then a short spell of people. The people made noises with their mouths. No one understood her, or one another, or anything. The world was out of reach. A chasm opened up above her head. She raised her arms up into it. She wanted to be gentle. The professor called time.

She sat in the back for the rest of class, feeling defeated. For no reason other than her own suspicion and tendency to think this way—because they had in fact clapped for her, and stared at her, and made room for her on the floor whispering "slide over"—Molly believed she had failed. The performance had not come off as she had wanted it to. There were several disastrous beats, a too-large motion here and there. She'd been too much in her head.

"What planet are you on?" her friend Denise asked her. "All you thin, beautiful girls . . ."

"I'm just saying—"

"A bunch of crap," Denise said. "If I'd done what you did, I'd be walking around like, 'Suck it!' That was amazing."

They were putting their jeans on over their tights in the now empty classroom. Denise crouched down slightly and shook her ass like a girl in a Dr. Dre video. Molly was jealous of that ass. It was round. It was an actual ass. Molly thought hers was only okay. She imagined herself doing squats.

"You're thin too," Molly said. "You're beautiful."

"I'm cute," Denise said. "I'm healthy."

"You're beautiful—so shut up."

"What I am," Denise said, as she continued to gyrate, "is sexy as shit. I've got confidence. It's gonna take me places."

She waited for Denise to finish changing, to put on her big, furry boots and hat. School frightened Molly sometimes, the other students, their overwhelming confidence. Hers came and went. Eric said she was a classic narcissist.

"I hate that guy," Denise said, as they went down the stairs. "He's the worst. You know what he did the last time I saw him? He walked up to me at O'Malley's, slapped me on the ass, and called me a cunt. Who does that? What kind of a person do you have to be?"

"He was probably drunk."

"That guy's always drunk," Denise said. "You've got a real Freudian thing going on with him. You're having sex with your father."

"Disgusting. I am not," Molly said, although the thought had occurred to her as well. Her father was seven years sober. "Don't ever say that again, please. I'm gonna throw up."

"Relax," Denise said. "Everyone's had an incest dream or two."

The downstairs bubbled with students. The mood was celebratory. Finals exhaustion had lifted like a face peel. Their skin was young and bright. Half the seniors would be moving to LA for the spring semester. The college did an internship program out there. They lived in an apartment complex or something. It was a big selling point. There was a pool. Did NYU have a pool? Could they see Warner Brothers from their mountaintop? Had the Fonz gone there?

Molly would have to wait for all that. Even as a freshman she'd already made the decision not to do stage work, even though she loved it. She loved the high, and the rehearsals, and the feel of the wood beneath her feet, but, at the end of the day, she felt estranged from that particular dream of life. She didn't get off on the idea of being art poor. Her future was lit differently. It wasn't quite as dark or as neon. She didn't want to smoke forever. When Molly saw the seniors, she was reminded of the years that remained, of the never-ending credits, of the basic math course she would have to take, of the job she would need on top of school next semester, and all the semesters post that, and for how long afterward, and for what, and why? How would she even get to that future? What sort of loan would it take?

Alone, she crossed over Beacon Street at Charles and walked into the Common. It was noon, but the holiday lights were on in the trees. A golden retriever bounded through the snow as if auditioning for a catalogue. Over the hill, behind the monument, she heard the warbled speaker effect of the ice skating rink. Where the four paths met at the oak tree, she saw Greg Watson.

"Hey, jerk," Molly said.

"What? Why?"

He was coming from their building. They lived on the same floor.

"I waved at you earlier. I was saying hi. You were too cool."

"I didn't see you."

"Yes, you did."

They left it at that. Greg never wore a hat. His shaved bald head suited him. He wore a beat-up old leather jacket. She asked him where he was going.

"Speech final."

"Speech on what?"

"Raymond Carver."

"Jesus Christ," she said. "You guys and that guy. It's a lifestyle."

"He's great," Greg said.

"Yeah, yeah, yeah," Molly said. "Read a woman. Read a black person."

"I do."

"Sure," she said.

Greg never seemed to be in a rush. He kept a small notebook in his back jean pocket. He smoked a lot of pot. He hung out with another writer dude in his class who worked at a liquor store in Jamaica Plain. After workshop, they always sat on the low brick wall at the edge of the Common. They would smoke cigarettes, and tell each other to fuck off, like it was the funniest thing in the world.

Molly explained her entire life to him.

"Sucks about the holds," Greg said. "What time is he supposed to bring the movie?"

"Pretty soon."

"He's an awful person," Greg said.

"I know."

"I mean like really."

The wind picked up and blew into them as if from out of every direction possible. Both Molly and Greg staggered in it, a little two-step, and peeked at the other through lashes. Once upon a time, two weeks before, they'd been drunk at three in the morning, side by side on a stranger's top bunk. He'd kissed her. She'd called him sweet. It devolved into one of those moments where she had a boyfriend.

"I gotta do this thing," Greg said. He moonwalked away from her, his back to the wind.

"O'Malley's?"

"Where else?"

Back upstairs, her roommate was gone. Leslie had taken everything that belonged to her: the TV, the rug, the mini-fridge, the bean-bag chair, the microwave—even the phone. Molly wanted to be angry about it, about the phone, but what was poor, depressed Leslie supposed to do? She was seventeen, and seemed even younger than that, and she wasn't coming back in the spring. She was "taking the semester off," but Molly could guess what that meant: naps, masturbation, TV. It gave Molly the willies. It seemed like a long dark road.

She sat on Leslie's bed and contemplated her own side of the room. Molly liked her *Breathless* poster, and her giant Bette Davis smoking a cigarette. She liked the upside-down roses from after the freshman showcase. She loved the bookshelf she'd put up herself, and all the books upon it, their colors and titles, how she'd read them all, and the way she'd ordered them, not alphabetically, but by size, tallest to shortest, so that a tiny volume by Blake greeted anyone who entered. Near the foot of her bed was her desk. On top of her desk sat her computer. Above her computer was an old gilded mirror that had belonged to her mother's mother, and in the window a stained glass of an eagle made by her too. There was also her great aunt's jewelry box on top of her dresser. It was empty, but it was expensive. How much for all that? she wondered. What was all that stuff worth?

The short was about a girl whose father has a heart attack. She gets a phone call from her mother. It's not serious, the mother says. It's minor. She doesn't need to come home, or not now at least. He has to eat better, the voice of Rosanna Archer says. He has to exercise. The mother's been saying that for years. Molly goes ahead and throws her party as planned. It is a wild time in a small space. One guy wears a sombrero. A girl falls onto a table and flattens it. Someone brings their dog, and the dog eats the cake. After the party montage, Molly goes out onto her fire escape. She smokes a cigarette and looks through the window of the apartment across the way. A young father puts his tiny daughter to bed, turns the light off in her room, and goes into his kitchen, where he opens the window. He too smokes a cigarette, half his body hanging out into the cool, autumn night. He says hi. Molly does the same. She apologizes for the noise. Eric Os, portraying the father, says it's fine. It's karma. It's all the parties he ever went to coming back to him. Everyone gets a turn, he says, but could they wrap it up by midnight?

The party dies its drunken death. It's well past three. Alone again,

Molly's phone rings. She answers. She listens. Everyone decided it would be more powerful if she didn't cry.

She did her laundry and packed. By five o'clock, there was still no Eric, still no tape. They had an hour.

"Do you know how much money I spent on that crane shot?" Rosanna asked. She lay on Molly's bed and stared at Bette Davis. "The permit alone was fifteen hundred. I had to tell the city it was for a commercial. Do you remember how hard it was to get the crane in the alley? It was impossible. Impossible!"

"But you did it," Molly said.

"I did. I made that happen. Me. I did that," Rosanna said. "Whosoever can change the night to day. Whosoever can turn the sun to rain. She shall be the producer."

"What?"

"I don't know," Rosanna said. "Where is that asshole?"

They tried calling from the pay phone, but once again they got his machine.

"Hello, Eric. This is Rosanna. I am going to kill you with my bare hands. I'm not even upset about it anymore. I'm resigned to whatever jail time I do. I will kill you, and when the judge asks me if I feel remorse, I will say no, and that the only thing I regret is that I can't strangle you to death, every day, until forever. Molly's upset as well."

They would have to get the tape themselves. It was decided. They would have to run out of there, through the Common and the Garden, up Beacon Street to Eric's apartment at the corner of Exeter, and pry it out of his coke-over'd hands, no matter its state. That was all there was to it. It would have to be done.

In front of the dorm, as they pulled on their hats and gloves, Kevin Murphy, a marketing major with ill-advised dreadlocks who

Molly knew through Eric, said, "Hey, you two. I almost forgot about this," and yanked a thick, oversized envelope from out of his messenger bag.

The students had daydreams about the future in which they sat to be interviewed by entertainment news reporters. It was one of the things young lovers bonded over—the revealing of this fantasy. They kept journals and diaries and what some of them insisted on calling notebooks, and in these they admitted to a certain kind of anguish. They threw the word *genius* around. She was a genius. He was a genius. They were geniuses. Harvard was for shitheads. Fuck those kids, they said. The students walked around with guitars strapped to their backs as if they knew more than three chords. They called their parents and asked for money. They rehearsed. They went to Alaska the previous summer and PA'd on a documentary about Inuit tribes and then acted like it was the first time in the whole history of the world anybody had ever done that. They could not understand why that Harvard girl would not call them back. They dropped acid on a rooftop in Beacon Hill and saw the city stretched out before them like the glowing revolutionary concept it was. They watched endless amounts of television and wrote term papers comparing *Little Women* to *The Golden Girls*. Like anyone, they rolled big fat fatties that went straight to their domes. They had nervous breakdowns. They were shipped off to rehab. They went on tour with their band, a little van circuit, to Buffalo and back. They free-styled. They went to Miami over break and came back with crabs. They would not shut up about Bret Easton Ellis. They spoke of *Howl* like Ginsberg had written it yesterday. They said they had an idea for a play that was ten hours long, maybe twelve, and they were going to need *everybody*. They did a line of coke and went to the gym and passed out on the treadmill. They watched a movie being shot on Charles Street with a TV actor who was trying to break through. They listened to the Cure, to the Wu-Tang Clan. They went to the Middle East, the Orpheum, to that shithole in Inman. They rode the Red Line. The Green Line. The Orange Line if they were cool. They performed. They wrote. They rehearsed. They found an original print of this. Of that. They watched it in the Student Union and wondered if they should drop out. Should they drop out? They wanted to drop out. They got off on Cassavetes, Kieslowski, Lynch. Hollywood was full of crooks and liars, but they wanted in. Everything was for that. That was everything. This wasn't pretend. It was real. It was happening. They were going there. Or New York. Or San Francisco, if they were some kind of purist. No matter where, they were going. They were a movement, a motion, a force like a river overflowing its banks, and who could stop that?

The Vault was packed. It was a refurbished bank building with its namesake like an open mouth in the back, but covered up now by the projection screen. The purple and gold NHSFF logo wobbled on the canvas as if floating in a day old bowl of milk. Molly wore heels, a red jumpsuit, and a bra that pushed her tits up. She knew how good she looked: she looked amazing. It had been decided that if they won, Rosanna would accept the award, but Molly wanted to leave an impression up there on stage. Everyone clutched their voting ballots or had left them on chairs to save their seats. The little pencils were all over the place. Students circled one another, and then one member of the circle would splinter off and hurry down the row to another circle. They spent their lives on top of one another, and they were never not in competition, or on the verge of hating someone forever, but every occasion felt like a reunion, or a once-in-a-lifetime party.

Through the glittering air above their heads and onto the screen the movies played one after the other. A girl met a stray dog and took the dog home to her sister who was dying of cancer. A boy who was late for school ran through a series of obstacles including a drive-by shooting played for laughs. There was a music video with a choreographed dance, a mockumentary about a homeless super villain, a doc titled *My Summer with the Inuits*. A father explained in a voiceover what it had been like to escape Cambodia under Pol Pot as the camera panned over skulls from the killing fields. Men in full drag reenacted a scene from *The Golden Girls*, and then it was Molly's movie. She didn't recognize it at first. Eric had changed the title.

"*The Candle in the Window?*" she whispered to Rosanna.

The opening was the same. The camera swooped down from the tops of the buildings. Through the window, Molly is seen in her apartment. Her phone rings. From the audience, she watched herself on screen.

                    MOLLY
        Hello?

The voice track cut out immediately. The whole tenor of the short was lost, the entire plot gone. There was a jump cut to the B-roll, to what Molly had thought were extended establishing shots where she'd sat on the futon and mouthed nonsense into the phone. The next shot was of the candle. Watching the movie, Molly sensed the tonal shift. It wasn't the same story anymore. There wasn't a story, or not a good one. Eric had reshot his part. The young daughter was history. He stood alone in his character's apartment, staring out across the alley into Molly's living room. The next three minutes were a sequence of establishing shots reedited to look continuous.

These shots were intercut with new footage, and each cut to Eric was worse than the last. In one, he unbuckled his belt. In the next, he unzipped his fly. Eric's only decent choice for the following shot was that it was framed from the waist up, but everybody knew what that arm motion meant. The next shot was of Molly reaching out to put her finger in the candle flame. During the shoot, she'd done this as a gag. It was something between her and him, not their characters. Molly hadn't even known they were rolling. She watched herself pull her finger out of the flame and put it in her mouth and suck on it. She watched her character stare at Eric. She watched her finger slip out of her mouth and then slide back in. She did this twice more, and then she pulled down her bottom lip so her mouth was half open. The last shot was of Eric, a close-up, and everybody knew what that face meant. The moan was entirely unnecessary.

"At least it wasn't you getting off on camera," Greg said. "That's one good thing."

The Candle in the Window placed next to last. Molly and Rosanna sat through the award announcements and speeches in a trauma- tized stupor, their eyes dead and faces slack, like the last remaining survivors in a bloodbath. Greg had found them. He led them next door to O'Malley's, where the bouncer was a rageholic sophomore named Trevor. If you were cool with Trevor, it was cool—you could be there.

"I hate him," Molly said. She put her hands down on the table they had miraculously scored, felt the sticky beer, and lifted them back up into the air. "I feel like a whore."

"I would too," Rosanna said. "I just paid fifteen thousand dollars to watch you simulate a blowjob."

"How much?" Greg asked.

"You heard me," Rosanna said. "We aren't all fundamentalists, like you. This isn't art for art's sake. Talk to me in five years when you're living in squalor."

They sat there drinking. O'Malley's was not a college bar. It was for old men who drank during the day, and there shouldn't have been a hundred and thirty students in it. "Freedom" by George Michael played on the jukebox. A few of the older marketing majors, tall girls like her, but with blow-dried hair and a certain finish to their outfits, looked at her and laughed, but otherwise no one paid Molly any attention, or, if they did, it was only to briefly glance at her, a stupid girl who'd made herself look like an ass, one of a million, and not worth their time. This, finally, was the offense that revealed itself, and stuck. It wasn't that she'd been sexualized—she was used to that. It wasn't that Eric had ruined the movie—that almost made sense. What bothered Molly, hurt her feelings, and enraged her, was that she wasn't being taken seriously. Eric had turned her into a joke. It felt unforgivable.

"Did that thing really cost fifteen thousand dollars?" Greg asked.

Rosanna had gone to the bathroom. The line was seven miles long.

"Twice that," Molly said. "That was her half. Eric paid for the rest."

"For that?"

"What's it matter? You're all rich. You're all sitting on a pile of candy."

"First of all, Brando said that. And second of all, in what universe am I rich? How do I get there? I wanna go."

"You always have money," Molly said.

During the three and a half months she'd been friends with Greg, she'd noticed him noticing. He was not especially suave about this. It came off like a long stare, where he wouldn't blink, and simply look into a person, rummage around inside them for a while, and then come back out into the light of day with a bloody, incontrovertible truth in his hands. He'd shared some of this information with Molly. "Rosanna hates herself," he'd told her. "Your friend Denise is a closeted lesbian." "Eric's father never shows him affection." Across the table, he peered into her. She thought Greg was going to tell her something about herself she didn't want to hear.

"I sell weed," he said.

"Since when?" Molly asked. "I want some."

"I don't sell it at school. I don't want people knowing. I sell it back home in Newton. Not all the time. Just when I need the money."

Greg knew a guy who lived in Allston. The guy fronted him the weed. If they asked nicely, if they were cool, he would probably do the same for Molly, but only if she wanted to, and only if she could sell it back home. It would solve her money problems, Greg said. It would take care of the holds.

The thought crossed her mind in a serious flash, but, then again, she'd seen that movie and read that book. It was an exciting and entertaining story, and it was for those very reasons it kept getting made, but Molly didn't have time for a lunatic drug dealer, or the cold, hard fact of a gun on the table. All of that was totally not her. In the moment, her whole life felt that way. Everyone Molly knew wanted experience, and Greg was no exception. His life was research. He was in the pursuit of material. Molly admired this about him, but she was tired of experience. She wanted a life. It was a no-thanks.

After one more beer, she called it quits.

"Come see me," Rosanna said. "My parents would love you. They'd want to adopt you. You could stay forever."

"Let me know if you come down," Greg said. "I could give you a heritage tour. Those are always boring."

Molly hugged them both and promised them each she would do what she could. Crossing back over Tremont, she noticed the weather. One of those warm December evenings had been born. She smelled the earth in the air, and the garbage. It was early still, not even ten, and she wasn't tired anyway. She walked into the Common, and retraced those steps she'd made all year. Here, in its center, Boston was an old jewel of a town, a dark ruby, or a fortress made of brick and tarnished bronze. On the hill, the State House dome radiated light. She crossed the street into the Garden, where the pond had long been drained, the mud at its bottom rippled in ice. The city had dressed the Comm Ave lampposts up in Christmas boughs and ribbons. She went up the mall, between the brownstones, and then cut down Dartmouth in the direction of the river. Marlborough was spooky in the dark, and in the daytime too, the untrimmed weight of the apple blossoms deforming them into the street, and it was always a revelation, a feeling of having come through, when it was behind her. She took Exeter to Beacon, went a half block, and walked up the stairs at 309. At the top, near the front door, Molly leaned over the handrail. She steadied herself so as not to fall, and knocked on Eric's window.

After several long minutes, during which she rapped, and tapped, and shouted, "I know you're in there, Cecil B. Jerkoff," his shade went up. Eric was wrapped in a blanket, and his face had the bunched, dehydrated look of a dead white rose. The dim wattage of his desk lamp in the background completed the mood of existential hangover going on. He put a crooked finger in the air, and Molly watched him shuffle away.

The front bolt was tricky, but he finally got it.

"Not yet," he said. "I'm begging you, please. Let me lie down."

She followed him back into his apartment, and closed the door behind her. She heard him drop onto his futon. It was a cheap and familiar sound. The studio gave off whiffs of body odor and mold.

"I'm opening a window," she said. "When was the last time you were outside?"

"I don't know."

"Today? Yesterday?"

"Negative," he said.

With some effort, she raised the window. The cold air blew against her chest. She stared across the alley at the condos.

"You're a piece of shit," Molly said. "Do you know that?"

"Yes."

"Everybody hates you."

"I know."

"Everybody."

She sat in the chair nearest him, and examined his face. Eric had radiant blue eyes. In between them, above the bridge of his nose, a pair of tiny hairs grew. Molly knew he usually plucked them, but there they were, taunting her. She told him to stop crying, went into his bathroom, and came back out with a roll of toilet paper and his tweezers. She handed him the toilet paper. "Sit up," she said. "Blow." When he was finished, they looked down together at the blood. "Shhhh," she said. "It's okay." She wrapped the old toilet paper in a bundle of new and threw it in the trash. She told him to sit up straight, and to relax. With her left hand, she cupped the back of his head, and leaned in close. He smelled of sweat and gin. She narrowed her eyes, and plucked.

"*Ow*," he said.

"That's one."

"*Ow*."

"That's two."

She told him to lie down on the futon. She pulled a dirty blanket from off his bed and covered him with it. In his kitchenette, she poured him a glass of water, and placed it on the floor within his reach. She took the chair again.

"It was bad?" he asked her.

"Yeah."

"How bad?"

"Bad," she said. "Was it real?"

"Yes."

"Jesus, Eric."

"I thought it'd be flattering."

"You're an idiot," she said.

There was a poster for *E.T.* on the wall, the boy on his bicycle against the moon, E.T. hooded up like Eric on the futon. He was from Chicago, or from one of the John Hughes–style towns outside the city. His father worked in the top floor of a very tall building.

She drank from her own glass of water.

"I don't think I can come back next semester," she said.

"What are you talking about?"

"Holds."

Eric asked her how much and she told him.

"You're a dirt-poor country girl."

"Yut," Molly said.

"That's hysterical."

He sprang up all at once and ran to the bathroom. Molly listened to him vomit.

"You okay?" she asked.

"No," he shouted. "I'm not. This is my whole life right here."

Eric stood in the doorway, and wiped his mouth with a washcloth. If he tried to clean himself up and make a move on her, she was going to kick him in the movie star. She looked at him and felt sad. He believed her kindness meant she had forgiven him. He didn't understand women at all.

"You can't go," he said. "Look at me. What would I do without you?"

"The same thing," she said, and smiled.

"Seriously," he said.

"Seriously what?"

"You can't go. We have movies to make. People will forget about this one. People forget everything. That's all they do," he said. "I've got a screenplay idea where you're homeless. We could do method research. I know a Harvard guy who works at a shelter. We could sleep there. We could really get it."

"Tempting," she said.

"I'm serious," Eric said. "When do those loan checks come in? It's a lump sum, right?"

He went to his desk and pulled open a few drawers.

"I don't want your money," she said.

"Just hold on."

His back to her, Molly watched him find his checkbook. It was a joint account that his father dumped money into every few weeks.

"It's more than the holds," she said. "I've got a plan."

"One second."

Molly heard him tear the check out. He walked over and handed it to her. It was for two thousand dollars.

"Keep half," he said. "You can pay me back the rest when your loans come in."

"What are you doing?"

"I'm saying, 'I'm sorry,' " Eric said. "I'm saying, 'I'm sorry about the movie.' "

He was paying her off, was what he was doing, and she absolutely, positively could believe it. Eric was pathetic. She pitied and hated him. Her plan, the one she'd made on the walk over, had been to go back home to Vermont and work. If her parents tried to force her after the new year to go back to school, she would fake a breakdown or a depression or something. The symptoms would be easy to fake. She would work and save up and move to California in May, when Rosanna was home. After that, she didn't know, but she had planned it out that far at least, and now it was going to happen much, much sooner. She wouldn't have to work at all.

DUES

1997

2

"You're an absolute mess."

Sally was sitting in the front row of the theater, looking up at Molly on stage.

"You're completely devastated. You want to die."

"I want to die?" Molly asked.

"Yes."

"I'm going to kill myself?"

"No," Sally said. She had on black leather pants and a purple smock. She'd given up recently and had cut her hair short. "Wanting to die is different. We're in LA, for god sake. It's pilot season. Everyone in this room wants to kill themselves. Wanting to die is different than suicide. One's an action. The other isn't. Let's do repetition. Let's explore this."

Molly set her script down on the stage floor. She looked out into the small black box theater at the dark faces of her classmates. There were fifteen of them tonight. Abigail was still crying from two scenes ago. Roderigo was pounding his fist into his knee. Once again, he hadn't been able to be cruel. He simply couldn't call Justin a fag. It was right there in the character—it was all but in the character's mouth—but it was too loaded for him. It was too much. Justin sat beside Roderigo, and Molly watched him put a hand on his friend's shoulder. She turned away.

"Upset," Dominic said to her. Molly squared up, and looked at him—this beautiful, reprehensible man—and wondered where he got his frosted tips done. They were so light, nearly natural.

"Upset," Molly said.

"Wait! Wait! Wait!" Sally interjected from her seat. "What's 'upset'? What is that? 'Upset' isn't anything. Remember, keep it simple. What's right *here*, Dominic?" Sally tapped her diaphragm. "*Right here, right here*. What do you see when you look at her?"

Dominic and Molly stared into each other's eyes. It was like playing catch, except you didn't have a glove or a ball, and you weren't outside at all, but on the second floor of a strip mall off Ventura Boulevard down in the Valley.

"Sad," he said.

"Sad," Molly said.

"Hurt," Dominic said. "I want to help you."

"You want to help me."

"I want to hold you."

"Hold me," Molly said, feeling something, some small shaft open. She tried not to notice it.

"I need to hold you," Dominic said. "You're beautiful."

"*Okay. Okay. Okay*," Sally said, rising off her seat into a weird crouch. Over drinks once, she'd told Molly the only problem with Meisner was that for the first two or three months of class the only thing male students could observe honestly was their need to fuck everything. "It's their only accessible instinct," Sally had said. "It's pitiful."

"We know you find her beautiful, Dominic," Sally said. "We all do. But you've got to use that more honestly. Think about it: you're leaving her. She's just lost a child, and now you're going to *leave* her. Believe it! It's happening to you!"

Molly couldn't look at him. She stared at the space above his right shoulder. Why would she look at him? Why would she do anything? He was leaving her. She wanted to die.

"It's not Molly's fault," Dominic said, breaking character. "But I'm not here."

"Where are you?" Sally asked.

"I don't know," Dominic said. "Somewhere else. You know, I've had this thing lately. There's been a lot of . . ." he trailed off.

Molly was one of the class's beautiful people. She belonged to that company—her and Dominic and Justin and sometimes Lena— but she didn't like to take advantage of it. She didn't like to do this thing—this thing that Dominic was doing right now—where the beautiful person in question clogged up the whole room with their most recent drama. Sally's wasn't that kind of class, anyway. You couldn't get into it because you'd seen a flyer down at the Coffee Bean. You had to know people. You had to be vetted and recommended. You had to be serious. Molly had been telling Justin for weeks that Dominic should be sent back down to intermediate. He wasn't ready. He wasn't an actor.

But the thing was, Sally loved him. She thought he was sex on a stick, which was true. If Molly hadn't been sort of kind of engaged, she might have even . . .

"Let's try something," Sally said. "Bring that chair over. Put it in the middle of the stage. We're going to get you over the hump here, Dominic. Over the hump through humping. Do the lines, but as a sex scene. Okay? You need to feel how screwed up this whole scenario is. Take off your shirt, Dominic. Molly?"

"I'll leave mine on."

"Stay open to this, Molly," Sally said, before turning to the class. "Everybody! Stay open! This is the kind of thing you're going to run into in casting offices. You'll prepare for the audition one way, and then—*woof!*—it's something else. Be fearless!"

Sally instructed Molly to sit in the chair so that she was facing the audience. She told Dominic to stand up behind Molly. Each of them had their pages in their hands.

"Whenever you're ready," Sally said.

It was like dancing with someone who wasn't a very good dancer, but who could maybe become a good dancer if you led them properly, except you weren't dancing with them at all. Instead, you were in a softly lit room, pretending to have sex with them in front of fourteen people.

Dominic began to rock the chair back and forth so that the rear two legs came off the ground a few inches, then dropped, then rose, then dropped again. Molly caught his rhythm.

"I love you," Dominic read aloud.

"I know," Molly read.

"There's something wrong with me. I can't help how I feel."

"You disgust me."

"Don't say that."

"What should I say?" she asked.

Molly pulled her shirt off over her head. She felt her breasts shake in her bra. She tried not to care, but she cared, so she used it. She followed the feeling down. She didn't force anything. She let it come. Dominic had to put more and more weight into his motion to get the chair off the ground. She could hear him breathing harder.

"I hate you," she said.

"It's something I have to do."

"After this, I never want to see you again," she said.

"But what about—"

"Never," she said.

The scene was supposed to end there, but Molly swung her arm around awkwardly and grabbed the fabric of his pants. She pulled him into her, and caught his rhythm once again, and then took it over.

She wanted to make Dominic cum against the chair if she could. She wanted him to feel as ashamed as his leaving her was making her feel. She started to moan. She pushed harder against him. Instead of the rear two, the front legs began to rise off the ground. Molly worked toward her climax, and when she was done—when the last fake twitch had escaped her—she let her hand drop from his pants, and then sat there with her arms between her legs, catching her breath.

Sally turned to the class.

"If this were an audition, Molly just got the part."

After class, she stuck around to use the telephone. She needed to double check her call-back times for the next day. The office was behind the stage, in a room that had once been a darkroom. No one had ever bothered to take out the revolving door. When she was finished listening to her messages, Molly turned the window fan on above the desk Sally shared with three other acting teachers, lit a cigarette, and tried to figure out how she was going to get from Studio City to Burbank in five minutes the following day. Without traffic, it would take at least fifteen minutes, and then she would have to find parking, walk to the office, compose herself, make ten seconds of memorable chit-chat with the casting agent and the assistant producer, hear their notes on whatever changes they'd made, incorporate those, and do it. It was all completely impossible, but what other choice did she have?

Sally spun her way through the office door.

"Oh, Roderigo!" she said. "You're killing me!"

"I know. Breaks my heart," Molly said. "He's the sweetest, most wonderful man in the world."

"Too sweet," Sally said, taking a cigarette from out of Molly's pack. "Too wonderful. There's an angry monster in there, I know. He has to let him out. He's all blocked up. He's all constipated. I don't know what the problem is."

"We talked about it," Molly said. "Anger feels stereotypical to him. He feels like 'the angry *cholo*' when he gets angry."

"He has to get over that. Where in this town is there a script for a wonderful, intelligent Mexican American man who works two jobs, goes to night school, and acting class once a week?" Sally asked. "This is Hollywood. This isn't reality. He could do a one-man show if he wants reality—get it out of his system. In the meantime, what he should do is get a neck tattoo, shave his head, and start wearing those big khaki pants they all wear. He'd get a part like that."

"That's terrible," Molly said.

"Is it?"

"Yes," Molly said. "That's one hundred percent screwed up. That's not him."

"But who is?" Sally asked. "I mean really. What a presumptuous idea. He's an actor. He should act. Be the cliché. This is America. Clichés pay the bills. You think I like being the 'acting teacher?' 'Acting teacher' is how I make money. If it was up to 'Sally,' she wouldn't do a damn thing. We'd be living out on the street. Actors are weirdos who pretend to be normal—but we're accepted, thank God! We're accepted! People need us, and they know it. It's not like we're painters or something—or poets, for fucksake! We aren't embarrassing people to death. They know what to make of us, at least. That's a stroke of luck, believe me. If this country had its way, they'd round up all the artists and burn us alive."

Sally always spoke about herself as if she were a hundred different people. Molly only ever felt like who she was, and she found this depressing. She was twenty-four and often told herself that if she didn't make it by the time she was twenty-six, she would go ahead and kill herself. Most days she didn't mean it—not really—but the fantasy made her feel better. Then there were the other days.

"How about you?" Sally asked. "How was the deodorant audition?"

"Great," Molly said. "I've got a call-back tomorrow."

"That's so good."

"Yeah," she said, forcing the enthusiasm. "I've got a pilot call-back too."

"What?" Sally said. "That's huge!"

"Totally. It's totally huge," Molly said, although it didn't feel that way. To get a part, you needed to have been seen before, and Molly had yet to be seen. Casting agents remembered you from in-person interactions, but producers often didn't. Producers needed context, prior validation in the form of screen time. The role didn't have to be a lead, or a supporting even. You could have walked into the frame and handed someone a piece of paper. What was important was that another producer had approved of you, had said, *"This one's good. We can use her."* Everything in Molly's life was connected to the same question: If she couldn't get a part in order to be seen and get another part, how was she supposed to get a part? She couldn't complain to Sally, though. Sally was the only reason she had a manager at all. The woman was connected. She'd made some calls and still it took two years.

"That's tomorrow too," Molly said. "The pilot audition."

The show was about a guy who solves crimes of a historical nature by remembering his past lives. Molly was up for the role of GIRLFRIEND. The character didn't yet have a name. It was a small role, sure, the producer had said, but there was always room to grow. What could Molly bring to it? How could she aid them in seeing

GIRLFRIEND more clearly? Could she make GIRLFRIEND feel big? Could she make a seemingly insignificant, nearly worthless character come alive?

"Are you prepared?" Sally asked her. "Have you done the research?"

"Tons," Molly said.

Because it was a Wednesday night, which meant her manager wouldn't be there and they could eat for free, she met Jared at the restaurant where she worked. Parking was parking. She found a spot near the edge of a sloping driveway, checked her bumper two or three times to make sure she wasn't over, and then walked the two blocks to the restaurant. Through the front window, she saw Jared at the bar, nursing a Manhattan. He was seven years older than her. One of the fundamentally boring things she loved about him was that he didn't drink too much. Her first two LA boyfriends had been drunks—the usual, self-pitying sad sacks—and Molly wondered if she didn't have a bar sign on her forehead, some mark that attracted them. Since college, she had adopted a personal discipline that made her feel dull sometimes. She waited tables. She went to acting class. She worked out. She auditioned. She guessed the drunks had relieved her of that routine, but they were exhausting after awhile. She liked Jared's attentiveness, his trust in her, and his sense of humor, although Molly often regretted having fallen in love with another actor. She also wasn't crazy about the fact that he might be *it*. She had a secret vision of herself as coupled with a man who would elicit far more of the world's jealousy than this one did.

She gave him a big hug and a kiss.

"How was class?" Jared asked.

"Fine," Molly said. "Weird. The usual."

He kept his hair short because he was starting to lose it. He had a nose that was round at the tip. Watching television on their couch, Molly liked to put quarters on his chin and leave them there.

"How was your day?"

"Terrible," he said.

One of their problems was that he didn't complain enough. Because he didn't, it made Molly the complainer in the relationship. She had, in fact, asked him to share more, but upon hearing the whiny tone in his voice she regretted having mentioned it at all.

"The audition?"

"The audition," Jared said.

There was hardly anyone else at the bar. A few local regulars. Molly ordered a glass of Pinot from the new bartender, who was a dead ringer for Lorenzo Lamas. She was suddenly not hungry.

"It was the horror thing, right?" she asked Jared. She reached out and touched his shoulder. At some point, they had to talk about bills.

"Yeah," he said, annoyed. "The horror thing."

"What?"

"Don't call it a thing," Jared said. "Horror gets out there. Horror gets you seen. Doors open with horror."

"I know," Molly said. "I wish I'd auditioned."

"Then don't call it a thing," he said. "I don't call your auditions things. It was a horror audition. Horror. The working title's *Funhouse*."

"*Funhouse*?" Molly asked. "That's a terrible title."

"I didn't make it up," Jared said. "I didn't name it *Funhouse*."

"Sorry," Molly said, but she wasn't. She'd always thought older guys would be less touchy, but they were actually worse. A man in his thirties understood when his life was falling apart. A young one didn't care—he thought he had more chances.

"I got there on time. I was early even. There were a few changes, but nothing big. I was feeling good," Jared said. "Probably another seven or eight guys were waiting. That guy from that FOX show was there."

"Which guy?"

"The guy with the forehead. I forget his name. Anyway, I'm going over the new lines. They were okay. Not awful. I'm totally there, ready to go, and then this guy walks out of the audition room."

"The guy with the forehead?"

"No. Another guy. Some guy. I've seen him around," Jared said. "You know how it is. He comes out of the audition room, and everybody looks up, or pretends not to be looking, but actually everyone is. We're all looking up at him, and then this guy—this fucking guy—slams the door behind him so hard a picture of David Duchovny falls off the wall."

"*What?*"

"Wait. It gets worse. He slams the door, and then he stands there for a second, kind of hyperventilating, and squeezing his fists in front of his face. Then he tears the shirt he's wearing off of his own body. I swear to God. He starts shouting, 'Fuck this town! Fuck this whole motherfucking place! I've wasted my whole life! My whole goddamn life has been a waste!'"

"Total breakdown," Molly said. "What did you do? What'd the other guys do?"

"Nothing," Jared said. "He walks past everybody to the end of the hall, turns around, and yells, 'They cast the whole thing! The whole fucking movie's cast! It's all bullshit! Life is bullshit! You're all bullshit!'"

"Then what happened?" Molly asked.

"The producer came out, put David Duchovny back on the wall, and called my name."

"Oh my God."

"It was terrible. I was so there, and then it was just like, 'What the fuck? Why am I here? What is this?' It was the worst audition I've ever had in my entire life."

"What did they say?" Molly asked. "Was the casting agent there?"

"They didn't say anything. That was the worst part. They acted like nothing had happened at all. It didn't even faze them. They were like, 'Hi, Jared. What do you have for us today? We're all heartless-monster-psychopaths who don't give a shit about you or your time.' I could have been Daniel Day-Lewis and they wouldn't have noticed."

"They probably would have noticed—"

"You know what I mean," Jared said, putting his forehead down on top of the bar. "That guy was right. He was insane, but he was right. It's all bullshit. It's all pointless bullshit. How much longer can we do this? Really. I mean, how much longer?"

She didn't like that *we*. *We* did quick work in her brain. It eradicated any notions of suicide or self-pity. It made her hate him a little.

"And what would we do? Move back to your parents' house in Idaho? Work the land?"

"I can do things."

"Like what?"

"I could be a carpenter."

"Why do men always—" she started. "You couldn't be a carpenter."

"I'm handy. I can fix things."

"What things?"

"I fixed the lightbulb the other day."

"You changed it," she said. "You changed the lightbulb."

"The toilet," he said. "I fixed the toilet. That was impressive."

She could have fixed the toilet too, she knew. She could have stuck her hand down inside the top part and jiggled the whatchamacallit, but she didn't want to.

"You did," she said. "That's true. That was very impressive."

"Don't patronize me."

"I'm not."

"Yes, you are," he said. "What's the point of doing this if you don't make it?"

"Make what?"

"It," he said. "It."

There were times when Molly believed she had changed, that she had grown and matured as a human being. Living on her own since she was nineteen had forced her to grow up faster than most people her age. She'd had to be more realistic, more practical. It was all on her. If forced to, she would act in teen soaps for the rest of her life. Or infomercials. This was her top layer of thinking, the layer most immediately exposed to whatever bullshit rained down on her (rejection, disappointment, waiting tables). Whatever grew there (her smile, a kind word, a hug) made it appear as if she were humble. But beneath that humility, beyond the reach of the insults that leeched down into her, was the truth. And the truth was, Molly Bit thought she was the best young actress in Hollywood nobody had ever heard of. All she needed was a break.

"You will make it. You will," she lied. Molly could make herself smaller or larger. She could be beautiful, ugly, or in between. She could dial herself up and down at will. Jared couldn't. He worked hard, but he was all technique. It wasn't technique, she wanted to tell him. It was, but it wasn't. Molly knew her way around a scene, a partner; she'd learned all sorts of tricks—but so did dogs. It was something else. It came to her. It took her over. It wasn't anything she could explain.

"Honey, it's one day."

"Over and over again," he said.

Lorenzo Lamas brought over Jared's dinner, salmon and a vegetable called kale that everybody in LA was just exactly then beginning to talk about. Food always made Jared feel better. He was simple like that. She let him eat half of it, and then asked.

"How do I look?"

"Insanely beautiful," he said. "As ever. A classic."

They liked to talk about her beauty as if it were a car.

"Should we take it for a spin? Go to this comedy thing?"

"Sure. We can drive it over there. I wanna park it out front."

"I feel like it's getting kind of old."

"Shut up," Jared said, and kissed her.

They went to the Laugh Factory on Sunset and watched the Upright Citizens Brigade. Molly laughed so hard her face hurt. Afterward, she ran into Lena from her acting class out on the sidewalk.

"There's this thing," Lena said. She had a beautiful, spacey quality. She'd grown up on a commune. "You should come."

The party was up in Beechwood Canyon. The mansion had once belonged to George Harrison. No one knew what the party was for. Christian Slater was there. Each floor had its own DJ. The upper rooms had fragmented themselves into separate parties of young producers, agents, and creative execs. There was a piece of talk getting passed around about a special sex room.

Molly and Jared hung with Lena, who had a thing for comedians. Molly understood the fetish. For the most part, LA was shockingly earnest. Everyone was a striver. They chanted secret mantras. Comedians were the opposite of that. The most honest joke Molly had heard recently was during a female stand-up's bit about anal sex. "You know, I was down on all fours," she'd said, "and I was thinking about my day. I was thinking about my agent, who can't remember my name, and how my best friend stole my producer's credit, and how—even though I had been promised the part—it went to that other, dumber, prettier, skinnier bitch, and I said, 'Go for it, Jim! Ram it on home! Let's keep this theme going!'" As far as Molly was able to understand, *comedian* was only another word for working-class manic-depressive. Like Lena, she loved them.

She went upstairs to use the bathroom. It was the techno-floor. Standing in line, she felt the bass in her teeth. A conversation screamed behind her.

"Color has a problem with syncing!"

"It has something to do with the file locations!"

"I hate computers!"

"I have another composer! It's my roommate's ex-boyfriend, but they just broke up, so I don't know!"

"We don't know how any of this will work out!"

The bathroom interior shook with the deep throb of party life. After Molly peed and washed her hands, the door opened up on her. She said, "Hey-hey-hey, occupied!" but Abigail from her acting class was already inside, holding a script in her hands.

"This is weird, I know," Abigail said.

She was the tiniest, strangest little person. Abigail Kupchik was from the Midwest, from a little town with a German name outside St. Paul. Aside from whatever scenes Molly had performed with her in class, they'd had few interactions. She was a little over five feet tall. Molly loomed over her.

"I need to talk to you," Abigail said, staring up. "I saw you come in here. I thought, 'Here's my chance.'"

"Okay," Molly said. "Can we like talk out there? Get out of the bathroom?"

"No-no-no," Abigail said, speedily. Molly realized Abigail had done a little, or maybe a lot, of coke. "It's too noisy out there. That techno turns my brain to mush."

"Is it important?" Molly asked.

"Super important," Abigail said. "Super-duper-important."

Molly sat down on the edge of the tub. Abigail, as though she was assuming an actual throne, took the toilet. The script—who didn't know a script when they saw one?—was on Abigail's lap.

"I'm just gonna jump right in here," Abigail said, drumming the pages with her fingers. "I've noticed something about you."

"What's that?" Molly asked.

"You don't have a community," Abigail said.

"Is that so?" Molly asked. It was the first time in her life she'd heard her mother's voice come out of her own mouth.

"You don't have a community," Abigail continued, "and you need one to make it in this town. You need something. There's all sorts of girls out there, and they've all got three or four girlfriends who are all doing the same exact thing with their lives, day in and day out. They're going over lines together, and taking overnight trips to Ojai. They're doing all sorts of stuff all the time together, and each one of them is a member of another friend group, and so it keeps getting exponentially larger all the time, their community. They don't even know they're doing it, but they are. These women out there are helping one another get auditions and grocery shop and take care of their kids—some of them have kids—and little by little they're doing something in a really, really weird way."

"What weird way is that?" Molly asked. "What are they doing?"

"They're mapping this place," Abigail said. "They're mapping it like *'Tracy lives off Fountain and she can do this because she knows Lisa who works at this place and heard from Deborah about this woman named Charlie who's a lesbian and is plugged into this gay cohort of casting agents that pretty much runs a certain corner of Universal due to the fact . . . ,'* and it goes on and on like that."

"You're talking about networking," Molly said. "I know about networking."

"No. No, I'm not," Abigail said. "Men network. They shake hands and make contacts. They have buddies and business partners. *'Hey, pal. How are you, bud? Good to see you, man.'* Women make friends because their lives depend on it. They make communities, and you don't have one, and that's a problem. You're too alone. You can be alone later, if you want—or if that's what happens—but right now you can't be."

"What do you mean, alone?"

"I mean alone," Abigail said. "Alone. Maybe if you were in New York, you could do it. But this isn't New York. It's LA. You can't be alone in LA. It's the desert! You'll die! I think you're too good for that. Too good of an actress. You shouldn't die out in the desert without anyone knowing who you are."

Molly didn't care for people who were able to look past her beauty and charm to see the person she actually was. Abigail had hit upon a sensitivity—because Molly did prefer to be alone, alone or with a man, which was a better kind of solitude. She liked acting and acting class and the short films she'd done in part because those relationships were contained. Those friendships didn't get weird or too much. They didn't follow you into the bathroom.

"Are you asking me to be your friend?"

"Sort of," Abigail said. "More to the point, I'm asking you to be my actress."

"Your actress?" Molly asked. "Aren't *you* an actress?"

"I suck, Molly," Abigail said. "I'm the worst actress in the history of the world. We both know that."

"What are you, then?"

"A writer," Abigail said, lifting the fat script up into the air and then smacking her knees with it. "Obviously. But I'd like to be a director too. I need you for that. I've got the community. I need the lonely thing at the center of it."

"I'm not lonely. Who said I was lonely?"

"Sorry. Self-sufficient," Abigail said, holding the script out in the air. "Whatever you'd like to call yourself. Will you read it?"

It was as heavy as the first draft of *War and Peace*, Molly imagined, a hulking ream of ambition. The title was *Starcatcher.*

"Read it. You have to read it, and then you have to do it," Abigail said. "You have to. But read it. Will you read it? Will you?"

She would.

"Oh, thank God," Abigail said. From out of her purse, she took out a tiny bag of coke. "Do you?" she asked, shaking the bag.

"Not in years," Molly said.

"Want to?"

"Auditions tomorrow. But thanks."

"I love that!" Abigail shouted for some reason. "You're so serious! You're so focused!"

As Abigail tapped out some coke onto the top shelf of the toilet, Molly slipped past her to the door.

"Will you close that behind you?" Abigail asked. "I'm gonna camp out here for a while. See you in class!"

Molly went back downstairs past a line of twenty angry people who wanted to do their own drugs, and found Jared. He was yelling at a comedian: "I know! I know! That's so true!" The misery of his day had evaporated out of him in a way she hadn't expected. She yelled into his ear that she wanted to leave, and then they both yelled good-bye to Lena, and to the five stand-ups who had gathered around her. It was all so much joyful chaos. When they stepped out into the street, the near-silence of the canyon was like a curtain coming down across the play that was the party.

Driving alone in her car, she followed him. At more than a few stoplights, she looked down at the script on the passenger seat. Finally, after a mile or two, when she knew the way by heart, she picked it up and began to read.

I have friends, she thought in the morning. *I have a lot of friends.* But she didn't, she knew. Not really. She had acquaintances. She had people who she thought were nice, who she said hi to at the gym. She had contacts, but little true connection. Molly often feared she wasn't plugged into Hollywood enough, wasn't connected to it in the way one had to be: all at once and everywhere, on the tip of every tongue, fuckable and friendable, an actor/producer/writer/director who was part of a posse made up of the same, knocking on the door of the future, one big Sundance premiere away from taking over the world.

She was only Molly, Molly thought, staring at her reflection in the bathroom mirror, "and Molly looks like shit today," she said aloud. The skin under her eyes was puckered and purple. She had sleep lines cutting up and down her face. Leaning across the bathroom sink, she examined herself. She looked old. She looked thirty, or even older, ancient. *Was it all over? It was all over!*

She took a shower. She did her hair and makeup. She nearly

forgot her panic, but now she was sad. Her beauty would one day expire, she knew, and in a strange way she missed it—like it was already gone. Thinking this, vanity blended into guilt, and she hated herself. What was wrong with her? Her neck, for one thing. Her neck was too long. Her thighs were thicker than she wanted them to be. She hated her hands, her fat knuckles. And if she were being honest, she'd noticed the other morning her ass was starting to drop.

Feeling this way, she put on a pair of jeans that raised her butt up half an inch, chose a vintage Richard Hell and the Voidoids T-shirt, cleaned off her sunglasses, and hit the road. Her hair was thick and full and long. She didn't want to muss it at all, and kept the windows closed in the Toyota, even though the morning temperature was close to eighty, and the AC was on the fritz. At the long traffic stops on the 101, she rolled the windows down, stuck her head out, and inhaled the bus fumes. By the time she pulled off into Studio City, her back was all sweaty, and she regretted the tight quality of her good-butt-jeans, swamp-assed as they were.

It was a deodorant commercial, and she'd forgotten to wear any, not a swipe of Sure to speak of.

In the parking garage, she dug through the backseat and found a program from a Clifford Odets play, *Rocket to the Moon*. Molly used it to wipe her armpits, but all that did was streak the sweat around and make her feel disgusting and ridiculous. The underground parking garage was like a shallow region of hell, and she continued to sweat as she went up the dank, gray stairwell. She sensed, with each confident step she pretended to make, failure.

There were three other women in the hallway outside the office. She could have been walking into the opening scene of a movie about clones. All the women were white, five-ten, and perfect. An elevator-music'd version of "Shiny Happy People" by REM played over unseen speakers. Like Molly, each of the women wore tight boutique jeans and a vintage rock-'n'-roll T-shirt. None but her, however, were sweating like a seventh grader. The women were seated on Molly's right against the wall. Walking past, she gave them each her best closed-mouth smile. She spotted the silhouette of a lady on the nearest door, and went inside.

Molly looked, the mirror said, like a hooker, or like a groupie at CBGB's, and not in a good way. Fortunately, the bathroom was a single user.

"Okay, tramp," she whispered to herself in the mirror. "What are you gonna do here? What to do? What to do?"

Someone in her head began to ask her questions.

What is a commercial?

It is an advertisement for the people and things surrounding a product.

Who are you?

I am a sweaty, gross woman in need of deodorant.

How much money do you have in the bank?

Two hundred and thirteen dollars.

How should you behave?

Like myself.

No! No! No! Sally's right! Don't be yourself! This is a commercial! A national commercial!

How then?

Act!

She took a comb out of her purse and brushed away the mousse. She put her hair up in a ponytail. Turning on the faucet, she unrolled some toilet paper and dabbed it in the stream. Carefully, she removed her eyeliner. She used the *Rocket to the Moon* playbill to gently fan herself. She didn't want to look sweaty, but like a woman who could possibly sweat, or like a woman who knew exactly when to sweat—meaning only when appropriate, i.e., while working out or fucking. More preferably, she should look like the kind of woman capable of choosing not to sweat during either of those activities.

Okay?

"Okay."

It was that small little spot of her talking, the best actress in Hollywood nobody had ever heard of. As if possessed by the voice, Molly sat in the outer hallway with the clones, whom she no longer resembled. The other women were studying the promotional material. They perused laminated tri-folds, as if preparing for a test. Molly sat. She inspected her fingernails, and felt the resentment of the women, their frayed, frustrated nerves directed at her. *Well, she was frustrated too!* she might have said. *She didn't have any money either! Her boyfriend was planning a future for them in Boise! Boise! Can you imagine? Could you point out Boise on a map if you had to? If your life depended on it?* But she didn't actually say or even suggest any of that. Instead, she allowed a half-smile to slide across her face like a wall of sunlight passing through a row of window blinds.

"Molly?" a woman's voice sang out. "Molly Bit?"

There wasn't time enough to worry. She sped the Toyota down the curve of the earth into Burbank, past the creamy exterior walls of Warner Brothers, where beyond the gate her call-back time was fast approaching—there it was—and then it was gone. She pulled into the security lane.

"Molly Bit," she said to the guard. He was a young guy with cheekbones so high you could dive off of them.

He glanced down at his clipboard. "How do you spell that? The last name?"

"B-I-T. As in, 'I just bit it.' Bit."

"Memorable," the guard said, handing her a pass. "Park in the green lot."

She didn't see the green parking lot (its absence was like a madness passing through her) so she parked in the red lot, grabbed a few head-shots, and cut through the outdoor commissary, where suits, techni-cians, and tourists mixed together. Warners was a factory and a village and an amusement park. In the early afternoon, most of the enormous sound stage doors were open. A line of extras filed behind a girl in a yellow vest. Gaffers with utility belts strapped to their hips walked around like cowboys. Molly found the building. She shot up the exte-rior stairs to a sign on the door that read *Back to Life Auditions*, took a second to get her shit together out on the landing, and opened the door.

The same junior assistant sat behind a table, a woman named Erica. Since Molly had last seen her, she'd dyed her hair blond.

"They're running long," Erica said. She was filing her nails. "You're fine. There's new pages, though." She handed Molly three sheets of paper.

Hunger, for whatever it might be—food, love, a part—makes one less choosy. She had read scripts so underwritten as to appear mal-nourished, and yet she'd managed to read these without judgment. She'd hunt out her beats, the arcs of scenes, motivations, and hardly give a thought to critique, or to whether or not the script in her hands was good or bad or something in between. But this one was abso-lute garbage. Some writer had pumped it out in five minutes. Sitting down to read the new scene, Molly experienced the acute pang of the professional, where it feels as if no one else in the entire world but you is bothering to do their job.

GIRLFRIEND was blander than ever. Hardly there at all.

                    GIRLFRIEND

Oh, honey.

                    GIRLFRIEND

That's so strange. What do you think it
means?

                    GIRLFRIEND

All I know is, I love you, and that means
we're together forever, babe.

                    GIRLFRIEND

I wish I could do that!

She'd been up until three in the morning reading Abigail's script. The experience had spoiled her. That character had nuance. She was neither virgin nor whore. Neither boring nor over the top. She was real. Once you explored a character like that, went down into a person as true to you as anyone in life, you couldn't go back. To go back would be impossible. You were ruined.

"They're ready for you, Molly," Erica said.

The room was darker than she'd expected it to be. The only natural light came in from a half open side-door. The same five men sat behind a long table. A sixth man, someone she'd never met, stood in the corner of the room. He was very short. Maybe five-five, if he was lucky. He spoke into one of those new satellite phones. His black suit fit him perfectly. He didn't wear a tie.

The show's creator and prospective showrunner, Roger Mills, sat at the middle of the table. He said, "Hi, Molly. Water? You remember everybody, don't you?" He said the name of each man.

They nodded at her. When Molly smiled, it felt like her face might break in half.

"Hi, Roger. Hi, Dave. Hi, Sam. Hi, Tom. Hi, Mike. I'd love some water, thank you." (You always took the water if they offered you the water.) "Nice to see you all." A sudden blast of nervous fear hit her in the bowels.

"That's Ian," Roger said, pointing at the man on the phone. "He's at Warners. He's hiding from his boss. Isn't that right, Ian?"

"No," Ian said, all business. "It's not." He pushed a button on his gigantic phone. "That's over. Whenever you're ready." The power coming off of him reminded Molly of the Berlin Wall, of a moment in time she'd witnessed on television where a thick slab of it fell to the ground.

"So you've had a chance to read the new pages," Roger said. "She's still—we're growing her, as you can see. We're growing her slowly."

"Glacially," Ian said.

Roger ignored him.

"Any questions, Molly?" he asked. "We're looking to see what you can bring."

"Anything at all," Ian said. "Anything."

All Molly had were questions, but she didn't have one that would make Roger Mills feel smart or talented or as if he were really on to something.

"No," she said. "No questions. I really like the new pages."

Earlier, there had been too much aggressive feedback in the room for her entrance to have made a ripple. This lack of attention was something Molly wasn't used to. More often than not, men turned toward her. They looked. They glanced over their wives' or girl-friends' shoulders to catch a glimpse. They rolled down their car windows. They scoped her out in the gym mirror. Men were drawn to her, but they were also drawn by her, as if the movement of her body was the hand that sketched them into being. For several minutes, these particular men had been too distracted to recognize who they were dealing with. Having finally gained their full attention, she flicked her switch on. She felt her power dilate like a pupil. To say "she smiled" or "she gave them a smile" would rob the world of its very improbability. It would be a sin, like murder.

The red eye of the camera clicked. She went through the scene with Roger as her partner. She tried to give the lines some mystery, some depth. She ignored the exclamation marks, and showed the writers how the one-note-ness of them was too constraining. During the scene, without realizing it, she folded the pages in half, and then that half into another half. She couldn't have glanced down at them even if she needed to. In three minutes' time, they'd come to the biggest bloc of dialogue. She tried to be a cipher, a tree, no one. It was that bad.

GIRLFRIEND

```
Who could imagine? I mean you? I don't think
I've ever met anyone with a special . . .
what would you call it? Ability? Is it like
déjà vu? Déjà vu always reminds me of a
time when I was a little girl. My mother
took me to a park. It was in the fall. I
remember, I was on top of the slide, and
I had this feeling that something bad was
going to happen, like something bad had
already happened, maybe, and that's what I
was feeling, the memory of it. I went down
```

```
the slide. I was so little. I shot right off
of it. I came off it funny and broke my leg.
Ouch. Thinking about it makes it hurt. Is
that what it's like? Is that what remembering
your past lives is like?
```

She'd done the best she could. It was over.

"Thank you, Molly," Roger said. He betrayed nothing. "We really appreciate your coming in. We'll let you know."

To depart an audition, to hear those words—*thank you*—was the most rapey part about the whole thing. Molly grabbed her purse, politely said who knows what to the men, and went out into another perfect Southern California day. She walked in a daze down the exterior stairs and across the appallingly clean asphalt of the Warners lot and weaved her way through a pack of Rosie O'Donnell audience members. When she got to the red lot, she saw her car was gone.

"No, no, no, no, no," she said. She stood in the empty space. "No."

Above her, the sun was at its *High Noon* peak. She had work in an hour. She didn't have any money. If she hadn't been so angry, she would have cried.

"Did they tow you?"

She spun, her purse twisting around her legs, and saw the tiny man, Ian.

"Yes."

"They love doing that. What's the license plate number? Maybe we can catch it."

He had his phone in hand.

"What?" she asked.

"The license plate number."

Her face said, *I don't know what my license plate number is, and I feel stupid enough already, so don't . . .*

"What's the make and model? What kind of car is it?"

"A Toyota Corolla."

"What's the color?"

"Tan?" she asked. "An ugly yellow? It's the color of an old mattress."

He was a member of that small male minority who still knew the power of a suit. There were maybe five of these men. Six, tops. Grunge had definitely passed him by.

With his pointer finger, he stabbed numbers into his phone.

"This is Ian Brewster . . . Yes. Me. Put me into parking, or maintenance . . . I don't know. Put me into whoever the fuck it is who tows car around here." He looked at Molly. "Nice audition . . . Yes, this is Ian. You towed a car. I need it back . . . Call the driver then . . . Then call him on the CB . . . It's a tan Toyota Camry—"

"Corolla," Molly corrected.

"*Corolla*," Ian Brewster said. "A tan Toyota Corolla. I'm guessing old and shitty." He was asking Molly. "Is that right?"

"The oldest and shittiest," she said.

"They put me on hold," he said. "A very nice audition. But too bad, because when that asshole Roger goes home tonight he's going to get a call from his agent telling him the show's dead. Am I still on hold?" He was back with the operator. "What? The red parking area . . . Yes. Right . . . They wouldn't have given you the part anyway . . . Right, right, yes . . . The writers in this town are fucking idiots. Once they're done writing, they should be shot in the face. They annoy me more than the actors . . . The red parking area."

He hung up.

"It'll be here in five minutes," Ian said. "I love this phone. I make up reasons to use it all the time."

"Thank you so much," Molly said.

"Don't thank me," he said. "I mean, thank me, but not for the car."

She didn't know who he was, or what he did at Warners. She desperately wanted answers.

"I'm casting something," Ian said. "Actually, I did cast it, but I'm thinking of making a change. I don't like the lead."

"Who's the lead?"

"She's nobody," Ian said. "Like you. It doesn't matter."

"What is it?"

"Horror. Working title's *Funhouse*."

Jared was going to kill her.

"Great title," Molly said.

SUCCESS

2001

3

MOLLY HADN'T BEEN TO SAN FRANCISCO IN YEARS, NOT SINCE the spring of '97, when she'd shot a commercial in a Sequoia grove just north of the city. That was her first real gig, and with the money she'd bought a new car, another first. As she waited in the security line to board the plane at LAX, she thought of the commercial, how she had to crouch on the roots of a Sequoia tree, smiling and sweating through eight consecutive T-shirts. She remembered the line like she remembered her own name. "*I need an antiperspirant that's tougher than nature.*" MaxWoman had been a terrible product. Since then, she'd advertised for far worse, but those commercials had only ever aired in Japan. It turned out the Japanese loved horror. They couldn't get enough of it. In every commercial, whether it was for noodles, or for kitchen cleaner, or for a home pregnancy test, she said her big line from *Funhouse*: "Time to die . . . clown face."

She was four hours early. The world had changed since last she'd flown. State troopers and Marines and what looked like private security guards were everywhere. There were an endless number of leashed dogs. She had never seen so many rifles or handguns. A feeling of tense closeness pervaded the country. Every room felt crowded with memory. The passage of time had been replaced with the voices on the television, with images of first the one plane, and then the other; of the buildings as they collapsed; of the crowds running through the streets, of the dust and the debris; the falling man;

the press conference. Over and over again, the anchors said "9/11" like they'd been saying it for years.

She moved forward in line, heading toward the small arches of the metal detectors. The thick, watery light of the day poured through the airport windows, illuminating the dust of the terminal so that the air looked smoky. More often than not, Molly took it for granted, but it was true: the light in Southern California was freakishly perfect. Years ago, during those first months in Los Angeles, she liked to drive on her days off—just drive. She'd go up and down the coastal highway, winding herself along Mulholland and through Topanga Canyon, thinking that the city, and her life in it, didn't seem real. It wasn't until she understood that it was the light doing this, the sunlight lying down upon everything with a plasma-like sheen, hazing and burning in a soft glow, that Molly was able to say to herself: "I live here. This is my home." She'd passed through that strange, certain knowledge that California is the woozy aftershock of a dream.

There was a woman a little ahead of her in line. She was not beautiful in any natural way, but attractive in terms of the Hollywood standard. Her blond hair and exercised body were of the type. Her short-shorts were pink. As the line moved forward, the woman kept looking back at Molly, her mouth forming something like a smile.

At first, she wasn't sure if she was evaluating the situation correctly. In a Walgreens once, buying paper towels, Molly smiled and said hello to an old man she thought was staring at her. "I thought you were somebody else," the old man said, before walking down the foot cream aisle.

A critically acclaimed independent movie, a minor supporting role, and some industry chatter about a rom-com whose release date had been pushed back to October, hadn't made her a celebrity. Hers was one of a thousand eerily familiar faces. If anything, people couldn't quite place her, but knew they remembered her from somewhere. High school? College? Who the hell was she?

For more than an hour, the woman kept turning around and looking at her. When Molly reached the front of the line, the detector went off—one long, high pitched beep—and a Marine told her, "Step to the right, miss." A female security guard patted her down: stomach, legs, and ankles. "Turn around." The guard ran her hands along Molly's hips and inner thighs. "You're good."

Molly found a metal bench, and went about the irritating process of putting her shoes, earrings, and belt back on. She looked up, and the blond woman was standing directly in front of her. The woman held her clutch bag in the crook of her arm. She nervously stroked it as if it were a small dog.

"Hi-ee."

"Hi," Molly said.

"Sor-ee," she said. "But I was just . . . *bleh, God.* I was just wondering."

She said nothing after this.

"Wondering what?"

"Were you in *The Matrix*?"

"What?" Molly said, shocked. "No."

"Oh, okay," the woman said, and walked away.

Later, Abigail said, "*The Matrix*? That movie came out like two years ago."

The two of them were in Abigail's car, driving out of SFO. South San Francisco looked like an old, broken dollhouse.

"Who were you supposed to be in *The Matrix*? That doesn't even make sense. Did she think you were Laurence Fishburne? You look nothing like Laurence Fishburne."

"That's not the point," Molly said. "The point is, she stopped talking to me afterward. I mean, I'm glad she did, but it was like, 'You weren't in *The Matrix*? Okay, by-ee.' Not another word. Like I didn't exist."

"You're in the pop imagination now," Abigail said. "You're haunting their vapid nightmares."

"Shut up."

"I'm serious," Abigail said. "You're floating around out there. You're not a person. Or you sort of are. Half of you is in limbo, or wherever. You know when somebody dies? It's like that. No one knows what to say. There's no frame of reference. It's this unspoken thing, and then all of the sudden it appears. That's what it's like to be a famous person. Expect awkwardness. Expect the weirdest, strangest shit."

"You're high," Molly said.

"That's true. That's what I am," Abigail said. "And you're an actress."

Molly was there to talk preproduction. In a month's time, Abigail was set to direct their third movie together. Their first, *Starcatcher*, had whiz-banged through a single Canadian film festival and was never heard from again. The second fared much better. Titled *Trust*, the film was set in New York City. Reviewers had called it a "dark independent comedy." In it, Molly played a struggling actress named Elle. She becomes the unknowing mistress of a married man. It is only after the man's death that Elle learns about his wife and family. She attends his funeral, and later the post-funeral luncheon at the family home. The wife, as it turns out, had known about the affair all along. "You're not a woman," she lectures Elle. "You're a girl. Go over there. Eat some cold cuts. Then leave."

Back in '98, handing the script over to Molly, Abigail had said, "Most of this shit happened to me."

Abigail was wild, a strange talker of nonsense with the unique ability to always hit upon, after awhile, the absolute truth. She was the person in Hollywood whom Molly most owed her career to. She was also a drug addict.

Raising the money for *Starcatcher* had felt like begging for change. Neither Molly nor Abigail were in any position to secure so much as a meeting, so for a year they "fundraised," which actually meant having dinners with the parents of their rich friends. In the end, they managed to raise *Starcatcher*'s minuscule budget. But then, like a girl abducted, Abigail vanished. She called Molly two weeks before the start of the shoot to say she was in rehab.

"For what?" Molly had asked.

"For all the coke I do," Abigail told her. "Duh."

Clean, Abigail kept *Starcatcher* under budget, and would later manage to sell the film rights to a Danish production company. They recouped all of their investors' money on *Starcatcher* (an eighty-minute movie about a heroin-addicted librarian), and the impossibility of this fact—that they'd somehow managed to break even with an unwieldy, poorly reviewed, mostly silent art film—caught the attention of real producers, who then wondered how much money they could make if Abigail wrote and directed something audiences would actually want to see.

Abigail lived a few blocks southwest of Chinatown. She parked her BMW in her private driveway, and the first thing the women did was take the elevator up five floors to the roof of her apartment.

Trust had made Abigail something close to a millionaire. Two purchased, yet unproduced screenplays had officially put her in the upper tax bracket. She'd left LA to become one of those San Francisco people, Molly thought, one of those people who never seem to do anything but who have a ton of money. When Bay Area people came down to LA, Molly never quite knew who she was talking to. She couldn't tell if Mr. Ponytail was a hippie or a dot-com billionaire. She didn't know if the nerd in the Polo worked for a think tank or Pixar. Molly had come to enjoy the transparency of Los Angeles. There at least people lied to you up front about what they claimed to do.

Four white hemp couches formed a loose square in the middle of the roof, and in the center was a black marble coffee table. Abigail said the floor was quadruple-reinforced bamboo. She went to the coffee table, pulled a joint from a porcelain jewelry box, and lit it. She pointed at the bay.

"Look."

Molly stared out across at the water.

"Alcatraz," Abigail said.

There it sat: the working lighthouse, the fenced-in buildings, the little white boats speeding by.

"I've never been," Molly said.

"There's a tour, but tours are for tourists."

Abigail coughed and coughed and coughed. When she was done, she said, "People up here take their weed very, very seriously. Everybody does now, I know. But honestly I'd never thought of it as a real drug until I moved north. And then I was like, 'Yeah, okay, I get it.' It's all about cross-breeding and mutations. The whole twenty-first century is. Nothing will ever be left alone anymore. Everything has to change constantly. Otherwise it's forgotten about and tossed aside."

One way or another, and because she was a writer, Abigail was always talking about herself. The two unproduced screenplays, both dramas, had combusted in development hell. Abigail had signed a two-picture deal with Hydrogen, a production company founded by Emily Roth and her brother, Leonard. The Roth siblings were notorious for their taste, charm, and pathological need for total control. Abigail had refused Hydrogen's rewrite suggestions on the grounds of artistic principle. "No one lives at the end of anything," she'd said in an interview with *Rolling Stone*. "Why should they in a movie? Why should the couple—who clearly don't belong together—get together? Why should I pervert my vision?"

"Your vision?" Leonard Roth had screamed at Abigail in their final meeting. "Your fucking vision?" Everywhere she went, Molly heard about the incident. For a few days it was all anyone could talk about. It started to feel as if she'd been in the room. "Here's your perverted vision: it's dead. You're dead. Fired. You want to know how badly I can pervert someone's 'vision'? I'm gonna turn your movie into a cartoon and make a hundred million dollars off it. And, just because I can, I'm gonna ruin you."

It wasn't an overt destruction campaign. Leonard let Abigail's downfall come about slowly—like the afterthought it was to him. At first, the Hollywood rumor mill only described her as difficult, temperamental, an auteur. Three months after that she was effectively blacklisted. Finally, no one spoke of her at all. She claimed to prefer it that way.

"I feel free up here," Abigail said to Molly. She closed one eye, and pointed at the island. "The prison's a nice little reminder."

It occurred to Molly, and not for the first time, that she might hate her friend. Ever since *Trust*, Molly had felt indebted to Abigail, but Abigail's career implosion had reflected poorly upon her. In meetings for the two studio roles she'd been up for, executives had asked her if, like her friend, she possessed an aversion to traditional publicity.

Leonard Roth hadn't been so direct. On the fourteenth of September, three days after his sister died while on board United Airlines Flight 175, Molly read for a part in a Hydrogen production called *The Human Variable*. Molly's agent, Irene Neidecker, had assumed the audition would be canceled. Molly was surprised to get a call that morning. Feeling the old fear, she drove to the Universal lot, and read to a room of distracted execs. Although he himself had insisted preproduction on *The Human Variable* continue as planned, Roth sat expressionless throughout her reading. When she was finished, the executives turned to him. Leonard's face was the worn-out color of a dry-erase board.

"I don't know," Roth said. "I don't know about you. I don't know about anything."

"I'm sorry," was all she could think to say.

Staring past her friend at Alcatraz, Molly watched the last of the cool morning air evaporate. Inside her purse, her cell phone rang.

"How many of those do you have?" Abigail asked.

"Phones?" Molly asked. "Three."

Digging through her purse, Molly kept her eyes on her friend. Abigail mumbled through the smoke curling around her face.

"They must be a-ringin' all the time," she said. "Just a-ringin', and a-ringin'."

Alone in the guest bedroom, she listened to her voicemail. "Hi, Molly," her assistant Diane said. "So . . . seventeen messages. I've emailed you a brief recap of each and the required contact info. Leonard Roth called eight times. Also Jared. He didn't seem to have your new number. I gave it to him, which I'm assuming is fine. Hope your trip is going well. I'll check in later."

Her agent, Irene, had told her from the start, "You show up to these things. You be yourself. End of story. I am the fame-whore-engine. I'm extra bad all year so I'll get coal for Christmas. But if you're one of those sluts who doesn't believe in compromise, who doesn't believe in lying, or smiling when you would rather die than smile, then don't get on the train." Irene was the sister of Cleo Neidecker, a casting agent who'd fallen into Hollywood-love with Molly, getting her into room after room, audition after audition. Because of these two women, Molly had started to happen. She'd landed the romantic comedy *Make It So*, her first big role. Based on that, she'd been given a part in the smaller, but more prestigious *Initiation*. Through her publicist, she managed to secure a three-page photo spread in *Vanity Fair* titled "Girl from the Future: Why in Six Months Everybody Will Know Who Molly Bit Is." By the time shooting on *Make It So* was supposed to begin, she was exhausted. What hadn't happened to her in the last year? The clearly drugged wife of a Sony executive had inquired if her tits were real. An Italian photographer had shouted, "Look more dirtier!" at her. She'd recorded and sent in eighteen audition tapes. She'd gone to a fundraiser for Children's Leukemia Research and spoken to the parents of children who had died from the disease. She'd held some of their hands, but could not divorce herself from the fact that her sympathy—which was real—was also false. Standing in a backless ballgown, Molly understood she wasn't there for these people. She was there for her. She was there to be seen.

On the eve of their second wedding anniversary, Jared had said to her, "You have a negative outlook on life."

"What? Why?"

"Can't you just enjoy it? It's a good thing," he said. "You're raising money. You're meeting people. You're doing great."

"I'm not raising anything," Molly said. "What money did I give?

All my money's tied up in this house. And I know it's a good thing. I know I'm meeting people. I'm not saying I'm not doing great. I'm just saying . . . it's weird."

"You think everything's weird."

"Everything is weird," she said.

They were in their house, her house, which was in Coldwater Canyon. The realtor had called it modest, but there were five extra rooms that Molly had no idea what to do with. Irene had suggested a screening room. "For when, you know, you wanna go to the movies." Molly didn't know who you called for something like that, and wrote it down on her "Questions for Diane" list.

"You think I don't appreciate this?" she asked him.

They were unpacking books in the large back room that overlooked the unfilled pool.

"I'm not saying that," he said.

"What are you saying, then?"

"I'm saying," Jared said, "you could get someone to unpack these books for you. If I were you, I'd enjoy what was happening to me a little more."

"The thing is, it's not happening to you."

As soon as she'd said it, she regretted it. Jared had been supportive. He'd listened. He'd sidled up to her at premieres. He'd stepped aside when the photogs asked. He'd gone over her lines, feigned a good attitude at his own abysmal career, attended the meetings she'd set up for him which had come to nothing. At events, he'd made chit-chat with the wives, the girlfriends, the other husbands. He'd done everything she'd asked him to do, and if what he felt toward her wasn't exactly resentment, it was then maybe something much worse: the refusal to acknowledge it.

"That's true," Jared said. "It isn't happening to me. You're right."

"I'm sorry," she said.

"For what?" he asked, and walked into the next room, like always. "What do you have to be sorry about?"

Unpacking her overnight bag in Abigail's guestroom, Molly felt terrible. She'd forgotten to give Jared her new phone number. He'd called her old number, hoping to say hello, or to let her know how the play rehearsals in New York were going, and had reached Diane instead. Jared's month had been harrowing, terrible, the sort of month he would speak of—or not—for the rest of his life. He'd arrived in New York on the ninth of September in order to begin rehearsals for an off-Broadway play called *Mr. Tomlin's Angry Daughter*. The first rehearsal had gone well . . . but then Tuesday. That Tuesday. The Tuesday.

"Where are you?" she'd asked him that afternoon.

"In a bar," he'd said. He was drunk. The world was out of the ordinary.

"I was freaking out. I couldn't get a hold of you."

"You were?" he'd said. "You were freaking out? You were?"

For a week and a half, rehearsals had been canceled. Instead, he'd gone to Ground Zero. He rode down in a school bus every morning. They gave him a mask, a bottle of water, and a red flag attached to an iron rod. He moved cement into dump trucks. He called out hello. Most of the steel he touched was still warm. Jared was a hero. What was she?

"I'm an asshole," she said into his voicemail. "I'm sorry. I forgot about my new number. It just happened. Things have been crazy. Call me."

Then she took a breath and tried Leonard Roth.

As expected, she got one of his assistants, Langdon, who Molly had never seen in person. He sounded nineteen.

"Hydrogen Productions."

"Hi, Langdon. It's Mol—"

"Oh, Molly. Thank God. Where are you?"

Roth's assistants always sounded as if they were being hung upside down over a cauldron of bubbling tar.

"He was slamming doors all morning when he couldn't get you on the phone. He screamed at the head of Warner Brothers. And he fired two people. This old guy started crying."

"Jesus."

"Where are you?"

"San Francisco."

"Fun," Langdon said. "But not fun. God, San Francisco?" Hydrogen's main office was in New York. "Okay. Let me figure this whole thing out."

Molly heard Langdon typing, and mumbling, "Cock sucking motherfucker" under his breath.

"Langdon?" Molly said. "Hello? Hello?"

"Still here, Molly," Langdon said. "Sorry. Sorry. It's just . . . It's just—"

"What's going on?"

"I don't know!" Langdon shouted. "All of the sudden this morning it was, 'Where's Molly Bit? If I don't get Molly Bit on the phone pretty soon, I'm going to start cutting people's heads off!'"

"Where is he?"

"I don't know!" Langdon shouted again. "He saw a screening of *Make It So* last night, came in here this morning, starting screaming about not being able to find you, and now he's gone. Can I call you right, right, right-right back? Is this your new number? I mean, like yours?"

Hydrogen had put up a small stake in *Make It So,* a few million dollars, some scant points on the gross as their return. It wasn't their kind of movie. They weren't exactly art house, but they weren't rom-com, either. They were movies like *Trust*, which they'd picked up at Sundance, reedited, and marketed the hell out of. *Make It So* promised to deliver what movies like it had always promised to deliver: the feel goods, the fairy tale, the unmitigated horseshit of a happy ending. "I know you want to make art, honey," Irene had said to her after the contract was signed. "But first you have to make money."

The script was like Nora Ephron minus the talent and nuance. On the page, Molly's character was your standard advertising ex-ecutive type-A blank. At first, this fact frightened her. The woman's name was Christine, and Molly hunted through the script for clues to her life. What had Christine's childhood been like? *Sweetly happy*. What about past boyfriends? *Affable*. What were her flaws? *A case of mild yet charming neurosis*.

Finally, Molly found a line that, with some imagination, was mildly interesting.

CHRISTINE
When I was a kid, I went to clown camp.

Like a big red nose, the line honked at Molly, taunted, and dared her. Molly played the character as if she was a warm-up performer at a Poconos resort in the 1950s, or a slightly deranged kindergarten teacher—anything other than an ad exec. Christine liked to toy with objects. She would turn a watercooler cup into a tiny house, wield a butter knife like a sword, knot her boyfriend's tie into a noose, and then laugh hysterically about it. After what should have been a scene's end, Molly would mumble miniature asides. ("Benefits to living alone: less concern over personal hygiene.") On set, she felt great about it. The crew loved it. The other actors loved it. The director, who'd cast her for this very reason—for her particular take on Christine—loved it.

But maybe everyone had been wrong.

She'd seen Leonard Roth on the *Make It So* set a few times, knew him of course from when Hydrogen had purchased *Trust*. They were "hello" people. They said "hi." In the role for *The Human Variable*, he'd cast Helen Wheeler, a more established actress. At first, Molly wanted to go to his Malibu home and throw a brick through his front window, but after a few weeks she'd stopped taking it personally. Business was business. Until they met again, Leonard Roth was finished with her.

So why the phone call? She reached the worst conclusion. Maybe Hydrogen had more money invested in *Make It So* than Molly first realized. Leonard had intended to broaden Hydrogen's product base with the movie, and now he was calling Molly to let her know she'd ruined his first foray into major market suburban mall cinema with her goofy ad-libs, and that her career was officially over.

Her phone buzzed. Area code 212. Hydrogen.

"Molly," Leonard Roth said. He sounded like a schoolboy. "How are you?"

His sister, Emily, had been the prominent one. Magnetic, unstoppable, she'd been the company face. Throughout her audition for *Human*, Molly noticed how Leonard seemed to be bobbing in his grief, the little brother, suddenly grown.

"I'm well," Molly said. Was she a "well" person now? "How are you?"

"Maybe you heard I threw a shit fit trying to get a hold of you, but now I feel much better," he said. "Much, much better."

She wanted to say something about his sister, at least acknowledge it, but there didn't seem to be room—or there had been, but it passed, sealed itself off.

"*Make It So*," Leonard said. "Have you seen it?"

She had, a rough cut. The movie was supposed to have been released in mid-September, but after the eleventh, all the schedules were in flux. The new opening was the first week of October.

"And have you talked to anyone over there at WB? Nick?"

Nick Perlman was the president of Warner Brothers. *Make It So* was a mostly WB production. She had not spoken to him.

"So that makes me the first," Leonard said.

"The first to what?"

"The first to congratulate you." Molly could feel him relax. It felt like the electric charge after a storm. "That seems appropriate. I think about *Trust* every day. You're part of the Hydrogen family. And family always gets first crack, right? First dibs. First congratulations."

"Depends on the family."

Leonard Roth's laugh was so practiced it sounded almost genuine.

"You're upset," he said. "About Helen. What can I say? I was under a tremendous amount of . . . you know. I still am. Mistakes were made. I'm sure you've heard about her. About what happened."

"Yes," Molly said, but she hadn't. Helen Wheeler was a good actress. A little bland, but a good actress. Molly had no idea what Leonard was talking about. "It's too bad."

"Yes, well, here's the thing, Molly. That's in part why I'm calling. *Make It So*—incredible. I couldn't take my eyes off you. Nobody could. I was at a screening last night in New Jersey. It tested"—he lit and exhaled the smoke from a cigarette—"high. But it's not about the numbers. It's about the quality of feeling that was in that theater. You know what I mean? The pulse."

Molly tried not to feel excited. She commanded it of herself.

"You're sure you haven't spoken to anybody at Warner Brothers?"

"No," Molly said.

"Good," Leonard said. "Good for us. So what I'm going to do, Molly, is get on a plane tomorrow morning—very early tomorrow morning—and come see you in San Francisco, if that's all right?"

He understood her silence as something.

"Obviously, with Helen's situation, we need to replace her. I'm interested in having a conversation."

Again, she lacked the words.

"Molly?"

"Shouldn't you be talking with Irene?"

Every time Leonard took a drag off his cigarette, Molly dreamt of the one she wasn't having.

"Come on," he said. "We both know you're not going to be at Neidecker much longer. I know that. You know that. I'm sure they know that."

She'd had one meeting at CAA. She had been assured it was private. She was only exploring her options. She wasn't even positive she—

"You're practically gone already, and that's good. It's a small pond over there. As I see it, you're currently without representation. Listen," Leonard said. "It doesn't have to be anything more than a hello."

He asked about Warner Brothers again.

"No."

"And where are you staying?"

"With Abigail Kupchik," Molly said.

"Right-right. How do you like that," Leonard said. "Good old Abby."

•

Abigail stared through a foggy eye at the alarm clock in her bedroom and did the math. She had been "napping" for three and a half hours. Her sheets and underwear were soaked in sweat. She was cold. The darkness of the room implied one a.m., but it was 5:30 in the afternoon. She heard Molly in the kitchen (was she doing the goddamn dishes?) and said quietly but out loud, "A fucking movie star."

Her head gonged. Today was the wrong day to get so drunk the night before that she'd forgotten where she'd stashed her Valium. Abigail tried to think it out logically. She must have come home last night and thought to herself: *I'm not doing any more Valium, my whole problem is Valium,* and then hid the rather (in the end, compared to everything else) harmless little pills somewhere. She definitely would not have flushed them down the toilet because even in her blacked-out state she would have known that, come tomorrow, she would want a Valium, and anxiously need to find them. If she hadn't been in such a hurry earlier, late for the airport and Molly Bit, none of this would be happening. In a way, it was all Molly's fault. There was too much time in between last night and this afternoon to remember where she'd put her pills. Abigail turned on the table lamp. She dug her hand inside her cluttered nightstand drawer and pulled out a loose Percocet. She blew on it once, twice, and swallowed that down instead.

She missed the good old days, when she was able to pretend that she wasn't a total fuck-up, but the time for that sort of denial had long since passed. Even in rehab (all three times) there was still a nagging part of her that whispered, *You don't really belong here, you're just having fun, you'll grow out of it.* Then time passed. She was twenty-nine years old now. She was not ancient, but she was beginning to resemble it: her face, her saddlebag hips, her tiny beer gut. Simple subtraction told her she'd been doing this to herself for fifteen years. There was no getting around it. She had a problem. Everything was the same as it had ever been.

Inexplicably, like a little present she'd left for herself, there was an unopened beer in the middle of the shower. It was a twist-off even. Drinking the warm beer as the cold water soaked her hair seemed necessary. It cleared her head. Life was putting together the fragments of memory and intent into some sort of appreciable order, into some sort of form, and then presenting that form to the world. You had to remember, Abigail remembered, why you were doing the things that you were doing, otherwise people sniffed out the fact that you were a total failure. Not everyone needed to know you were barely a person, especially not your soon-to-be-movie-star-friend washing dishes in the kitchen. It was her fault your shower was cold. The whole scenario made Abigail wonder: Who exactly were you narrating to when you narrated like this? Who was the audience for this type of voiceover? What sort of movie were you in? Comedy? Drama? Thriller? What was the mother-fucking genre?

She couldn't write—was absolutely unable, blocked—but her mind still worked that way, like a screenwriter's, because she was one, whether she produced a single word or not. The last script she'd written was *Echo Chamber*, all set to shoot in a month's time down in Los Angeles. Molly had been attached to star since before a single word had been written, and her name (Abigail would say it, "Molly Bit," as if she were sprinkling pixie dust on the small-time producers she was able to wrangle) was the only reason the movie was getting made at all. Without Molly, there was nothing. No movie. No career. No life. *Considering all of that*, the voiceover asked, *was it any wonder Abigail was annoyed with her?*

She finished her shower, made up her face, and found Molly in the living room, laid out on the couch, reading scripts.

"When was the last time you saw *Days of Heaven*?" Abigail asked.

It took her twenty-five minutes to find a parking spot, and, by the time she paralleled into a space just shy of a fire hydrant, the fog was back, particled and drifting through the air like slow-motion spit. At dusk, San Francisco grew cold, assumed the color blue. Walking into Foreign Cinema, the Percocet hit, and suddenly her eyes felt rubberized in some way. She'd slept with the host a few months back, and he greeted them immediately. Most of the Foreign Cinema staff were film people, or at least film buffs (some of them were Bay Area actors), and they all—down to the bus boy's turned head—recognized Molly, probably from *Initiation*, or maybe even *Trust*. It wasn't so long ago when they'd been impressed by Abigail too.

The handsome front waiter led them through the crowded restaurant out into the alley. The movie was being projected onto the wall of the adjacent building. Thanks to the space heaters, and Terrence Malick's color scheme, the outdoor dining room glowed. Brooke Adams and Sam Shepard were as tall as the three-story building to the right; their projected arms and torsos wavered like grass against the pocked gloss of the cement. There was no sound, but it didn't matter.

"A good tattoo would be of Sam Shepard's face," Abigail said.

This was an old game of theirs.

"Young Sam Shepard or old Sam Shepard?"

"It doesn't matter to me," Abigail said. "I would jump his dead bones."

"Where would you get it?" Molly asked.

"On my face."

"Like your whole face?"

"Yes," Abigail said. "Then my face would be Sam Shepard's face."

Molly gave a stranger across the room a closed-mouth smile.

"Or maybe you can get it on your neck," she said.

"Right," Abigail said. "Like a Latin King who went to the Actors Studio."

"Or on the inside of your bottom lip," Molly said.

"Totally," Abigail said. "So every time I made out with a guy it would be like I was making out with Sam Shepard, but only I would know."

Maybe it was the fact that they were only a half-day into the visit, but their patter felt forced, like an imitation of what it used to be. Abigail stared at Molly and could not see the girl she once knew. Molly was thinner. Her wrists and arms appeared more delicate. Someone on Beverly Drive was styling her hair now. She wore a sheer green top with a short collar, and a four-hundred-dollar pair of jeans.

When they'd first met, Abigail had seen herself in Molly Bit. *Trust* had been a love letter to the girl Abigail had once been. As Molly crossed her legs, and leaned confidently back in her chair, Abigail no longer saw the resemblance. When the waiter came with their first drinks, she asked him to go ahead and bring her another Stoli martini.

"To the future," she toasted.

"And the past."

"Tell me everything," Abigail said.

Her role in *Initiation* was small, but important. Molly had had four scenes in the movie, three of them with Harrison Ford.

"He spoke about you, you know?" Abigail said. "In *Interview*."

"I read that, yes," Molly said. "That was nice."

"What about the other guy? The young guy?"

"Jean Philippe?"

"Yeah, him—the sexy French guy who looks like Marlon Brando. Who do you think I mean? Did you? You know?"

"I'm married, Ab."

"Come on."

"No."

"You're missing out on all the perks! It's your God-given right to fuck your hot French costars," Abigail said. "How is Jer-Rod, any-way?"

"*Jared* is okay, thankfully. I mean, he's in New York. He was there."

Abigail listened to Molly's 9/11 story, but heard it as only that, a story, one of the hundreds she'd listened to in the last two weeks. Molly's was about a man named Jared, who was her husband. The scenario was that he was in New York to do a play. The subplot was that he resented and maybe hated his wife. The inciting event was 9/11. He goes down to Ground Zero and finds courage and self-worth among the rubble and destruction. Abigail would have to set the ending elsewhere, she knew, maybe jump ahead in time to when he's with his new wife, the one who's better suited for him. The last shot in a movie like that is always the ocean. The audience sees the man's back. There's a little kid running out to him maybe—or the new wife's pregnant. One or the other. Death is rebirth and all that shit.

Her second martini came. They ordered salads. The waiter lingered awhile, filling up their water glasses. Clearly, Abigail thought, he was now fully updated on who was at his table. In some ways, the film and theater scenes in San Francisco were more up to speed than in Los Angeles. Molly was an actress who was entering the mainstream from the cooler, more independent fringe. That sort of outsider status appealed to SF, a city eager to absorb the new thing a moment before it hit the wider culture, before whatever it was—a band, an actress, a writer—"sold out," a term Abigail herself now often used.

Molly smiled at someone again. Her full lips stretched across her teeth.

"Is that happening a lot?" Abigail asked.

"Is what happening?"

"Go fuck yourself."

"Yes," Molly said. "More often. Since the profile. Sometimes I'm wrong."

"Are you wrong now?"

"I don't think so," Molly said. "There's this mother-daughter over here."

"Should we tell the manager?"

"Ha-ha," Molly said. "You're funny."

"Who's joking?" Abigail asked.

There might have been sound to the movie after all, Abigail realized, only the restaurant was too loud for her to catch it. Her head went dizzy for a second, and then it felt as if her brain was wobbling inside her skull—or as if she had died, donated her body to science, and now her brain was inside a jar of formaldehyde, bobbing, bobbing, bobbing. Molly appeared to Abigail like someone beyond the glass.

She asked how Irene Neidecker was.

"She's fine," Molly said.

"Does she know I hate her?"

"She's aware. Although I don't quite get it."

"You 'don't quite get it'? Her agency dropped me. That's the same thing as her dropping me."

"She's been good to me," Molly said.

"Who isn't good to you?" Abigail asked. "I'm not talking about you."

There were times when the words that fell from her mouth surprised even her. The worst were cruelties shot out like dislodged pieces of corn. What could she do about that, though? I mean, seriously. What could she do besides shut up, and hope the person across from her hadn't noticed? Now it was her turn to watch the movie.

"Whatever happened to Brooke Adams?" Abigail asked. "Is she a cautionary tale, or just a regular person? Where's the waiter?"

Once upon a time, Abigail had been able to chart her drunkenness, mark her different moods like they were colors on a wheel. Nowadays, her mind resembled the industrial-grade espresso machine she owned and didn't know how to work. Steam would shoot out from here, water from there, grounds went all over the place, and it kept making a clanking sound while pouring out sludge. After *Echo Chamber*, Abigail knew she would never direct again. All of that was over. They couldn't stop her from writing, but what did that matter?

She understood everything now. Movies, Abigail thought, were only images, and maybe a little bit of sound, and they would go on being made with or without writers. Movies were dreams, and the dialogue in dreams was either nonsense or nonexistent, half-mumbled sentences blown out into the darkness and forgotten.

"Who needs a writer?" Abigail said. In her head, the machine started shaking violently.

Their salads came. They ordered entrées. Molly wanted to know what she'd meant.

"About *what*?"

"About not needing a writer."

"My mind's not right," Abigail said. "I don't want to get into an argument about the crap being made today in Hollywood. I hate people who say that. I'm a person who says that. It's pseudo-intellectual garbage. I'm full of that. I hate people who go to the movies and say how much they hate the movies. I hate people."

"I need writers," Molly said.

"You need a camera pointed at your face, is what you need. You need a camera pointed at your face like I need a gun pointed at mine."

Molly pretended that she didn't understand her.

"I want someone to shoot me, is what I'm saying," Abigail said.

She was getting very drunk, and it was almost fun, watching Molly's memory work. It was sort of like watching her act. Abigail knew about Molly's father, and her father's father (drunks were like biblical characters: malicious Phil begetting stoic John begetting violent Sam). Molly wasn't going to rush in and try to save her. Abigail admired the way her friend's face grew hard, like a cooled piece of glass.

"You're a mess," Molly said.

"You don't even know. I have to go to the bathroom."

At the bar, Abigail thought: Where had all the money gone? There was so much of it, and now it wasn't there, like someone had pulled a bank heist. The forty-five-hundred-dollar-a-month mortgage had seemed inconsequential a year and a half ago. Bragging, hadn't she used the phrase "drop in the bucket" when talking to her mother? On what planet was fifty-four thousand dollars a year a "drop in the bucket"? She'd had to put up nearly as much to take the apartment off the market. Still, that left hundreds of thousands . . . but then there were the taxes, and the BMW, and her student loans, and her mother's chemo treatment, and the twenty-eight-day rehab at Hazelden for her brother, Paul, who had disappeared off the face of the Earth since then, and who was maybe—and just as well should be—dead. And then her own drugs, which were expensive, don't ya know, in the same way her Aunt Bernice might complain about the price of milk.

After all of that, after the million, Abigail had two thousand dollars in the bank, and nothing that anyone in the entire city of San Francisco could possibly refer to as a source of income. She loathed thinking about it. It was all so self-pitying, so hopeless. And it was all Leonard Roth's fault.

Those rewrites would have made her into something that she wasn't: a pusher of middle-of-the-road tripe, tugging on the heartstrings of suburbia. Her head swelled with the idea.

"I made the mistake all women make," she told the bartender. "I opened my mouth."

Abigail went to the bathroom. The vodka and Percocet ripped through her bloodstream. In the stall, she took from her purse a little bag of coke. She tapped some out onto her maxed-out Amex, and, snorting, tried to regain the focus a person needed to get from one room to the next.

"Good luck with that, sister," she said to herself.

Echo Chamber would put everything back together. All she'd said and done, all the bad will sown by Leonard—gone. Abigail had given Molly an opportunity she never would have had on her own, and it was time to be repaid.

Back at the table, the waiter was talking with Molly. Abigail looked up at his polite, gaunt face, and the blond fuzz on his cheeks triggered her hatred of the world.

"Get out of here, starfucker," Abigail said, as she took her seat. She looked down. There was her fish, head and tail. He'd been serving them.

"*Abby*—"

"*Molly*—" Abigail mimicked.

"Thank you." Molly smiled at the waiter.

"Right, right," Abigail said. "You have to be polite now. You're a celebrity."

"I'm not a celebrity," Molly said.

"You are," Abigail said. "You just don't know it yet. They don't even know it yet."

For reasons that were unclear, the waiter was still standing next to their table.

"*Hel*-lo," Abigail said. She shook her empty martini glass. "More drinky, please."

The waiter laughed as he walked away. His disdain for her was the one thing Abigail liked about him. She gave him a little clap.

Abigail watched her friend. Taking small bites, Molly looked out across the dining room. Counting the hours spent editing *Starcatcher* and *Trust*, the dailies from those films, being on set, the rehearsals, the meetings, the acting classes, and the time they'd spent together as friends, Abigail had probably stared at Molly's face for ten thousand hours. She knew it in some ways better than her own.

"You've become disturbed," Molly said.

"I've always been disturbed."

"This is something different."

"I've advanced."

A busboy appeared. He set Abigail's martini down on the table.

"See? If I wasn't with you, there is no way in hell I would have gotten this drink."

"I think your perception is off," Molly said.

"No," Abigail said. "I may be drunk, and on all sorts of drugs, but my perception is not off. Seriously, Molly. French costars, being a bitch whenever you want—you should start enjoying the perks."

Abigail drank her martini. In the end, she realized, what set Molly's face apart was how well she thought with it. She emoted full sentences from out of the bones in her face.

"Two weeks from today, millions of people are going to sit in the dark and look at you. You acted with Harrison Ford. You shot a movie in Paris. Those are perks."

Abigail pulled the olive from her empty glass and placed it in her mouth.

"Enjoy it while it lasts," she said, chewing. "Before they take it from you."

Molly carefully wiped each corner of her mouth with her napkin. She clicked the rage on.

"I don't want to hear about Leonard Roth again."

"You don't understand," Abigail said. "My life is impossible."

"There's a reason for that," Molly said.

Yes, Abigail thought, it was definitely Molly's face. It was a wonderful mask. It said everything. For instance, the muscles as they went taut and then eased along Molly's jawline told Abigail that her friend was done with her. She turned away. She noticed *Days of Heaven* had started again from the beginning. Richard Gere was on top of a train, riding through the middle of the land.

Molly watched too. "I know this movie by heart," she said. "This is the part where the little girl says, '*I met this guy named Ding Dong. He told me the whole world is going up in flames.*'"

The next morning, Molly dabbed and smoothed her face with concealer. Done with that, she sat down on the edge of the bathtub and rubbed her bicep. Her right arm was sore from all the dragging, and holding, and keeping Abigail upright the night before. Inside her skull, her brain felt swollen. It was a contact-hangover. She felt panicked and nervous, as if Abigail's fate were contagious.

One good thing was that she wouldn't have to make up an excuse about where she was going that morning. Through the wall, Molly heard Abigail snore. The choking honks were wet and arrhythmic, somehow mechanical. She wondered who could possibly stand such a sound? She imagined Abigail's one-night stands, still drunk men tip-toeing through the reverb, making their way out into the safety of dawn, never to be seen again.

Molly did not miss that kind of sex. As she stepped into Abigail's elevator, she thought of Jared. Nearly against her will, she daydreamed of his body up against hers, of his hips slowly rolling against her own. She wanted him to make her head knock against the wall—to have it hurt a little. Afterward, in the fantasy, they lay in bed for ten minutes, and then they went into the kitchen and drank orange juice from tiny glasses.

She stepped out of Abigail's building. San Francisco smelled of salt and urine. She'd called Irene the night before, waking the older woman out of a deep sleep. "Make sure he's there first, honey. He should be waiting on you," Irene had said, and then, to the fact it might be their last professional exchange, "Don't worry your pretty little head about it."

Wearing a green Donna Karan blouse and a high-waisted, tan linen skirt that flowed around her knees, she hailed a cab on Columbus. Five minutes later, she stepped out of the cab onto Market Street and walked into the Four Seasons.

The foyer was old school, with drapes on the walls, and carpeting. The angles that otherwise defined San Francisco, the gleaming edges that seemed to tip the whole city toward the future, were absent here. It was eleven o'clock in the morning, and the patrons were mostly old white ladies. A few men of similar age were among them. Aside from Molly, Leonard Roth was the only other person under fifty in the restaurant. He was a short man, with a body like an oil furnace.

He stood up to hug her.

"It's good to see you, Molly. You look beautiful, as always."

One of the things Abigail had mumbled to her last night as Molly dumped her into the passenger seat was, "Don't you just hate it when men tell you what you want to hear? It makes me feel so average."

"Good to see you too," Molly said.

To herself, she sounded strange, a little robotic, but it was a tactic she had learned to employ in order to get through those first few minutes, even hours, with the sorts of people she was dealing with now. When she was first introduced to Harrison, it was the only time in Molly's life where she felt as if she might actually pass out. Telling the story to Abigail, she'd played it cool, but the truth was, shaking his hand in the Eighth Arrondissement, she'd started to have an out-of-body experience. Not only did she feel as if she didn't belong on set with him, but wondered—and not for the first time—if this was what she wanted at all? She was slipping through a membrane, entering into a relationship with the world that afterward could not be reversed.

Leonard Roth wasn't Harrison Ford, but he was still Leonard Roth. She knew why he was there: to give her everything she ever wanted. It terrified her.

"Can I confess something?" Leonard asked. They were seated. He drank a cup of black coffee. "I kind of hate San Francisco. It's cold. I'm always cold here. And the people are ridiculous. I was in the car coming over, and my driver almost sideswiped this guy on a bike. You know what the guy on the bike yells? '*Please, be more mind-ful!*' What is that about? And you can't smoke here. That's the first sign of fascism, you know. Hitler hated smoking."

"You can smoke here," Molly said. Saying it, she felt like she'd wasted her turn. It wasn't exactly a conversation she was engaged in.

"Where? Outside? It's too cold outside," Leonard said. "Did you fly here?

"Yes, I—"

"They're gonna take away everything. You just wait. First, it's you can't smoke. Then it's you can't travel. Then you can't communicate. And last you can't think. Listen, I want to kill this Osama bin Laden with my bare hands. I would love it. I would relish it—tear his arms and legs off and watch the blood spray. I am full of a murderous rage that contaminates my life in a way I could never explain to you, or to anyone. But do you know how I got to where I am today, Molly?"

"How?"

"By not being a short-sighted asshole. Don't get me wrong. I'm an asshole, but I've got vision. Just like your friend Abigail."

Men saw what they wanted in you. This was especially true of powerful men, who spent most of their time imagining scenarios and then watching those scenarios become realities, so that the difference between their private desires and the world was almost negligible. As soon as a powerful man had an idea in his head, he expected it to be. Her life in Hollywood, Molly knew, would be easier to navigate if she were an idiot, some sort of hollow-eyed vessel. That was why the town was filled with girls who had IQs that peaked at 70. A girl that dumb was easy to make into something else. The powerful man said, "You're like this. This is you," and she said, "Okay-ee." The old adage was wrong. The world wasn't harder if you were a woman.

The world was harder if you were a woman with a brain. A brain was friction, and that kind of friction wasn't the sort of friction that a powerful man, or maybe any man, wanted.

Leonard didn't say anything. The microphone was apparently hers.

"I'm sorry about your sister."

"Thank you. That's nice of you to say. I appreciate that," Leonard said. "It hasn't quite hit me yet. It comes and goes. It came on there for a second. Now it's gone. I won't apologize for that. I'm physically incapable of apologizing."

From across the room, a copper-skinned waitress came to take their drink orders. Directed at Leonard, her face held in it the dull recognition of fame.

"More coffee," Leonard said. "And I'd like an ashtray."

The girl was beautiful. Molly could imagine the tips. Was she Brazilian? Argentinean? Chilean?

"You can't smoke in here, sir. I'm sorry," the waitress said.

"Okay, then. You're sorry. Everybody's sorry. The whole world's sorry."

The waitress paced back to the host stand.

"I assume you've spoken to Nick by now," Leonard said.

Earlier that morning, Molly had had a very brief conversation with Nick Perlman.

"And what did he say? That he was just pleased as fucking punch with your performance and wanted to do business with you again? Only Nick needed to wait on the box office, right? He didn't say that exactly, but you knew what he meant. Did he remind you of Warners' history? Did he use the word 'storied'?"

It was almost word for word. Perlman, like Roth, was a talker, although he lacked Leonard's charm, the boyish street-corner bluster that made his arrogance palatable, entertaining. Perlman was like the father of one of Molly's high school girlfriends. He had spoken to her as if she were fifteen, stressing cautious optimism, patience. Molly needed to think about her future, Perlman kept saying. She needed to make intelligent choices that would ensure optimum returns. "You're in the big leagues now," he'd actually said. Had Perlman finished the phone call by reminding her to wear her seatbelt, she wouldn't have been surprised.

"There's nothing like being congratulated for the work other people have 'allowed' you to do, is there?" Leonard said. " 'Allow us to say you're welcome for all the difficulty you've encountered. Be patient with us while we don't pay you enough and fuck you over.' I never could have worked at a studio. Thank God for Emily. At a studio, I would have pulled a *Temple of Doom*. I would have ripped hearts out. And the young guys—all respect to Nick—don't know anything about film. I mentioned Fellini once to Nick Perlman and he thought I was talking about pasta. Shouldn't you know a thing or two about history if you're going to hang it over the talent's head?"

Leonard pulled a pack of cigarettes out of his jacket pocket and set them on the table, his lighter on top.

"Listen, Molly. *Make It So* is going to do well. It's going to pull in numbers next weekend. That's the popular vote. And then some fucking fucknut who thinks he's the next Ebert is going to write a piece about your choices, about how brilliant you are, and so the very small percentage of people who give a shit about that sort of thing in this country are going to love you. On the level now, Molly? All bullshitting aside? None of that is going to mean a thing to Nick—in terms of you as a performer. He'll say it does. They'll run an ad in *Variety*. He'll get six of his producers to send scripts. You'll be up to your eyeballs in meetings. And that's just Warners. It'll be everybody. Every fucking studio in town. But those meetings will be to pitch *Make It So* II, III, IV, V, fucking piss-poor copies of lightning in a bottle. That's what it'll mean to Nick and to everybody like Nick— which is all of them. It'll mean, 'Here's a product I've got. How do I market it?' They have no understanding of history. They don't understand talent, or how to take care of it. They don't get the magic."

Molly didn't need Leonard Roth to tell her that she was in a rare and enviable position. She didn't need him to say anything. The fact that he was there meant she didn't need him.

"Did he mention specifics to you?" Leonard asked. "Did he talk dates?"

"No."

"Really?" Leonard said. "Interesting."

He picked up his cigarette and flicked the filter with his thumbnail.

"Sorry to hear about Helen," Molly said.

"Why? I'm not."

"Her back? It's broken?"

"Fractured two vertebrae," Leonard said. "It's fine. She'll walk again. The lesson here is: famous people shouldn't ski."

"She won't be ready by February?"

Leonard lit his cigarette and inhaled. Molly couldn't believe it. It was as if she expected the police to come banging through the dining room, or for the old ladies to stand up from their seats and athletically pounce upon him. But no one did anything. Not the waitress at the host stand, nor the short manager wearing glasses beside her. No one. Leonard had gone ahead and tested the rule, and he'd been right: it didn't apply to him.

"February?" he asked. "The shoot's in three weeks, Bit. Twenty days, actually. We've taken advantage of a timid job market. It's why I'm here."

Molly's brain clicked into place. Knowing that the shoot would start in three weeks made Leonard's California trip understandable. It wasn't that Molly was his one and only, his dream girl. The forces that blew her life in one direction or another suddenly revealed themselves to be more practical. Leonard had walked out of that screener for *Make It So* and asked himself three questions. 1) How much do I want her? 2) How much would she cost? 3) Would she dump the other movie?

"But you've got this Abigail thing, is that right?"

"Yes," Molly said. She lifted her purse from off the floor. She unzipped it, and reached inside for her cigarettes. "She's my friend."

"Is she?" Leonard asked. "Is that woman capable of having friends? Is she an actual human being? I don't think so. I think she's a drug addict, and, all respect to drug addicts, they aren't people."

"What are they?"

"Needy," he said. "Manipulative. Full of shit where their hearts should be."

"Sounds like a person to me," Molly said.

"No one would blame you," Leonard said. "It would make sense."

Molly lit her cigarette and moved a bread plate into the middle of the table. Drawing, she didn't have a chance to respond. She wasn't deliberately stalling, but Leonard was used to immediacy, to things happening *right now*—or yesterday. Perhaps a second had passed.

"You're right," Leonard said. "This is a conversation. I said we would have a conversation."

Two cigarettes seemed to be the limit. The manager approached, a short man in dark chunky glasses with a certain delicate wobble to his voice.

"I'm sorry," he said. "This is just—we can't have this."

"Can't have what?" Leonard asked. "What can't you have?"

"The smoking, Mr. Roth. I'm sorry. And you," he turned a kind smile on Molly. "Hi. You're wonderful. I loved *Trust*."

"Isn't she amazing?" Leonard said. "Isn't she the best?"

"She is."

"Thank you," Molly said, putting out her cigarette. "I'm sorry."

"What are you doing?" Leonard asked her. He turned his face toward the manager. "I paid thirty-eight dollars for a BLT that still hasn't come yet, and you're telling me I can't smoke? What is it with this city? Why is it so afraid of death? It's gonna come for you. It's gonna come out of the sky one day, and take you, and swoop you up to heaven with a bunch of virgins. Tell me those guys aren't disappointed. Who wants to sleep with a virgin? It's like fucking a hole in the ground."

"I'm sorry," Molly said to the manager.

"It's the law, is the thing. If it was up to me—"

"What's San Francisco's heaven like?" Leonard asked. "Is it just like San Francisco? That would be the worst. Is it fifteen assholes in beanbag chairs writing code? Why the fuck are people dying in planes that crash into buildings, and you're telling me I can't smoke? Who the fuck are you?"

"I just work here," the manager said.

"That's a Nazi answer," Leonard said, suddenly out of breath. He put out his cigarette. "Do you see what I mean?" he asked Molly. "It's a moral lockdown."

"Thank you," the manager said. He snatched up the ash-covered bread plate, and walked away.

As if for the first time, Molly looked at Leonard. He was in pain. The skin on his face was loose with anger, as if his body had tried to pull away from his bones.

"My sister is why you had the audition," he said, staring back at her. "It wasn't because you were in the movie with Harrison. Emily remembered you from that horror movie, that *Funhouse*. She had a Rolodex in her head of untapped talent, and you were at the front."

"I only met her once," Molly said.

"She was a force. You would have liked her. If it weren't for her, I'd be selling cars. She kept saying, 'Get her in for an audition. I'm telling you. Get her in. I'm telling you. That's the one.' What do you want me to say? I had a moment of weakness with Helen Wheeler. I was in shock. She was what I thought I needed. Her reliability turned me on. Her competence. I'm glad she broke her back."

"That's a terrible thing to say," she said.

Some smoke lingered in the air. Molly blew it off with a wave of her hand.

"Maybe," Leonard said. "But I've been in the mood for truth lately. It's my new thing. All truth, all the time."

"Is that so?"

"It is."

"Answer me something then."

"Say it."

"Do you want me for the part, or am I the only one you think you can get?"

It had been a long time, maybe even years, since someone had asked Leonard Roth a specific question related to intent. She could see it on his surprised face, in the way his skin tightened around his mouth and eyes. Molly could tell he wanted to come back at her— *Temple of Doom* her—but her other gut feeling, that she was becoming something other than what she was, registered with him too.

"Both," he said. "The answer to that question would have to be both."

He took another cigarette from the pack and slipped it between his lips. He was a wonderful smoker. He looked beautiful with a clean, unlit cigarette dangling from his mouth.

"I'm gonna to talk for a while," Leonard said. "I wanna tell you a story, so don't interrupt me. Okay? The story goes like this . . . I grew up in the middle of nowhere. Gray winter sky, people who don't talk too much, no culture, right? I didn't go to a concert until I was twenty, and what about you? I think you know what I'm talking about. We grew up with a loneliness that doesn't exist anymore. These kids with their internet are going to grow up and feel loneliness for the first time and they're gonna wanna kill themselves. My parents worked all the time. I hardly saw them. I had three things: TV, books, and the movies. You with me? You following? I was a fat kid with bad skin, and no friends, and the only reason I knew about those things—the books, the movies—was because of my sister, cuz she said, 'Hey, Len. Look at this. What do you think of that? Isn't that cool?' She had a natural love and curiosity for art. It was inexplicable. There was no genetic reason for this. It infected me. She read everything. Saw everything. I've got nothing without her. Absolutely nothing. Then she dies. She gets blown apart by jet fuel and metal and fire and, every time I see a television, or hear anyone speak, or think a thought, she dies again. So now let me explain something to you. Emily told me about *Make It So*. She told me I should see it, that you were the girl. I'd seen you in *Trust*, but honestly I'd thought 'dime a dozen.' Emily knew who you were, but I didn't listen. Helen Wheeler's boring ass plows into a pine tree, and later that day I get an email: 'Come to this screener in New Jersey,' and I go. I go even though I never go to New Jersey. Never. And when I get there, the theater is packed—it's like everybody forgot about the movies and then all at once they remembered. It's like I forgot about them too. Like I forgot about my life. About what made it. If I don't go to the movies, I know something is wrong with me. It means I'm depressed. I knew that, but I didn't realize I'd forgotten I was alive. It's you on the screen. That's part of it, and you're part of the reason why I felt alive for the first time in a month, but it was more than that. Do you know what it was? Do you?"

"What?"

"It was my sister talking to me. I don't care if you don't believe me, or if nobody does, and maybe you're the only person I'll ever tell, but it felt like my sister was the dark, and that my sister was the projection light, and that she was the seats, and the popcorn smell, and all the other people in the theater. You know the pulse when the houselights go down? It kind of sucks you into the dark? It's like heroin—you ever done heroin? It's the best feeling in the world. It's like that. It's like getting junk shot into your eye. That's when it started, and it didn't stop for two hours, like the air was charged with her, with her ghost or spirit, or whatever the fuck you want to call it, kind of talking without talking, like a big bubble of light and dark swirling around and in and out of itself and going bam-bam-bam-bam-bam on their faces. It was a spiritual moment that I will not apologize for, and do you know what my sister said to me? What she said to me without saying it, because she can't?"

Molly didn't.

"She said, 'Get her, Len. She's the real deal. Don't let her say no. She's the whole shebang.'"

Leonard was right: it was always cold in San Francisco. Standing out in front of the hotel, Molly wished for a sweater, or some sort of shawl—black, simple. She walked north into Union Square, found Neiman's, took the escalator up to the second floor, and bought the first thing that caught her eye. It cost three hundred dollars, and wasn't it a simple pleasure, declining the receipt? She found a coffee shop on the square, ordered a cappuccino, and sat down in a chair by the sun-beat window to call Jared.

"Hi," he said, flatly.

In the background, Molly heard the repetitive crack of hammer blows.

"Hel—loo," she said, dragging out the sound, hoping to break him early. "How are things?"

"Fine," he said.

"What is that?" she asked.

"I don't know. I'm out on the street. Something's always pounding into something else in this city. You don't notice it after awhile. The building across from my hotel caught on fire last night."

"Jesus," she said. "Was anyone hurt?"

"Yes," he said. "Of course. It was a fire."

Molly took a sip of her cappuccino. It was the best fucking cappuccino she'd ever had in her entire life.

"Maybe you miss sleeping next to me," she said.

"Maybe."

"I'm sorry. Okay? Don't be mad at me. I've got news."

"I think I'm calling you, and I get Diane."

"I know."

"It was embarrassing."

"I'm sorry."

"Don't you think that's telling?"

"Of what?"

"What do you think?" Jared said. "Hold on."

An ambulance or a fire truck sirened past Jared loud enough that Molly had to move her phone away from her ear. She wanted to end the phone call. She could pretend later that her service had been bad.

"Hello?"

"I'm here," she said. "I want to tell you something."

"I don't know."

"You don't know about what?"

"Nothing," Jared said. "What is it? What's the big news?"

"*The Human Variable*. I got the part."

He was confused, and she explained it to him: Roth, Helen Wheeler, the dead sister who was a movie theater. She explained the catch to him as well, the new shoot date, how it would probably hurt Abigail's feelings.

"Hurt her feelings?" Jared said. "It'll destroy her. I mean actually."

"We'll reschedule," Molly said.

"Reschedule? That girl's barely hanging on," Jared said. "There is no way she'll keep it together another three months. I hate her fucking guts, but I don't want her to be homeless."

"She won't be homeless," Molly said.

"Come on. No you, no movie," Jared said. "What about the crew? You know half of them."

That was true. She and Jared had babysat for the director of photography last year. But that was before everything. Back when there'd been time.

"Why are you pretending to not understand this?" Jared asked.

"Why are you pretending to not understand *this*?" Molly asked. "You read the *Human* script. You know how good it is. I'm perfect for it. And Hydrogen does a major awards push. I could get nominated."

"For an Oscar?"

"Not for an Oscar. I'm not saying that," Molly said. "But a Globe maybe."

From behind the front counter at the other end of the coffee shop, the barista was staring at her.

"Is this about the phone? Is that what this is about? I said I was sorry."

"Oh, fuck you," Jared said, and hung up.

Molly wanted to say it as soon as she got back, but Abigail was still asleep—or her door was closed, at least. Molly heard the house phone ring, and either the person on the other end had hung up, or Abigail had answered in a whisper that Molly couldn't hear. She wanted to tell Abigail when her door opened, but then the shower came on. She wanted to say it when Abigail approached her in the living room, but talk of food intervened. Finally, the time to tell had passed, or so it seemed, and she decided to wait. The moment would present itself eventually, and then she would say it.

They chose the new Mexican place.

Walking in the neon dark of the neighborhood, Molly felt alive again. It was a moneyed street, and chic. In the elaborate facial hair designs of the men, and in the short little boots of the women, Molly saw the excesses of fine arts degrees. It seemed to her that every stranger they passed glanced her way. She was not being paranoid. These people had the time and the money to go to the movies. They knew who she was. Hers was the ambition they whispered about. Molly had spent years wondering what it—fame, or the first creakings of the machinery of it—would be like, and the answer was simple: it was fantastic. It felt like something you wanted to hold onto.

Abigail ordered a Corona, and when it came she said, "Please, a toast. To being the worst hostess of my generation."

Molly raised her glass to that.

In the slightly green light of the Mexican restaurant, Abigail looked as ill as she claimed to be. Her left eye twitched, and her lips were thin and purple, like worms. The night was good, though,

Molly felt, one of those early fall evenings when the air seems to get warmer in the city as the sun goes down.

"Where'd you go this morning?" Abigail asked.

"Down to Union Square."

"For what?"

"To shop a little," Molly said. "Move around."

"That sounds nice. That sounds like just the thing."

Abigail finished one beer and then drank another. The color in her face balanced, went from splotchy to a low throb of even red. Before Molly could stop her, she started in on the preproduction talk. She said that all the locations, but for two, were secured. Molly would have to meet with the set designer next week, and there was a conference call on Thursday they'd both have to be in on. They needed to make a casting decision on the last two supporting roles. Did Molly have any idea about who she might want for that? There was still the matter of the third act to think on, because that version certainly wasn't going to cut it. Did she and James want to rehearse at all—or just get in there, and do it? How were they going to find the money for the crane shot on the bridge in Pasadena? Abigail had an idea. Molly might not like it, but Abigail wanted Molly to hear her out, let it sink in, take effect.

"Why don't you just ask Leonard Roth for the money? Since you're friends now. Since you eat lunch with him in my city and lie to me about it."

Molly didn't say a word. She wanted Abigail to disappear, to cease to exist entirely.

"I know the manager. Short little gay guy? Glasses? Him."

"Okay," Molly said, in that curt way people do, as if the evidence brought against them remains insufficient for indictment.

"Are you doing a movie with him?"

"Yes," Molly said.

"When?"

She looked down at the table. There was a cartoon donkey with protruding front teeth. The teeth were almost horizontal. Squiggled lines of laughter blew out between the top and bottom rows.

"When?" Abigail asked again.

"Three weeks," Molly said. "Less than."

"You cocksucker."

"It's a matter of recasting," Molly said. "There are other actresses."

"*There are other actresses.*"

"There are."

"This is the story you're telling?" Abigail asked. She wore the sad, confused face of the sold-out bad guy in the movie—the one who goes in for the hug, but gets a knife in the gut.

"It's not a story."

"It is. You're telling yourself a lie, and you want me to believe it. You're deluded."

"Me?" Molly asked. "You're not even here. You're out of your fucking mind."

"Do I need to say that you are the movie? That you're everything?" Abigail asked. "Is that the kind of shit you need to hear now? Is that what this is? Fine. Fine. You're a gift to the world, Molly. Please, oh please, be in my movie. I'm nothing compared to you."

"You can reschedule," Molly said. "I'm still co-executive. You should be happy for me. Why aren't you understanding this?"

"Because you're ruining my life."

"You can't blame me for that," Molly said. "You're doing a fine job of that on your own."

Abigail let out a small, creepy laugh. She hopped up and went to the bathroom. Like a mind reader, the waitress brought over the bill. The waitress stood and waited as Molly placed her credit card down inside the black plastic tray, and then she stepped back to run it through the machine. The whole process took no more than a minute, but Molly sat there for another five. Finally, she went outside, and lit a cigarette. There was some metal and plywood construction scaffolding attached to the front of the building, and Molly was glad for the cover. The night had turned to fog. A steel bar ran horizontal between two posts. Molly put her elbows on it, and looked out into the street. In her body there was something like sympathy—there was the feeling of it, like heat—but her mind pressed down upon it with the weight of a promise she'd long ago made to herself. She had set out to do something, and she was going to do it. She breathed in the Pacific air. She smoked.

Abigail came out of the restaurant, her eyes like two eight-balls.

"*You're out*," she said. "I'll get another actress by tomorrow, and then I'll shake off all the absolute shit you've put on me over the years. But I want you to know something. You think that you've done this for your career. You think you've done this because it's business. It isn't business. It's personal. Everything is personal. Movies are. I am. I'm a wreck, but I'm personal. You used to be. But not anymore. What are you going to be if you aren't personal? What will that even look like?"

Abigail stared Molly down.

"Give me a cigarette."

Molly handed her one.

"I need a lighter."

Molly handed her that too.

Abigail put her hands on the cross bar, and jumped up onto it. She twisted in the air, so that her back was to the street. Using both hands, she went to light the cigarette. Molly saw the whole thing coming. Abigail said, "Uh, oh"—her balance was gone—and then she went backward down off the cross bar four feet until her head cracked against the greasy road.

Because all Molly ever did was watch movies and television, and because she spent most of her time with other Hollywood types who, like her, confused the manic pulse of drama with the feeling of life, she thought Abigail was dead. She quickly fantasized about the morgue, the police inquiry, the Minnesota funeral home. But Abigail wasn't dead. There was only a lot of blood. It poured out of Abigail's head like wine. The kitchen guys knew what to do. They were even casual about it. Towel to the back of the head. Phone call. Didn't otherwise touch Abigail.

The ambulance started and stopped, and then weaved south. Molly sat beside the EMTs in the boxy deadlight.

"Six staples."

"Five."

"Six. Possible hematoma."

"No way. Five and nothing. Maybe a concussion."

"You look familiar to me," the one said to Molly. "I'm telling you six. Maybe seven."

It took nine. The waiting area at SF General was not exactly clean. Around midnight, they let Molly into Abigail's room.

"I'm not allowed to sleep," Abigail said. She sat up in bed eating applesauce out of a plastic cup. Whatever fluids they were pumping into her arm had her looking almost human. "I have a level-three concussion. If I sleep, I die."

After that, Abigail refused to say a single word. Molly took a seat. They seethed there for two hours watching television until a nurse came in and did some bloodwork. She was a black woman in her late forties, pretty and exhausted. She looked at Molly.

"Am I supposed to recognize you?" she asked. "Is that what this is?"

Through the booming sound of infomercials (Abigail kept turning the volume up on the TV), Molly read tabloids until she was bored and soul sick. There was a picture of Leonard in *US*. In it, he wore the same button-down shirt he'd worn to lunch with her. The tagline under the blurry photograph was "Leonard's Grief." He was smoking a cigarette in front of a restaurant in Manhattan. She didn't bother to read the article, but it shouted at her anyway. All the important words were capitalized and in bold. SADNESS. VICTIM. TERROR. PLANE.

At four in the morning, Molly wandered the halls and found an empty conference room. She stretched out across a couch, but soon a janitor arrived. He ran a feather duster over the blinds, waking Molly from a dream that, as soon as she reached for it, escaped her. The man was formless in the dark, like she'd made him up, and it took a blink or two, a drowning moment, for her to realize he was saying, "I know who you are."

VENICE

2006

4

THE BODYGUARD WAS VERY HANDSOME. OUT OF BOREDOM MORE than anything, during the long prep hours in Venice before the media offensive, Molly would fantasize about having sex with him. Not actual sex, but the pre-sex stuff of dreams. She would talk with Zen near a window and let his arm rub against hers as they looked down into the Statue-of-Liberty-colored water. They would say various things. It was a mood situation, a movie sort of flirting. Eventually, the two of them would pull back into the palazzo. She would ask him about Switzerland, where he was from, and wonder out loud if that was his real name? After he said no, Molly would undo his belt, and then it was back to reality, if you could call her life that.

"Zen!"

He was reading *The Bonfire of the Vanities*, which he'd found under her bed during his first security sweep. It was the same taupe hardcover copy her father owned. Molly knew exactly where it was on John's bookshelf back in Vermont. Zen sat in an oak dining chair positioned against the door. He was large and the chair was small. The phrase was perhaps legs and arms akimbo.

"Miss Bit," he said.

She folded the day's itinerary in half and placed it in her lap. Every time she moved, the leather wingback she sat in creaked like a ship.

"How's the book?"

"I just started," he said. "I don't know."

"But do you like it?"

"Gun to my head?"

"Gun to your head," she said.

"Gun to my head, I like it," Zen said.

Over the past day and a half, she'd taught him a few American phrases. Almost all of the phrases were violent, Molly realized. *Gun to your head. Killing time. Skin of my teeth*, even, was gross and aggressive. She couldn't get a sense of whether or not Zen liked this. She couldn't get a sense of whether or not he liked anything, really, unless she said, "Gun to your head." Then he was forced into opinion.

Molly pointed two fingers at him and cocked her thumb.

"Are you bored?" she asked.

"This is the job," he said, and went back to reading.

Zen had been employed at the insistence of Andrew Kessler, her husband of two years, who was coincidentally directing a movie down in Rome, and having an affair with his lead actress. Molly was pretty sure of this. It was sort of Andrew's thing: exotic location, stressful shoot, a tryst with the talent. It was how they'd started in Hungary three years before, when they'd both been married to other people. Molly remembered the exact moment when she knew it was over with Jared. She'd been hanging upside down by a guidewire off the side of a building. She'd held a twitching robot-baby by its foot. "Fantastic," Andrew had said into her earbud, his voice a combination to a lock. "Now smash open that window."

"I want to smoke a cigarette," Molly said.

Zen raised his shoulders, uninterested.

"Outside," she said. "On the veranda, the balcony—whatever that is."

Zen stood up, and set down the Wolfe. He didn't sigh, but pulled in a long, slow breath, as if he was about to go diving.

"*Balcone*," he exhaled.

"*Balcone*," Molly repeated. "How many languages do you know?"

"Six."

Molly stood. There was a full-length mirror next to them. Zen pulled open a set of double doors. As the canal scent of sewage waved in, she looked at herself. She had on a short gray Nehru jacket with green trim, a low-cut blue silk shirt, and a pair of off-black jeans that were tight enough to feel like rubber. She liked how she looked, but she wasn't crazy about it.

"This whole outfit is *blech*," she said to Zen.

He was out on the *balcone*, staring into the buildings across the canal. His blond hair was cropped close in boutique military fashion. He stepped back across the slight rise and looked at her sandaled feet.

"Heels," he said. "The red."

She gave him the eyebrow. It had once been compared to the Gateway Arch in St. Louis.

"A short marriage," he said.

Molly took the heels out from underneath the wingback, and slipped them on. She tried her weight on one foot, and then the other.

"How's this?" she asked, raising the gun.

"Good," Zen said. "Tall. Italians like to fear their women."

"Out there?" she asked.

"Clear," Zen said. "Kill your time."

The rain had stopped earlier that morning. In the air above her, seagulls went berserk. Molly put the itinerary in her back jean pocket and took the letter out of her purse. It was a photocopy, maybe the eighth or ninth reproduction, a number far away like that. She'd received letters before, thousands maybe, and she'd had to change her email address at least a dozen times. The fact was people wrote to her.

They weren't necessarily crazy. A PA, or an assistant at the agency, some anonymous twenty-something, copied down her information off a list. Then they gave it to a friend. Who gave it to another. All they wanted to do was say hi, or mention how they thought she was great. Three wrote, "You suck." It was an invasion—annoying, unprofessional—but it wasn't uncommon. It was like when she called a restaurant and a host said, "Yeah, okay. Sure. How do you spell that?" Some of the letters were creepy. They were blatantly sexual. "I want to do [*specific position*] with you." "You look like you need a little [*fill in the blank*]." Most of these people were easy to scare off. They were lonely, hospitalized, unstable. When the police reported back to her it was always to inform her that so-and-so wouldn't be bothering her anymore.

But this letter was different. The police liaison for the famous said so. It was consistent with a certain type of pattern. It was actually better, the detective said, if they mentioned killing you straight off. That was rage, and rage was brief. Rage was sloppy. He could detect then, he said, make an arrest maybe, put out a restraining order. Shame worked wonders. People moved back to Toledo or wherever. But when they mentioned love, you were in trouble. Love was bad. Love was something you had to worry about. It thought in terms of fate. It was screwed up like that.

"That's why it comes every week," the detective had said. "He thinks he's being considerate. He's in it for the long haul."

The photocopy was part of the dossier Diane had given Zen. Molly had taken it out of his briefcase when he went to the bathroom. She hadn't read one in months, even though it had been sent to every house she owned but for one. The Coldwater mortgage had been in Jared's name, but there was no way he could afford the payments, and she'd taken that as well. It was small, but she liked it.

It was cozy. She used it on the rare occasion when Andrew, rather than she, was out of town. The ocean blared like static all night long at the Malibu place. And she hated the Bel Air mansion—it was ridiculous. Part of her had only bought it because she could. Molly wondered what good money was if you didn't spend it? Andrew had said that this way of thinking proved she'd grown up poor. Real rich people don't spend a dime, he'd told her. Not if they don't have to.

She loved him, but she hated him. She hated his goddamn guts. Their marriage had to be reestablished every two or three months, when they actually saw each other. The rest of the time he didn't seem real. She might have preferred that. She loved him out of habit: out of an instant attraction that had never abated, and had never grown calm.

The letter hadn't changed, it was exactly like the first and the twentieth version, and she reacted to it as she always did. She was afraid, afraid for her life, and then she willed herself to forget about it. Molly had compartmentalized her fear of the letter into a strip of film three scenes long. She would hear a knock at the door. She would open the door. A man with a blank face would be standing there. As always, she put the film strip down inside her body, and once it was there it started to break down and spread throughout her. It was a private thing, slow and true, like another life.

She lit her cigarette and read the itinerary. In an hour and a half she had a store appearance in Piazza San Marco. She would sign autographs for the first three hundred fans. Reporters would be there as well, but it was bound to be soft-pitch stuff. How was she liking Italy? Venice? The food? Flashes would shutter in quick succession like water coming to a boil. Then it was the boat ride. First, they would make a quick stop at the Guggenheim. It was the last interview with the woman from *The New Yorker*. After that it was Lido and the jun-

ket. She'd do the big press conference first, and then the individu-
als. After the premiere, there was the after-party. Molly checked her
phone. It was ten a.m. She had a fourteen-hour day ahead of her.

The exterior of the building opposite her own was black with
soot. Molly imagined the centuries of fire and recalled a twenty-
million-dollar insurance policy Universal had taken out on her skin
for *Tribes II* and *III*. There had been a lot of fire in those, a number
of explosions. But she was done with that sort of shit. She didn't
even care. Her filmography was balanced. Her contracts had been
honored. She was the whole shebang.

Half the cigarette smoked, she rolled the cherry's edge on the steel
balustrade, and watched the small gray ash drift into the canal. In the
distance, she heard the deep growl of an outboard motor rev. Over
the last five years—since *Make It So*, and all the films that followed—
Molly had developed a sixth sense for money. She knew what it
looked like, and felt like. She knew when people were pretending to
have it, and when they were pretending not to. More than anything,
she knew the sound of someone tracking her down to get paid.

The first boat full of paparazzi came down the canal. Another boat
trailed behind it. When they saw Molly, they cut their engines. At a
distance of two school buses, the two boats rocked inside the waves
they'd created, their sterns taking on water, the anonymous men
aboard falling this way and that. They were like old slapstick extras,
with the same clenched faces, and the same blank stares. There were
never any women, and there were none this time. The men seemed to
swap voices as they climbed on top of one another. They were German, Spanish, Japanese. Their accents were pitchy and erratic.

"Mol-lee!"

"Mooly!"

"Millee!"

She kept her eyes on the water, or on the buildings, or the sky. Never them. Early in her success, she had made that mistake, and never would again. To look at even one of them, to stare into the lens, had felt similar to bad luck, or, worse, as if a curse had been put upon her.

Molly gave them a moment from her life. She quarter-turned. She waited a beat. Then she stepped back inside.

There was a quick knock at the door. Zen checked past the horizontal chain. Once he undid it, the girls banged in. The two faux-hawk'd stylists were first, and then the hair and makeup girl, Victoria, who looked exhausted, as if she'd partied so hard the night before her right eye was now lower than the left. Last was Paula, Molly's publicist. She had on a man's blazer with shoulder pads.

"Are those paparazzi outside?" Paula yelled. She walked toward the *balcone.* "Who tipped them off?"

"Relax," Molly said. "Zen's on the case."

"Who?" Paula asked.

"Zen," Molly said.

"That guy?" Paula nodded at the bodyguard.

"Yeah," Molly said. "Him."

"Jesus," Paula said. "That's terrible. That's a terrible name."

"I think it's kind of hot," Victoria whispered. She held her makeup kit under one arm, and handed Molly a cigarette.

"Where's Diane?" Paula asked.

"Gondola tour," Molly said. "She'll be back in a half hour."

Paula was clever in an angling for position and power sort of way. She possessed the usual take-no-prisoners, I'm-a-world-class-bitch attitude, but what she truly excelled at was choosing who, and who not, to give a shit about. She didn't give a damn about the stylists, or the hair and makeup girl. Diane, on the other hand, was to be placed on a pedestal. Not only was Diane Molly's assistant, but, having navigated the last five years together, her best friend. Paula knew that to make Diane happy was to make Molly happy. Both Molly and Diane found Paula to be a total fake, and wondered if she wasn't a sociopath, but agreed that she did her job extremely well. This fact confirmed their opinion of her character.

"A little break is good," Paula said. "That's nice. That's nice of you."

"She's not my slave," Molly said. "She's my assistant."

"Of course not. Of course she isn't."

"I have another assistant for the slave work," Molly said.

Zen crossed the room out onto the *balcone*. He gave a warning in Italian that involved the word *polizia*, and the boats took off.

Victoria and Molly smoked, and then Victoria started in on her makeup.

"There's no sense in going all out right now," Victoria said, applying foundation. "You're just gonna get on the boat with all that wind, and water, and the sun's no help at all either. I'll have to do you again at the Guggenheim."

With some makeup artists, you could tell it was their whole life. They had given themselves over to it completely. They blinked in the face of other worldly matters. This meant they were invaluable but boring. Not so with Victoria. She seemed to have other interests, although Molly didn't know what they were. It wasn't yoga. It wasn't vegetarian dining. She didn't know Victoria at all, and never would, but Molly liked her. She liked how she was always having sex with somebody.

"What did you do last night?" Molly asked.

"I think his name was Emil," Victoria said.

Diane entered. There was something off about her, Molly noticed. Her usual bright, open quality was dimmed like emergency lighting. A Styrofoam bowl of melting gelato overflowed in her hand. Molly didn't like Diane's short cut. The humidity made her hair all frizzy. She looked like a kooky librarian.

"A little early for that," Molly said.

"Weird, I know." Diane threw the gelato into a trashcan. She started wiping her fingers with Kleenex. "I just sort of walked into the store. 'Gelato, per favore.' Walked out."

"How was the gondola?"

"Nauseating," Diane said. "But now I've done it."

"What's going on?"

"Not now."

"We are ready?" Zen asked.

They went down the steps and crossed the empty cobblestone bridge to the other side of the canal. She and Diane grabbed seats in the far stern under a canopy, and soon the boat departed. Venice was a half-sunk music box made of stone. It was cold as a shadow. The canal walls, the buildings, the flesh of the people—everything was the lifeless shade of dead canary. She could not get enough of the green on the water. It was oil, she knew, sludge, but she liked it.

"What happened?" Molly asked. "Is he with her?"

"Yes," Diane said.

"She's twenty years old."

"Nineteen," Diane said. "There's a photo."

"A photo of what?"

"They're in a café."

Molly saw the image in her mind. Her husband, Andrew Kessler, Mr. Hot Shit Director, and the British actress, Kate Uppley, are seated at a table. They lean into each other, eyes closed, about to kiss. It's not a full-on lock. In these sorts of photographs a little space is good for mystery. The space between is where the action is. The window absorbs the street light. In the background, waiters blur.

"Which magazine?" Molly asked.

"*OK!.*"

"*OK!?*"

"We're in Europe," Diane said. "They're in Europe. This is Europe."

"Does the Queen of Darkness know?"

"Paula doesn't know."

"I don't want it out there."

"That's why I haven't told her," Diane said. "How much are you willing to spend? I'm talking to someone."

"At the magazine? Who?"

"This asshole," Diane said. "Everything passes through her. I floated the idea of thirty, but it's going to be more."

"Because pounds?"

"Because we're in a kind of bidding war."

"Kind of?" Molly asked.

"We are," Diane said. "But I don't know with who."

Their boat moved through the center of the city. Motors gurgled, sputtered, and smoked. A cloud bank slid east, and here came the sun. The canal water went from green to aquarium blue. The bridges appeared to be white marble. Exterior fixtures—railings, lampposts, shop signs—were gold. Everything was Gucci, Rolex, Dior.

"It's like Rodeo Drive meets the Lost City of Atlantis," Molly said. "Pay them whatever."

"It's not that easy."

She knew Diane would say that. Diane was always saying that.

"I talked to the accountant."

"And what did Albert say?" Molly asked. "How is Albert?"

"Albert's fine. He says hello," Diane said. "Everything is tied up. Do you know how much this Zen guy is costing you?"

"How much?"

"Fifty-thousand euros."

"*Jesus.* For four days? How much American is that?"

"I don't even know," Diane said. "Everything is nuts right now. The Bel Air contractor needs to get paid. I don't know why you bought that thing in Malibu. Jared's alimony is killing you. You didn't get any money at all for *Lowlife*. And Hydrogen owes you one bajillion dollars. You're cash poor."

"Can't I do a commercial?" Molly asked. She looked at one of the stores. "How about Chanel?" She noticed a familiar restaurant. "What about Burger King?"

Molly was joking, but she also wanted to throw herself overboard, and let the motorboat blades do what they would. Andrew was scheduled to arrive that night in time for the premiere, but she knew he wouldn't come. She remembered how he went about these sorts of things. In Budapest, speaking about the wife he would soon leave, he'd said, "I'll give it some time, some radio silence. That way she won't be caught off guard." Even then, in their early love, she knew he was a coward.

"A commercial would be a good idea," Diane said. "Or another rom-com."

"No way," Molly said. "Romance is dead. There's nothing funny about it. As soon as they mention love, you're ruined. You're doomed."

"Maybe."

"Maybe?"

"I mean, I can understand why you'd feel that way," Diane said, and pitched her gaze out to sea.

Molly inspected her friend, her assistant, her whatever. Diane could get terribly morose. She was a vulnerable person. About her own feelings, Diane was honest to a fault. She was often surprised when other people didn't respect this about her. It was one of the reasons Molly loved her—this vulnerability—but it also drove her insane. Diane was too sweet to be so open. Only the cruel can afford to be totally honest, Molly knew. The rest of us have to lie.

"What's going on with you?"

"We need to figure out this money," Diane said. "We can go to forty with *OK!*. Anything after that, I don't know."

As the boat entered the lagoon, the wind ripped apart the canopy. The captain tacked against it, but the wind persisted. It blew Molly's chignon out. Her hair went everywhere.

"Call Victoria!" she yelled.

They docked the boat near the tourist and commuter ferries. Victoria boarded. "This is what I mean," she said, combing out the tangles. "The wind, the sea, the sun, the air. The goddamn elements. The world hates women."

"Time," Molly said.

"Fucking time," Victoria said. "You should see some of these faces I work on. I mean up close. I did a seventeen-year-old last month who gets horse sperm injected into her lips. I couldn't understand a single word she said to me."

"*Who?*"

"She's not famous," Victoria said. "She's nobody."

"What about Kate Uppley?" Molly asked. "You ever work on her?"

"*No*," Victoria said. A hardness reconfigured her voice. "But I know her."

Molly looked over at Diane, who'd stopped tapping into her phone.

"My brother parties with her," Victoria said. "He's emotionally disturbed, but I love him. I've met Kate a couple of times. She makes him seem normal."

"This sounds like gossip," Diane said.

"It is."

"Don't let us stop you."

Victoria's brother was on the scene. He was the image of Holly-wood as witnessed from a passing car. Outside unmarked club doors, he smoked cigarettes among his cohort: C-listers, the inebriated children of television stars, "producers." He hovered at the edges of pure excess, and swooped in from time to time, as if heeding its call.

"The one time I really met her," Victoria said, "like really, was at the Chateau Marmont. It was five in the morning or something, in one of the bungalows. You can imagine what was going on. Scott Weiland was there. Kate Uppley is like—What is she like? She's like someone you look at and think, 'What the hell happened to this person? Who hurt her?' She's weird looking, too. In person, I mean. Her head is enormous."

Victoria, her brother, Basel, and Kate Uppley sat on a couch. At some point in between lines, Victoria noticed there were a number of teenage boys in attendance. They had long, skater-boy hair, and terrible skin. Kate Uppley ordered them around. " '*Get me a juice, stupid. Bring me a cigarette, you little moron.*' It was weird," Victoria said. "I thought it was pretty obviously some kind of sex thing, and then I didn't, but then I did again, because I saw they weren't wearing any pants or underwear."

"They were naked?" Molly asked.

"No. They wore shirts. They just didn't have pants on," Victoria said. "They also had little tails."

Nobody had to ask.

"Yeah, tails," Victoria said. "They were hanging down between their legs. When I asked Kate about it, she said, 'Oh, those are anal beads. Aren't they great?' "

They stepped off the boat to join the others. At the end of the short wood dock were fifteen police officers. They wore tight blue uniforms and had brown eyes. Twenty feet beyond them were the paparazzi. Some were undoubtedly the same as from before. A few aimed their cameras at Molly and took practice shots. She showed her teeth to Diane.

"Is this a smile?" she asked.

"No."

She relaxed, tried again.

"How about this?"

"Even worse."

They walked around the corner of a nine-hundred-year-old building to find the square flooded with a foot of seawater.

"Why wasn't I notified about this?" Paula screamed into her phone.

Zen took Molly's hand and led her down a raised walkway. The basilica was to the right, hovering above its own reflection. Molly admired the building. They skirted by tourists, some of whom noticed her and gave off little gasps. They made their "oh my" faces. Pigeons swooped around like tiny aerialists. Set back inside the arches, the storefronts lit up the gloom. A cloud front had moved back through.

The store was in the northwest corner. As they stepped off the walkway, they met a crowd of fans, mostly young women, lined up in tight rows of fours and fives. The human length of them stretched back eighty yards starting from the boutique entrance. Like someone able to build and start a fire in the pouring rain, Molly gathered her natural forces and threw herself into the edge of them. She posed for photographs, she shook hands, and hugged, and did it all as if in a trance, or like someone under hypnosis. She felt only the pure energy of giving herself away. She forgot every moment as soon as it was over.

The boutique was practically empty. Whatever looped ambient music that normally played had been turned off. The store rep, Auggie, a short and slim Marc Jacobs clone, handed her a towel.

"For your feet," he said, in a thick accent. "They are wet."

Molly looked down. She hadn't even noticed.

Molly sat at the table. At any signing there was a one-to-one ratio of weird to acceptable. Molly found it strange that she should be signing posters with her airbrushed face and body on them; old headshots that sellers extorted people for on the internet; action-figure boxes; video games; magazine covers that announced her engagement; a paperback tell-all that told exactly nothing; DVDs; an old issue of *Entertainment Weekly*; a stand-alone film festival info sheet for *Lowlife*.

She hated audiences. She said she loved them, but she hated them. Her role in *Lowlife* was a minor supporting one. She'd agreed to the part because without her the movie wouldn't have been made. The attached lead was her friend Angela, who, even though she'd starred as Diana Ross in a bio-pic that netted eighty-five million dollars, and had played Denzel's strong, no-nonsense wife in not one, but two movies, couldn't get a studio to pony up. Waiving her fee, Molly signed on as the beleaguered common-law wife of a white supremacist, and suddenly it was a go.

The next couple of fans were nice. With a Sharpie, she signed the necks of two fourteen-year old Parisiennes. She held a Polish woman's infant son. An American woman, a brunette with a pleasant face like cut-glass, stepped up.

"I dated your high school boyfriend for a while," she said. "At UVM. We were there together. You remember him?"

Molly tapped her right hand twice on the table. It was the sign for *Get this person out of here*.

"Of course I remember Luke."

"He was all broken up about you," the woman said. "It was a problem."

"I'm sure he's fine now."

"He isn't."

Auggie came out of nowhere.

"This way, miss."

British husbands heeled a foot behind their wives.

They let the preauthorized photographers in and herded them behind a rope. "Look here, Molly! Molly! Look here!"

A German woman asked, "Have you ever been to Kazakhstan? You must shoot a movie in Kazakhstan! You must! You must!"

Near the end, she tried signing with her right hand, but it wouldn't work.

"Anal beads?" she whispered to Diane.

In Italian first, and then in English, Auggie announced, "*Allora.* Thank you for coming. This concludes our event. Miss Bit has a press conference. We thank you, Molly!"

The information passed back through the line, and then returned as seven hundred moans. She smiled her fake smile at them, the condescending one. Molly sat down in a chair, and it was like falling through a hole in time. For a moment, no one spoke or looked at her. The fans turned their backs in silence, as if honoring a pact. She felt the constant threat of love, or, worse, its absence, drain away, seep out into the flooded square, and mix among the particles of filth in the Adriatic. To hell with all of it, Molly thought. For one entire second, she felt calm. And then one more. Molly blanked out on it. It was like a drug. But then someone tapped her shoulder—*who? who was it? who was there?*—and it was time to go.

•

Diane stood on the Guggenheim boat landing. Out here, away from the city, the water was shot through with light. The color was like a translucent key lime. The waves *thwa-thwapped* against the palazzo foundation and sprayed into the tall hedgerows. Earlier, the gondolier had said, "There's four hundred bridges, one hundred and seventy canals. It's a maze," and Diane had felt, gliding through the shadows, the extraordinariness of her life. She had sensed, as if a girl again, that it was a remarkable thing to be alive, to feel the light pass between two buildings and warm your face, to smell the soaked world. This feeling bloomed in her. It expanded. She'd been happy. On the landing, she searched it out again. She tried to call it up out of herself, or see it in Venice. She did deep yoga breaths where she imagined her diaphragm was the center of the world. She wanted to know exactly where the stress was in her body. Was it in her stomach? Her hips? Her shoulders? Could it be everywhere? Was it possible to be more stress than body? What would her therapist say to that?

"Taking a moment?" Paula asked her.

She didn't want to dislike Paula. It was occupying too much room. She'd taken to rehearsing angry monologues directed at the publicist. Hate was exhausting.

"Sort of," Diane said.

They each turned and looked into the Guggenheim courtyard, where Molly sat on a stone bench with the writer. The two women were engaged in what seemed to be a serious conversation. Molly's hands waved in the air. They did karate chops and pirouettes. They conducted.

"She seems off today," Paula said. "I wish she had let me cancel. We could have done it tomorrow."

"She's done a thousand of these," Diane said.

"A writer can turn on you," Paula said. "Intellectuals don't know what they want from other people. It's why they're always disappointed."

"Molly's got the whole world wrapped around her finger."

"That's the problem," Paula said. "A writer is a person with a grudge."

"Against who?"

"Everybody," Paula said.

They watched as Zen appeared from around the corner of the museum. He stood beside the dog tomb and scanned the horizon. Diane guessed she understood the appeal.

"She's completely fine," Diane said.

"Is she worried about the movie?"

"No."

"Not even a little?"

"Maybe," Diane said. "I don't know."

Paula thrived on stress. She was one of those women who live forever, who keep their ships tight, who openly say they're right all the time. She was the kind of strong, confident woman other women loved at first but then grew to hate. The affair, the whatever-you-would-call-this-idiotic-thing-Andrew-was-doing would have pleased her. Paula didn't like the look of *Lowlife*. It wasn't sympathetic. She plays a racist? Did Molly think she was Edward Norton? Did she think—like they did with men—audiences could separate fact and fiction when it came to her? Who would see this thing anyway? *The New Yorker* article had been arranged to get the all-important art angle out there. Remember, people, Paula was saying via the press, Molly thinks she's an *artist. Ar-tiste.* We have to forgive her for that.

Diane knew exactly what Paula would think of the photo. For her, it would be a tool. It would even the field. It would inspire great heaps of sympathy. It would excuse Molly's character-actor turn.

"There's nothing wrong with her," Diane said. "Everything's tip-top."

"Tip-top?"

"Tip-top," Diane said. "I have to make a phone call."

She walked in the direction of Yoko Ono's *Wish Tree*, a large olive tree covered in scraps of paper, and called the new assistant, Tiff. This was the third time Diane had called Tiff, and once again there wasn't any answer. In the salt-air breeze, Diane heard the writer laughing. What grudge? she wondered. The woman had seemed kind. She could have used a haircut, a blow-dry, something, but she was otherwise very nice looking—beautiful, actually. She'd apparently written a novel. Diane wondered if she knew Greg Watson, Molly's old college friend. Diane had his novel, *The Last Century*, in her tote bag. Molly claimed there was a feature in it, but Diane didn't know.

She called her girlfriend, Stephanie.

"I'm at work," Stephanie said.

"Okay." Diane said. "Hi to you too."

"I'm really busy."

"I just wanted to say hello."

"Hello," Stephanie said.

It was exhausting. The whole thing was exhausting. Diane was exhausted.

"What time is it there?"

"Who cares?" Stephanie said.

"What's the matter?"

"*What's the matter?*"

"Yes," Diane said. "What's the matter?"

She could picture Stephanie moving down one of the production office's hallways, any number of muted gray colors surrounding her, swallowing her—her short, quick stride tapping out against the carpet.

"I had to put fifteen thousand dollars into your boss's bank account last night is what's the matter," Stephanie said.

"It's not your money," Diane said.

"It's *our* account."

"But it's not *your* money."

Diane listened to Stephanie compose herself. She was a small person, with a sexy, frantic quality. The way she moved had always suggested excitement, a kind of welcome recklessness, but of late Diane had felt otherwise. She understood it now as a pointless, nervous energy. It was oppressive.

"*What kind of a movie star is she?*" Stephanie asked. "Who borrows fifteen thousand dollars from their personal assistant?"

"It's complicated," Diane said. "The money's tied up."

"What the hell does that mean? She's using you. They're all the same, Diane. I'm sick of it."

Diane spun around and took in the Guggenheim. A bat flew out from under one of the museum's eaves. She saw its screeching, hideous face. She had only wanted to say hello. She'd meant that.

"I asked you to do one thing," Diane said. "I put your name on the account so you could buy a car. I helped you. I'm helping her. It's difficult over here right now. There's a bodyguard. There's everything with Andrew."

"I don't care about the bodyguard," Stephanie said. "I don't care about who's sleeping with who. These people are deranged. All they do are horrible things to one another. It's making me physically sick. I'm ill. She's your whole life. I don't want her to be mine."

"What does that mean?" Diane asked. There was a call trying to come through.

"What does *what* mean?" Stephanie asked.

"Can I call you right back?"

"*No*," Stephanie said. "*I'm working.*"

Diane hit Accept. The *OK!* woman's name was Bronwen. She was a terrible human being.

"There's an offer at sixty."

"From who?" Diane asked.

"I can't tell you that," Bronwen said. "I've said that already. Why are you asking me that? What do you say to sixty?"

Diane heard a London street scene in the background. In her head, it was like a science fiction novel as written by Virginia Woolf. A double-decker bus passed by in a cartoon flash of red. All of the pedestrians walked in straight lines. They had deeply serious and bureaucratic faces. The city buzzed with their consciousness. Souls flew about, having taken the form of pigeons.

"I say I hate your accent," Diane said, and hung up.

She'd spent half her life in the Coachella Valley, where her father was the custodian/full-time resident at any number of meditation retreats. Her parents had never been married. Her father was too far down the road of his own journey to entertain the idea. Because of that—because he loved her and listened to her and absorbed her as much as he could into the wandering quality of his life—she had never held it against him. It was simply how he was.

Sometimes, on long weekend visits, he would borrow one of the retreats' permanent cars, and they would drive southwest through the fertile, Mexican-worked plains until they reached the Salton Sea. Her father would rent a cabin for something like twenty-five dollars a night, and at dusk they would walk along the low tide edge of the sea, the bones of ten thousand fish cracking and splintering under their shoes, the salt smell gag-worthy at first, before their noses shut themselves off to it. The next day they would rent a boat and fish. It was perfectly safe, her father would say. It was only salt. And because he said this Diane believed it too. The boat moved slowly in the sodium-rich water; they would let their lines drag and pull the fish in all day long. Once she caught a fish that had three eyes and her father threw it back. They grilled out at night. The fish were always delicious.

In the mornings, her father would meditate for three hours, and Diane would explore on her own. The sunlight was a blinding experience. There was no shadow. It was only the white light of the sea and its edges and the rocks and shells and fish bones. The temperature was perfect enough to feel like nothing at all. Diane walked alone in the all-white blankness, and it would seem to her after awhile that maybe she had forgotten all about color, and that she would never again see red or green or blue, and even though she knew this thought was a kind of daydream, it filled her with panic. It was only on these trips with her father that it occurred to Diane a person could go crazy and stay that way forever. She didn't know why this was so—he had yet to go mad. She only knew this happened to people sometimes. She only knew she was afraid for him. When this particular thought hit, she always ran back to the rented cabin as fast as she could. The fish bones would explode up all around her like shrapnel. She'd enter into the calm daylight of the cabin's interior. Indian-style, she would sit on the floor across from her father and quietly wait for him to open his eyes.

The light on Peggy Guggenheim's little island wasn't nearly half that obliterating, but it was constant. It was heavy and everywhere. It wanted in bad.

Zen approached. Beneath his feet, small pebbles crunched like something being eaten. Diane had tried, like Molly, to forget about what Zen represented. She had attempted to ignore the letters, but in the end she couldn't. She wasn't like Molly. She used her feelings for her life. She experienced them. With Diane, there wasn't some weird alchemy at work where her fear and anger showed up in the manner-isms of a white supremacist on sixteen millimeter.

"We're behind," Zen said. "She needs to stay on the boat when we get to Lido. I need to confer with the security there."

For two days straight, all Diane had said to the man was, "Okay. Okay. Okay."

"Okay," she said. "Did you meet Andrew?"

"Pardon?" he asked.

"Did you meet her husband?"

"He hired me. We had a meeting in Rome."

"She hired you," Diane said.

"She pays," Zen said. "He hired."

Zen didn't get angry, Diane saw. He suggested it. He tipped his head down at a nearly imperceptible angle. Otherwise, he was all sunglasses. Her reflection irritated her enormously.

"Can I ask you something? I don't want you to get offended."

"I don't get offended," he said.

"Ever?"

"Ever."

"You've never been offended in your entire life?"

"Is this what you're asking?"

"No," Diane said. He made her feel off-balance. She was sensi-tive. If you were a native of California, you could feel an earthquake before a transplant did. "Do you think you need to be here?"

"This is not something I ask," Zen said. "I don't think about it. It is not important."

"What is important?"

"The job."

Did all men with guns speak like they were in a David Mamet play?

"I get it," Diane said. "The ocean is vast. Never trust a dame."

"I'm sorry?"

"Nothing," she said. "It was just a question. I'm sorry I asked."

What she wanted to know was whether or not her own concerns were warranted. She needed her own feelings to be validated for her. This had always been true, but it was especially true now. The letters had been coming for over a year. Nobody seemed to know anything. They were treated like the normal consequence of fame. Because of this treatment, their potency, their effect, had been diluted. The letters, and the paranoid worry Diane experienced over them, had somehow been folded up into the nature of business as usual. But they weren't a script in need of a rewrite. They weren't a new young star with her nose in a mound of coke. You couldn't simply throw money at the problem in the form of a handsome Swiss bodyguard and clap your hands free of the whole mess. Didn't the truth persist? Or had it stopped doing that?

"The job is the answer," Zen said.

She stared at him in disbelief.

"Is this the language barrier?" she asked. "Is that what this is?"

"It does not make sense to ask why or if," he said. "Molly is the job. The threat could be anything, everything. For someone like her, the threat is always. This is why I am here. I mean: *Keep it away. All of it. Every last little thing.*"

"What about the letters?" Diane asked.

"What about the letters?" he asked. "The letters are not important."

"But that's why you were hired."

"I was hired because the threat exists."

"But the letters are the threat."

"No more than anything else," Zen said.

Molly had never gone out much. She did what she had to do—premieres, certain parties attached to the ends of certain events, dinner soirees thrown by somebody's wife or boyfriend—but other than those afternoons and evenings, she kept to herself. Not in any real way was Molly Bit a social person. If anything, she used her charm to keep people at a distance. She used it to get jobs. For the last year, she'd worked constantly. Everything was a location. Morocco. Singapore. She'd kept the world away. It wasn't any big surprise about her husband.

"Everything is a threat?"

"It is."

"Should I be worried?"

"No."

"Why not?"

"Because the world is as it always was."

Diane knew this wasn't exactly true. The world had changed. It was different. For instance, Stephanie believed Molly was a narcissist. While this was probably true, at least Molly had gone about earning her adoration. It was an old fame she'd sought. Molly had been born in the '70s. She'd had to learn what www. was. She'd had to invent a reason to be looked at. It hadn't been invented for her. She wasn't famous because she'd taken a picture of herself with her phone.

"Here she comes," Zen said.

It was one thing after the other. Action zinged Diane this way; it zanged her that. It was never her life. She wanted a better love. She wanted someone who knew her.

Molly and the writer came quietly chuckling out of the garden.

"Hello," the writer said. She gave Diane and Zen a little wave.

She had long, slender fingers. Her hair was a mess. "I'm the lady novelist."

Molly laughed her actual laugh. It was an inside joke. How long had that taken?

"I'm Susan," the writer said.

"Diane."

"So I've been told," Susan said.

"Ah."

The women shook hands. They looked at each other. What passed between them didn't feel like ruin at all. It wasn't anything close to doom.

She hadn't eaten since seven-thirty that morning.

"Here's the thing: I know what it's like to be a person," Molly said. "I know what it's like to be a woman. I started from there."

"But this woman is—I want to be careful," the reporter said. From *Film Comment*, he was the first and only black reporter she'd seen all day. He was also the only reporter who'd gotten right down to it. The others, the white ones, had applauded her for her "courage," lobbed a few soft questions, and then asked her what it was like to work with this one, and that one, and who's-a-what's-its.

"She's in many ways an awful human being," he said.

"Yes," Molly said.

"She's a racist," the reporter said.

"That's true," Molly said. "She is."

He was very slim, and wore an old, ripped up jean jacket in a New York/LA way. If he'd been from anywhere else, it would have looked ridiculous. There was something about the precision of his haircut, the clean shine off his glasses, and the cuffed ends of his slacks that helped him to pull the jacket off. The hotel suite was bare and white and modern. The curtains against the windows had been opened. Molly glanced out to the sea. It was early evening on the Adriatic. The distance was blue. Then bluer. Then bluer still.

"What kind of preparation did you do?" the reporter asked. "How did you get down to that level? She's gruesome."

It was the sort of question Molly both wanted to answer and hated to. It was an actual question, and for that she was grateful, but it was also a personal one—more personal than any other perhaps— and it brought out her defensiveness. The question touched off in her a series of insecurities and worries and superstitions. Its answer was always the same: she didn't quite know how she did it.

"I like your jacket," she said.

"Thank you."

"I don't think of it as 'down,' first of all," she said. "I'm not in any position to judge her."

"Right," he said, and wrote that in his small blue notebook. "But you're able to get there. It's a frightening performance. It was difficult for me to watch. Not in a bad way, necessarily, but still. I'm going to assume there's very little of you in her."

"That's maybe fair to say."

He uncrossed his legs.

"But not entirely fair?"

"No. Not entirely," she said.

Paula came in from the other room. She said hello with her eyes, and went to a nearby table, where she pretended to look through the mail, as if there was any. She'd been on high-paranoid alert all day. Her publicity sense smelled something in the air.

"I'm American," Molly said. "I grew up in a very white part of the country. A very white and very poor part of the country. I know any number of people who remind me of this woman."

"And they're racist?" he asked.

Paula tore a piece of hotel stationery in half.

"Yes," Molly said. "But my character doesn't think of herself that way."

"How does she think of herself, then? How do they?"

"As not racist," Molly said. "What racist thinks they're racist? They think what they think. That's what they think."

"And that's accessible to you?" the reporter asked. "To think like that?"

"It's accessible to most people, apparently."

"To most white people?" he asked. "In America?"

"Yes," Molly said.

"How many do you think? Percentage-wise?"

"Seventy-five?" Molly asked.

"You think seventy-five percent of white people in America are racist?" he asked.

"Is that too low?" she asked. "Eighty?"

"Okay! Enough!" Paula shouted. "This interview is over."

"Well . . . I mean," the reporter said, already gathering up his tape recorder and pen.

"Over," Paula said. "We love *Film Comment*. Don't we, Molly? Don't we just love it? Don't we love its dedication to true criticism? Isn't it the *Cahiers* of today?"

"There's still *Cahiers*," the reporter said, heading out of the room. "It's still published."

"Good to know," Paula said, closing the door behind him. "Bye."

Paula spun around with her hands up in the air and her mouth open wide.

"That was bad," Molly said.

"That was very bad!" Paula shouted.

How had Diane put it earlier? *"The picture's out of our hands?"* That was certainly one way of describing the situation. Another way to put it was that her husband was having sex with a teenager, and soon the whole world would know. Another way to say the other thing was that maybe someone wanted her dead. During the press conference, Molly had sat to the left of Angela, and had politely deflected all questions to her friend. She'd played it easy breezy. She hadn't wanted to come off as magnanimous, or as if she were doing anybody a favor. After awhile, it became a running joke—Molly Bit wasn't going to answer any actual questions today. Everybody got it. It had then fallen to Angela, a fellow charismatic, and so private sufferer, to work the room.

She told Paula about the photo. The publicist stood there for a moment. She didn't say a word. Molly couldn't take it.

"Hello?"

"I'm thinking," Paula said. "I'm thinking many things."

"Like what?"

"Like blah-blah-blah, *I'm so sorry for you, I'm furious you didn't tell me*, yada-yada-yada. But none of that matters. What matters is that this could be a good thing. You just called every white person in America racist."

"That's not what I said."

"That's what they'll hear," Paula said. "Trust me. That's going to go international. We need damage control. We need to put that 'white people are all racists' thing in context."

Like certain other kinds of businesses—hardware, plumbing supply, animal control—the entertainment industry trafficked in certainties. Problems were meant to be solved. You ordered the part, you put the raccoon down, you let the photo do the work you could never do. Only then, once the customer was happy, once the water danced and flowed, once you'd had a little more nosh off the lavishly stocked food cart, did you walk the red carpet at the Venice Film Festival.

Zen hung back. The resort air crinkled with camera light. Molly tilted her head in slight degrees. She stepped the left foot back. She put her right hand on her hip and made a triangle with her arm. In the lulls, when their attention turned off, she spoke quick asides with her costars. *How were they? They were doing what?* Her life was a series of meaningful gestures. Andrew was in Rome, she told them, but they already knew that. Zen stepped forward at a certain point. He touched her arm. There was someone in the crowd. He stepped back. It was nothing. Her costars pretended like he wasn't there. A green firework exploded in the sky above the island and sizzled down in twenty or more sulfurous, trembling arcs.

While the movie played, everyone who was involved in its production ate dinner in the hotel restaurant. They were seated at a giant table. Molly whispered to Angela what had happened with the *Film Comment* reporter. She said she was sorry.

"For what?" Angela whispered back. "I'm sorry for you, but . . ."

"But what?"

Angela had a face like a church. It was perfectly balanced like that.

"I hope they run the interview. Do you know how little money marketing will put into this? It's pitiful," Angela said. "But that's bad for you, Mol. I'm sorry. If you call white people racist, they go insane. They lose their goddamn minds."

Molly ate a piece of bluefish and looked around the restaurant. Diane sat with Susan at a corner table. They weren't exactly laughing, but they weren't exactly serious either. Molly hoped Susan was forward. Diane needed to be pushed into her true self. The two of them should get a little drunk. If infidelity was in the air, it should at least help get rid of Stephanie. Dreaming of this (that she finally wouldn't have to look at Stephanie's stupid face ever again) and taking one sip, then two, then knocking back the rest of her wine, something strange happened to Molly Bit: she started to relax. She was a movie star, after all. She knew how to shake it off.

"Who's the tall bloke?" the Irish actor Dylan Laughlin asked her. He nodded at Zen over by the entrance door.

"Security."

"Lovely," Dylan said. "The world's piss. Cheers."

Dylan was drunk, which was part of his charm. If he was like Peter O'Toole or Richard Burton—except Irish—who was Molly? He was at the festival to promote a detective thriller he was the star of. He couldn't quite remember the title. They were in a corner booth with Angela.

"Mine's around here somewhere," Dylan said.

"Security?" Angela asked.

"Oh, yeah," he said. "But he's shite."

"What's going on?" Molly asked.

"A woman," Dylan said. "Either it's a woman, or it's a man—or it's something else. This one's a woman. She broke into my house in Dublin. I wasn't there. Gave the maid a start. Who's the big detective, eh? Who's the big crime fighter?"

Dylan took Molly and Angela by the arm and paraded them around the dining room. They said hi to a table of middle-aged directors, the last traces of their wonder-boy charm evaporating off them, the pressures of the marketplace and various drug habits having wrinkled them into a sudden old age. Through Andrew, through being around them, Molly knew the kind of shit they talked on actors. She wanted to moo at them, like a cow. She resented their auteur-ness, but at the same time wanted to be one of them. If she was crazy, and narcissistic, and too much trouble to bother with, and a vapid idiot, and a whore, and if she'd somehow fucked her way to that role, and sucked this one's cock, and if a trained monkey could do what she did, then they were a bunch of assholes. The directors laughed and smiled and said how incredible she looked, and she laughed and smiled and said the same. It was the same wonderful, usual lie they performed. It was guilt-free, a little drunk, and splendid.

Like assassins, high-powered executives were everywhere. At best, their lives and livelihoods were tenuous. At worst, they were doomed. In private, Molly called them Humpty-Dumpties. Bloated with fear and need, each even minor gesture or decision they made could be the end, could be the failure that sent them toppling over the edge. She and Angela and Dylan said hi to all of them too. They were tough little pigeons who fluttered at the actors' touch. One you had to stroke. One you had to coo at. One you had to tease. One you had to flatter. One you had to sit there with in near silence and wait for him to bless you with his word.

When Leonard arrived, the room expanded. Molly saw him pass through the entrance that connected to the hotel. She tried to get Diane's attention. She waved her arms around. She clapped her hands together. Nothing. Diane was lost over there. Finally, she sent a text.

"Here," Diane said, and gave Molly the book. It was in a shiny black plastic bag.

"How's it going with you two?" Molly asked. She raised her eyebrows a few times, Groucho Marx style.

"*What?* We're talking. She's a very nice person."

"She's pretty," Molly said. "I like her laugh."

"I guess."

"You *guess?*" Molly said. "Don't be like that."

"Like what?"

"Oh, brother."

The night went on this way for a while, voices low to pollinate business deals and sexual misadventure. It was a good place to be, in a room full of people who aimed to please, who hoped for love more than understanding, encouragement more than faith. As the hour stretched to two, the dinner evolved quite naturally into the after-party held in the top-most suite. Through the window, Molly stared past her own reflection at the sea, and caught sight of Leonard Roth's white pants striding through the door.

"White pants?" she asked him.

"I'm confident," Leonard said, and kissed her on the cheek. "You look like all the money in the world."

"And yet I haven't any," Molly said.

"How's Andrew?"

"He's in Rome."

"Right. Right," Leonard said. "How's that going?"

"I don't know," Molly said. "I haven't read the trades lately."

They caught up for a minute. They spoke real things. How was his son? His wife? What did she mean she hadn't read the trades lately? How was Andrew, really?

She didn't tell him a goddamn thing.

"And what's this?" Leonard asked. He touched the black plastic bag with this thumb and forefinger.

"Your next project," Molly said.

She watched him pull *The Last Century* from out of the bag.

"Greg Watson?" he asked. "Never heard of him."

"We went to school together. He's good."

"You went to school?"

"Read the novel," she said.

He said he didn't read anymore. He paid a kid for that. "He sits in a room all day," Leonard said. "Who owns the rights?"

"Me," she said. "I want *you* to read it."

"*Me?*"

"*You.*"

"What's it about?" he asked.

"A brother and sister. You're already saying yes. You're personally invested. You just don't know it yet."

"And you'd star?"

"I'd direct."

"*You?*"

"Me," she said.

Leonard didn't appear pleased by the idea. He rocked back and forth on the balls of his feet. He pushed his hands into his pockets.

"It's nonnegotiable," Molly said. "It's the deal."

She looked across the party. Standing by the door was Zen. Standing next to him was Dylan Laughlin. Every time a woman passed by, Dylan would jump behind Zen in pretend fear and laugh. To him, the whole thing was hysterical. It was one big joke. It was the funniest thing in the world.

INTELLECTUAL PROPERTY

2009

ONCE, BACK WHEN THEY WERE STILL FRIENDS AND SPOKE TO one another, Abigail Kupchik said to Molly, "It's kind of a shame you have a father. It does you a disservice. It's like, 'Her too? Is that really necessary? Why?' You shouldn't have one. It would make a better origin story."

But Molly did. She had a father. And it was Father's Day. She decided she would give him a call. She was with Andrew on the western edge of Washington state close to where the Pacific Ocean flowed into the Strait of Juan de Fuca. The rental's sea view was a chronic navy drizzle overlayed onto a barrier of fog. She had one week before she was due in Vancouver. It was a detective movie. Molly was the detective. She'd been inhaling books on procedure, protocol, the right angles of law and order. Every thought was a flash of certainty in need of hunting down.

"When was the last time you spoke to him?" Andrew asked.

A spot of gray had taken root in his beard. It was on his chin, to the right. She hadn't made up her mind yet as to whether or not she liked this. She was leaning toward not. For some ill-advised reason, he was dicing an onion on top of a plate, but she decided to let it go.

"A few weeks ago," Molly said. "A woman I went to school with was in a car accident. He thought I should know."

"Were you friends with her?"

"No. She was a few years younger than me."

"Weird," Andrew said.

"Weird what?"

"That he'd call to tell you."

"Why is that weird?"

"You didn't know her."

"I knew her," Molly said. "Just not well."

"Got it," Andrew said. He scraped the onion onto a cutting board. It was louder than it needed to be. He started dicing again, with more force.

He'd never made her an omelet before. It was a gesture. They'd spent a year separated, Molly on set much of the time, flying here and there for long arguments and recriminations. Then a year married, but still apart, sharing a house, trying to smile at the people they'd invited over. Because of this routine, her face felt like it was going to fall off. Her mind, if not the decision, was made. She had the papers all drawn up. They were in her safe in LA. Something both very common and perversely Hollywood was going on between them. They shared friends. An action franchise. A complex and mutilated love.

"What happened?" he asked.

"With what?" Molly asked.

"With the woman you didn't know."

Everything was a movie with him. For the last two years, Andrew had been buying people. This was more than his participation in an IP trend. It appealed to him on many levels: the creative, the somewhat noble, the deeply fucked. He owned the film and television rights to nearly a hundred life stories. Not indefinitely. These were handshake deals or two-year contracts with loose language binding the parties. He owned the story of an American who'd escaped from a Siberian prison. He owned the story of the first one-armed woman to swim the English Channel. When Andrew asked, "What happened?" it was another way of asking, "Is it a feature? Would it sell?" Molly was sometimes swept up in it too. Who didn't love the real? Who didn't want to mainline actual experience? The tagline "Based on a true story" was a kind of foreplay. People heard it and said, "*Oh, yeah. Give it to me.*"

"She died," Molly said.

"That's awful. How?"

From her father, she'd gleaned the bare information: a two-day storm; a stretch on Interstate 91 like the tilting, curving ramp of a pinball machine; the woman and her daughter hydroplaning through the guardrail into the granite wall.

"You can't stop," Molly said to her husband, the owner of lives. "It was instant."

"What was her name?"

It had required a Google search for the face to click, and even then Lindsay Ingram was hard to recall. In five minutes, Molly learned everything there was to know about her. Lindsay had been the director of a drug-prevention agency based out of White River Junction. Her master's thesis at UVM had predicted the opioid crisis. She'd been married to the same man for twelve years. She was a licensed EMT.

"You see," Andrew said. "That's why I buy these stories. People live these absolutely exceptional lives. They live these exceptional lives—and no one knows about them."

"What are you talking about?" Molly asked. "People knew. Her family knew. Her friends knew. The people she helped."

"That's not enough," Andrew said. "A woman like that should reach a mass audience."

"Why?"

"Why not?" he asked. "Why shouldn't she? Why shouldn't she get her moment?"

"What moment?"

"Her moment on the screen. Picture it: she's slamming her hand down on the oak table. She's shouting about the epidemic going on. Nobody gives a shit, but later she's vindicated. Let's give her a movie husband. Someone with rugged good looks who grief looks sexy on. Let's watch her resuscitate a small child in the back of an ambulance out in the boondocks. Let's all be inspired."

The omelet was lumpy and over-fried but functional. Molly ate standing up near the kitchen island. Andrew was seated at the table. He ate methodically. He would cut the omelet twice, fork it up to his mouth, chew eight times, swallow, and repeat. She started eating with her fingers so as to break up the routine.

"What else did your father say?" Andrew asked.

When her mother called, it was always with news of cancer or terminal illness. Her father covered accidents, arrests, and natural disasters.

"Nothing," she said. "I don't wanna talk about it."

"Was there a flood?" Andrew asked.

"No."

"Did the pharmacy get robbed again?"

"No."

"Did the police chief have an affair with his brother's sister?"

"You're an asshole."

Andrew liked to mock the place where she was from. He had an idea in his head about what it had been like for her to grow up there. It wasn't necessarily right. It wasn't necessarily wrong.

"A guy I knew was arrested," Molly said.

"What guy?"

"Jesus. An old boyfriend." She changed her voice to a country twang. *"Ma high skool boy-friend."*

"What happened?"

"He beat someone up."

"What for?"

"Money, a woman, maybe it was a Friday—I don't know."

"Okay," Andrew said. "But what's his story?"

In one way or another, this was always the question.

"Both of his parents are dead," Molly said. "First his father, who was a son of a bitch. Then his mother, who everybody called sweet because they didn't know the first thing about her. It was one long illness after the other. He took care of them as they were dying. You can't make a three-act structure out of hospital bills."

"Sure you could," Andrew said. "What are you talking about?"

"How?"

"Parents die. Bills arrive. He pulls a bank heist."

"A bank heist?"

"Sure. Why not?"

"No bank heist," she said. "Or sort of. But in reverse. The bank robbed him. They took his house."

She looked at Andrew. He'd been reborn, reenergized.

"This guy's a gold mine," he said. "I mean really. It's exactly the kind of movie I want to make next. Financial crisis. Medical insurance. Home foreclosure. It's relevant. It's happening. It's real life."

"It's sad is what it is," Molly said.

"Of course it is," Andrew said. "It's terrible. I'm not saying it isn't terrible. I'm not some sort of monster."

"Noted."

He began to clear the table. He wasn't very efficient at it. Andrew had never needed to stack plates on top of one another, race across the dining room, swing through the door, and shout "Behind!"

"You scoffed at bank heist, but bank heist is the way to go," Andrew said. "You can't do real human beings in straight-up melodrama anymore. *The Best Years of Our Lives* would tank at the box office. It wouldn't get nominated for a goddamn thing. If you want to get actual feeling across you have to wrap it up in genre. Thriller. Action. Heist. I'm partial to a good old-fashioned rags-to-riches story myself."

She had once loved this about him—his knack for filling up a room with the power of an arbitrary notion and selling it for fact. In this way, he had explained to Molly the story of who they were, and, in particular, the story of their last few years. Because of how aggravating Andrew found her anger and sadness—because her moods annoyed him—the reasons for those feelings, the things he had done, had to be forgotten. In their place, Molly and Andrew lived inside a needless dynamic that, he logicked, Molly insisted upon. It had reached the point where Andrew was removed from the situation, and Molly was left alone to wonder who she was, and why her life had made her like that.

She no longer mentioned Kate Uppley. Not to Andrew or to anyone. The story surrounding the girl was too sad. Kate was like a death in the Hollywood family so horrible no one could bring themselves to speak of it. The silence made Molly sick.

The rumor was Kate had suffered a nervous breakdown. After the breakdown, she went to rehab. After rehab, she got a lawyer and filed a civil suit against a children's show producer. She claimed the producer had raped her when she'd starred in her breakout series *Kid City!*, but nobody believed her (or if they did, it didn't matter, for the fear of contagion had swallowed her whole), and she couldn't get a job anymore.

Years earlier, when it was all said and done, when the picture of the kiss hadn't been published after all, Diane opened her inbox one day to find a JPG of a check signed by Kate Uppley to *OK!* magazine. The girl had been the one to kill the story, and while Molly refused

Kate's other overtures (lunch or a phone call was out of the question), she remembered what it was like to be nineteen—the fog one had to constantly squint through, the posturing—and Molly had forgiven her.

She told Andrew to leave the dishes.

After a period of time in which both of them went to separate rooms and performed small acts of privacy the other wasn't aware of, they took the long drive into the nearest little big town. Everything around them was saturated. A seething darkness pulsed in the mossy tree bark and inside the mud and in the brackish, gnatty water that seeped out of the forest side of the road. Molly couldn't see the mountain range through the trees, but she felt it out there, disrupting the air, pulling the earth out of its gravity. On the left, the sea view came and went. She saw a line of kayaks paddling by. She saw a sailboat. Andrew turned the radio down.

"Maybe it's not a bank heist," he said. "Maybe I'm wrong. For argument's sake, let's say I'm wrong."

"I don't want to talk about this anymore," Molly said.

"Maybe you combine the two story lines," Andrew said. "We've been thinking about it all wrong. What's your boyfriend's name?"

"*'We'* haven't been thinking about anything," Molly said. "His name is Lucas Hutton. Luke."

"Maybe Luke Hutton is Lindsay Ingram's husband."

"No," she said. "Luke is not her husband. He's not going to find himself. Her death will not be a catalyst for personal revelation. Half of everything is a white lady found dead in a field. *'Who killed the white lady? Let's find the white lady's killer. Let's make the white lady's death about us.'*"

"You're changing the subject," Andrew said.

"Am I, though?" Molly asked.

"Yes, you are."

"I'm swerving," Molly said. "I wouldn't say change. It's the same conversation."

They bumped onto a new kind of asphalt on the rural highway. She remembered to look out the window. She never tired of traveling to exotic locations and having encounters with different and more spectacular types of trees. They drove past a waterfall that was actually two waterfalls crashing into each other and having a total cataclysm in the air.

" '*Who killed the white lady?*' is the plot of your next movie," Andrew said. "It's the reason we're driving down this road."

"That's different."

"Horseshit."

"Horseshit?"

"Horseshit," Andrew said. "It's no different at all."

Maybe, baby, she thought, in the style of a PI novel she'd been reading to prepare. But maybe, baby, not. Wasn't it a different scenario if she were the one doing the investigating? Weren't the sympathies more aligned? The motivations? The end result?

"Can we get back to reality?" she asked him. "That would be great."

"You're in the wrong business for that," Andrew said. "The old question has been answered. Life imitates us."

Perhaps their entire marriage had been a series of idiotic statements like that, statements where he said it one way, and she refuted it and said it the other, and in the end who gave a shit, and who really fucking cared? Not Lindsay Ingram, no longer capable of questions. Not Luke, who'd bragged in high school about reading exactly one half of one novel, *The Red Badge of Courage*, in his entire life. He was not sitting around somewhere—was he still in jail? how long did you stay in jail for assault?—thinking about how he'd make a great character.

"He could be," Andrew said. "Who are you to say?"

"His life is totally messed up," Molly said.

"And that's too bad," Andrew said. "It really is. I feel sorry for him. But that doesn't stop the urge to be on television."

"Now it's a series?"

"Movies, television—it's the twenty-first century. What's the difference?" Andrew asked.

"I think there's a difference," Molly said.

"There isn't."

"I think there is."

"I think I wanna crash the car off the road," he said. "How about that?"

There was the mountain, closest to God. Andrew walked into the bookstore. Molly sat in the Land Rover with her Red Sox cap pulled down over her eyes. The most recent bodyguard had been left at home. She pushed her cap up and looked around. All the buildings were one- and two-story echoes of the lumber boom. Impossibly organized men had conceived of the design. The road the SUV was on drove itself right straight smack into the ocean and the end of the world. Families paraded their fathers, their grandfathers, their great-great-ones, across the street to brunch. They were so much trouble to convince. They didn't like to shop. He just sees a bunch of stuff, mother said. The kids were thrilled to have him. What was he thinking? Did he like his watch?

Molly loved her iPhone. Even though she knew the number by heart, she thumbed down to find her father's contact, felt the surge of unwanted memory, and thought of Luke, of the countless times he'd called her there. When her father had said Luke's name over the phone, when he'd told her about the incident, Molly realized she hadn't thought about him in fifteen years—at least not in any deliberate sense. She might have considered him as a matter of pure biology. She might have once told a girlfriend how he had blue eyes or described his extra-long eyelashes she'd always wanted to put mascara on. She might have said how he looked exhausted when last she'd seen him in Vermont (a Christmas many years ago, his father already sick), as if he'd been dragged through time by his ankles, hands behind him clawing at the walls. They'd sat together in his family's decorated living room with a plate of elf-shaped cookies on the couch between them. She remembered feeling sorry for him. They spoke about the town they'd grown up in as if it were a dead person. He'd never left. She wasn't yet famous. They could hear his father in the garage, coughing. She said California was a state of mind. She said it is. You don't believe me, but it is. She laughed and touched his shoulder, but pulled back when she felt how much he liked it. In Washington state, lifetimes later, she remembered this. She recalled the exact sensation of the precise moment. For each of them there had been a tremendous amount of shame. Hers in knowing she had come to visit him out of a sense of charity. His in understanding that and wanting her there anyway.

Molly tried her father, but no answer. She smoked half a cigarette and then went into the bookstore. It felt empty, but she knew it wasn't. The clerk, a man with a lumpy, unshaven face, was reading at the counter. He didn't notice her.

Andrew was in nonfiction, evaluating who to option.

"Did you get ahold of him?"

"No luck."

"I was wondering," Andrew said. "Who do you think he voted for?"

"It's not something we talk about."

"You don't talk about politics?"

"Nope."

"Not ever?" Andrew asked.

"Not in years."

"Why not?"

"It was a point of contention."

"So, who your father voted for in the presidential election is a total mystery to you?"

"If you want to call it that," she said.

"What would you call it?"

"I would call it something I don't know," Molly said. "Not a mystery."

When friends asked her about her father, she had a cute line stored up. "He's like Jack Nicholson," she'd say. "He doesn't do TV interviews." The line implied that John was distant and cool, but what Molly actually meant was that he didn't talk very much and that he scared her. People enjoyed the Nicholson reference to the point where they didn't notice she'd evaded the question. She wouldn't have to say how one time when she was six her father took her to the grocery store and forgot her there. She wouldn't need to explain how he used to drink, but sobered up, and blah, blah, blah, everything's fine now.

"Who did your parents vote for?" Molly asked.

"Obama, of course," Andrew said. "They were at the fundraising dinner we threw. They donated fifty thousand dollars."

"Well, there you go," Molly said.

"What does that mean?" Andrew asked, but she'd already moved on to the fiction aisle.

She went to the W's to see if Greg's novel was there. As usual, it wasn't. Because there was little demand, nobody bothered to stock *The Last Century*. It was only on Amazon, priced at a nickel. He'd done a terrible job promoting it. She'd told him via text he needed to get an op-ed in the *Times*. Didn't he have an essay lying around he could get published? Couldn't he show his ass a little? He'd written back a quote about silence, exile, and cunning. In reply, she'd *lol*'d for the first time in her life.

Molly turned the corner at the end of the alphabet, and went to the other side of the bookcase. She started over again at A. From high school, she remembered *To The Lighthouse*, remembered the father who'd conceived of his intelligence as an alphabet, like a scale, or an odometer, but with letters instead of numbers. What had been the letter he was anguished to remain at? R? M? She'd thought it was the saddest part of the book, that someone should think of his life that way.

The bell above the bookstore entrance announced someone. Molly browsed C, D, E. A tall woman with a giant forehead walked up to her. Molly stepped back. The woman was white with blue eyes. She was in her early forties. Her dirty blond hair fell to her shoulders. There were a lot of freckles going on.

"You think all white people are racist, huh?" the woman bawled at Molly. Old spittle the size of tiny Quaker oats dislodged from the corners of her mouth. "You think people forgot you said that? You think you get to say some stupid shit like that, and then go back to your fancy life, you Hollywood whore slut?"

Molly continued retreating as the woman shouted. She was two body lengths away. She jammed her shoulders, arms, hands, and the back of her head into the four shelves of the poetry section.

The woman hopped toward a nearby shelf. First, she pulled, then she knocked, and finally she swept all the books off the shelf to the floor.

"*Yes, we can!*" she mock-chanted. "Who are you callin' racist? That's on you! You're the one who's racist! Happy Father's Day!"

•

Molly wanted to jump in the Land Rover and get the hell out of there, but they couldn't.

"Technically," the bookstore guy said, "you're also a witness. It would be a different matter if the perpetrator was still around. But she was so fast. Did you see her? She was like a cheetah. Some of these books are—I mean, look at these covers. I can't sell these. They're all bent. That's property damage. I'm an employee. I represent the owners. I need to file a report. You can do what you want, but you have to stay here."

The bookstore guy's face had changed. The entire situation had given him his zest for life back. He looked ten years younger. His skin was taut and brilliant. Waiting around for the police was the greatest thing that had ever happened to him. Molly played second fiddle to heroism.

"I saw your last movie," he said, leaning across the counter. "It was pretty okay."

"Alright," she said.

The guy went to the door and flipped the sign to CLOSED: BE BACK IN 10 MINS.

"Who are you?" he asked Andrew.

The cop was young, white, and in possession of a firearm. It was right there on his hip. You couldn't miss it. He also had a lightning bolt tattooed in black around his right bicep, a pair of gold aviator sunglasses on, and a scar that ran down the left side of his face seemingly from his eye to his chin like a wobbly line a child might have drawn. His face made Andrew's face seem inert—like who was this husband? like what did he bring to the table?

"What's the story?" the cop asked. In Bono fashion, he kept his sunglasses on. They all did that. It was a neat little trick of the eye.

Who could look in? Nobody. Meanwhile, he was a camera. What sort of psych training did police go through? Were they like hairdressers? Did they attend classes concerning the aura of their power? In her research, Molly had learned the answers to these questions.

The bookstore guy explained the situation. The cop hated him. Everybody felt it. Every time he said anything remotely boring, the cop scanned around the store. He didn't seem to be paying the slightest attention. Andrew kept his mouth shut.

"And you're not pressing charges?" the cop asked Molly.

"No," she said. "It's—I don't know. It's—"

"Complicated," the cop said. He took off his sunglasses and looked right at her. From the scar, his left eye was slightly pinched in the outer corner. It was impossible that he didn't know who she was. "I understand," he said. "Why don't you show me where it happened. Show me these books on the floor."

She led him across the hard bookstore carpet to the scene of the crime. They looked at the novels scattered everywhere. Who were these people? Where did they come from? What did they want? The cop crouched down on his haunches. He plucked a dark red novel up by its cover using his thumb and pointer finger. It dangled in the air in front of his face.

"My sister's a big reader," he said.

"What does she read?" Molly asked.

"I don't know," the cop said. "She's twelve."

"Is she smart?"

"She's average," he said. "Maybe slightly above. What did this woman look like? Can you give me a description?"

Molly did. She said the word *forehead*.

"Big forehead?" he asked. "Lots of freckles?"

"Tons."

"Like all over the place?"

"Everywhere."

"Nose? Cheeks? Chin?"

"That's it."

"I think I know who we're dealing with."

They gathered at the discount table. To make an arrest, as the bookstore guy insisted, the cop said Molly would need to identify the woman.

"Since you aren't going to file a complaint for harassment," he said, "all you are is a witness to the crime of her knocking books off a shelf."

"Several shelves," the bookstore guy said.

"Whatever," the cop said. "I just need you to point her out to me. You won't even have to leave the car."

They put Andrew in the backseat of the SUV cruiser. It was a whole other world back there. He was like if luggage could talk. Nobody up front cared. The bookstore guy had wanted to come, but the cop gave him the face that said no fucking way. Molly loved the doo-hickeys all over the cruiser's dash. She'd done twenty ride-alongs with various cops in East LA. You could push a button and light up like a disco ball. They drove east on a road coursing through a forest of black and dark green. The channels of your brain underwent a re-org in a cruiser. The world deadened somewhat. You were more alive. All objects were isolated and alone against the backdrop of reality. Cars. Houses. Road signs.

"Lots of Confederate flags," Andrew said. "And totem poles. I'm seeing both out here."

The static voice of dispatch announced a 417K.

"Somebody has a knife," Molly said.

The cop turned his entire head to look at her. He kept it that way for a beat longer than was safe, and then he went back to the road.

"How about a 211?" he asked.

"Robbery."

"451?"

"Arson."

"5150?"

"A crazy person."

"602?"

"Trespassing."

"Okay. Okay," the cop said. "Here's one. I've got one. What's a 422?"

"A terrorist threat."

"Holy moly," he said.

He asked her about the movie she was going to be in. She told him the plot.

"Sounds good. I like mysteries. I'm always watching a detective show," he said. "But you know what I got into over there? *Classics*. Black-and-white stuff. A guy in my unit went to film school. He was a godsend. You can't just sit around watching *Transformers* over and over again."

Half the cops she'd been assigned to on her ride-alongs were vets. She'd had to quickly learn how to talk with them. It was a whole different language, much of it unsaid.

"Where were you deployed?"

"Two tours in Iraq. One in Afghanistan."

"Nice to see you."

"Thank you," he said.

Then you changed the subject.

"What classics?" she asked him.

"All sorts. But if you ask me who my favorite is, I'd have to say Bergman. That guy is super fucked up. Excuse me, ma'am."

He took the cruiser down what looked more like a horse path than a road. They rolled and dropped among the giant divots. The house was a very normal affair. It was one of those sea-green ranch styles a Mack truck had delivered. A blue minivan and a red Saab were parked at angles in the yard.

"I'm not going to arrest this woman," the cop said. "If you wanted to file charges, I would. But you don't. Is that right? Am I understanding you?"

"That's right," Molly said. "It would be a whole thing."

"Understood," he said. "Bookstore guy is only an employee. He's not the owner. If the owners want to press charges, I'll come back out here. I'll take five or six hours out of my day to arrest her, process her, and file the paperwork. I don't have time for that today. It's Father's Day. My kids are making me pancakes for dinner. I'm just gonna get her out on the porch and nod to you. I need to let her know that we know. If people do this sort of thing and get away with it, it's all they ever do."

He gathered his ledger and called in his position to dispatch.

"One last thing," he said, hand on the door. "Why was she so offended? Why was she so angry?"

"Because of an interview I gave a million years ago."

"In which you said what?" he asked. "Specifically?"

"In which I said seventy-five percent of white Americans are racist," Molly said.

"Sorry!" Andrew chirruped from the back.

The cop turned around and looked at Andrew. Molly still liked the scar on his face. She didn't know about his smile.

"For what?" he asked.

HOME

2011

HER MOTHER WAS IN THE KITCHEN. MOLLY LISTENED TO HER from upstairs. Sarah was loading the dishwasher, arranging and re-arranging the plates. She heard a series of beeps, a pause, and then her mother say "*Oh, dear. Oh, no. Wait . . . there we go.*" The machine went to work, and her mother began to hum. These were the sounds Molly had been hearing all week, and they irritated her in the easy manner of a grown child's judgment. She sometimes thought her mother had given up on complexity, had let go of a more demanding engagement with the world, and that this letting go had made her strange. Back home in Vermont, Sarah used an ancient Mr. Coffee every morning, even though Molly had sent her at least a dozen far superior machines, often two or three at a time, so that her mother could pick and choose from among them and send back those she didn't like. Instead, Sarah gave them away to friends or donated them to local businesses. The fact that she'd explicitly asked for a new coffeemaker never seemed to register; once they were delivered, Sarah was afflicted with an historically New England guilt. "What do I need those fancy things for?" she'd ask. And yet, whenever Sarah came to Los Angeles, she absolutely loved using Molly's "fancy things," like the German-made dishwasher and the Italian dual-shot espresso machine, and raved about them as if only movie stars like her daughter owned such luxury items, marveling every time, "Would you look at that," as the automatic window shades descended on the night.

Molly guessed it was only age, but she couldn't get used to her mother's gee-whiz behavior during these visits. Her behavior, and the fact that whenever Sarah came to California she liked to get drunk, but only once per trip, and only on red wine. That night, on the eve of the awards, she'd gone ahead and done that, invoked, as Molly had come think of it, her privilege. Sarah was in rare vacation form, and had developed, after a second glass of Malbec, a competitive, even mean streak. With a wave of her hand, Molly flushed the toilet, washed her hands, and went back downstairs to see what the hell her mother was doing.

"The Twelve-Year-Old shouldn't even be nominated," Sarah said. She was sitting on the couch, glass of wine in one hand, remote in the other. The TV was off because she couldn't figure it out. "Something like that shouldn't even be allowed. Doesn't the Academy have rules? They should. It should be eighteen and over. Or twenty-one. You shouldn't be able to get a nomination unless you can drink."

"That doesn't make any sense," Molly said. "Who would play those parts?"

"What parts?"

"The kid parts."

"The kids would," Sarah said.

"But they can't get nominated?"

Sarah shook her head.

"Not even if they're good?" Molly asked. "Like great? Like this kid?"

"No," Sarah said. "Not even."

They were sitting on opposite ends of a couch in the second largest living room. Below them was the canyon. Below that was Hollywood, and in the distance downtown LA. The skyscrapers glowed blue and dark green at their edges. This living room and the kitchen were the only two downstairs spaces Molly Bit occupied. There was another, larger living area, and the smaller one, and the two dining rooms, and five spare bedrooms with their own separate baths. There was a room that had nothing in it but old promotional items like posters and T-shirts and a large cardboard cutout of Molly in a red leather trench coat. There was also a special twelve-seat screening theater with a digital projector. The fact was, Molly only ever used those rooms when she had company, which wasn't often. One of these days she would move, she told friends. She was working on it. But who had the time?

At the end of the year—in between the divorce being finalized and the publicity swing before the nomination—Molly experienced a month off, the first of her adult life. Initially, she didn't know what to do with herself. She kept busy with meetings at the agency, or at one of the studios, and every day there seemed to be five or six new places to eat lunch. This involved driving out to Malibu or down into Beverly Hills, arriving at enormous fortresses. Molly realized these social outings were unified by the theme of driving around by herself for hours. When she thought of her private life, when she imagined its true parameters, this was what she saw, and maybe what she preferred.

Because it was expected of her, she went on a few dates. One had been with a late-night television host, the other with a young, ridiculously attractive actor she'd played opposite in a poorly received thriller. Both evenings felt weirdly official, as if they'd been staged for any number of cameras that weren't there. Molly was thirty-seven. Both men were younger than her. They didn't make her feel old so much as profoundly uninterested in youth. Although she looked twenty-nine, she felt eighty. She'd gone ahead and slept with the actor, and everything but for her orgasm seemed ridiculous. She kept waiting for him to say his mom was a big fan.

"It doesn't matter," her mother said. "The Twelve-Year-Old doesn't have a chance. All she did was die for two hours."

"People love that," Molly said. "They love dying kids."

"But she didn't even die!" Sarah said. "She got better! What's that about? She dies in the book."

"They always die in the book," Molly said. "Death's different in books. Who cracks a novel and thinks, 'Oh, yeah, this'll work out'? Name one great book where a major character doesn't die? You can't. They all die."

"She's not going to win, is what I'm trying to say," Sarah said. She topped off her wine and took a long sip. "That just leaves the other three. The Legend. The Nun. And The Prostitute."

"Who am I?" Molly asked.

"You're The Mother," Sarah said. "You're The Wife. What did The Nun say?"

"She wished me luck."

"I know that," Sarah said. "But what did she *say*?"

Molly straightened up. Her face morphed into the smiling, over-joyed mask of a doll's. In a Georgia accent, she crooned, "'Oh, hi, hon. How you doin'? I just wanted to call, and wish you con-grat-u-lations. You were just *sooo* good. I know you won't believe it, but I'm rootin' for you. That scene near the end where the husband's gettin' outta jail, and you're waitin' there with those two little girls. It just about—it just about broke my heart.'"

The Nun was a part-time Scientologist and a quarter-time mother to three adopted Senegalese children. She was also a person without shame. She lacked the required number of synapses needed in order to connect action and consequence, and she would do—on set or anywhere—anything, and it was this sort of moral dexterity that made her an excellent actress as well as celebrity. In the last three months, Molly had seen The Nun twice. The first was at the Golden Globes, where Molly had witnessed The Nun pantomiming a conversation with Robert Duvall. He was asking, "What? What? What are you saying?" and she was moving her lips without making a sound. An NBC television camera was on them, and The Nun didn't want to appear dull.

The next time Molly saw her was at a private luncheon thrown by a former CEO of a major multinational media corporation. The CEO was trying to get The Nun nominated by the Academy, and was doing everything within the scope of his almost unlimited power to make that happen. Molly had been invited as a guest of The Nun, and, although she didn't want to attend, she had to, because Molly as well didn't want to seem overly competitive or incapable of appreciating the talent of her peers.

A luncheon designed to get someone nominated was like a cross between a funeral, a wedding, and an Apple stockholders' meeting. A top Disney executive got up and thanked fifteen or twenty people Molly knew for a fact he'd fucked over in deals. Then a clip of The Nun from *The Nun*. After that, the exec said things a person should only say about a cult leader. ("I wake up some mornings gratified by the knowledge she's alive.") Then they served lunch, during which The Nun rose and thanked everyone in attendance. "Molly Bit," The Nun said, hand over her heart. "I'm just, I'm just," and then nothing.

"She did not say she was rooting for you," Sarah said.

"She did."

"What did you say?"

"I told her I was rooting for her too," Molly said. "What could I say? We lied to each other for a while. We're always up for the same stuff. She's fine."

"I guess," Sarah said.

In the month and one week since the nominations had been announced, Molly had spoken to all but The Prostitute. She'd watched the broadcast at 5:25 that Monday morning, and the feeling that overcame her as she heard her name was not unlike the reaction to news of a sudden death. She felt like she was escaping her body or as if it were falling away from her. And then, because it seemed like the thing to do, as if it would keep her limbs from shooting off, she locked herself into her safe room, slid the titanium bolt shut, and screamed with all her lunatic excitement.

At three o'clock, she called back The Twelve-Year Old. The girl's incoming ringtone was the opening to the *Goldberg Variations* as performed by Glenn Gould.

"Why, thank you," The Twelve-Year-Old said, her voice proper like a yardstick. "As I said in my message, congratulations to you as well." She was in New York, doing *Uncle Vanya*. Molly would have to excuse her if she sounded tired, the girl said. Chekhov was a triathlon for the soul.

"Aren't you excited?" Molly asked.

"As much as a person in my situation can be," the girl said.

"What situation is that?"

"What I mean is, it's ridiculous to believe that I'll win, so it's important to take that into account, I think. My manager says, win or lose, I need to conceive of this as a footnote."

"A footnote to what?" Molly asked.

"To my career, of course," The Twelve-Year Old said. "If anything, this could be a hindrance. It presents any number of obstacles. We all know the trappings of early success, the long list of clichés one would hope to avoid. Do I want a life ruined by drug addiction? Do I succumb to that tragic narrative? Or do I aspire for something more?"

The Legend, as was only right, was the one who called Molly.

"Oh, yes," the older woman said. "That child is strange. We had her here once. She kept asking me about working with Marlon, but very odd questions, like how much did he weigh?"

The Legend lived in upstate New York on thirteen hundred acres of land that included a helipad and any number of horses no one was allowed to ride. These animals instead freely trotted and grazed every spring, summer, and fall, and spent their winters in Florida, where The Legend kept another home. Her husband was a world-renowned photographer-turned-local-eccentric. Molly asked about him.

"James is fine. He's going around to all of our neighbors asking if he can take pictures of them while they shower," The Legend said. "I don't think it's going to work, but he has this theory about showers . . ."

She told Molly not to be nervous.

"It's wonderful," The Legend said. "It's simply the best time there is to be had. Everyone is thrilled to be there. Everyone is happy and kind. The first time you're nominated is, really, the best time, because it's all so new and fresh and exciting. You're a little girl again. The second time is far different. I would say it's even better. The third time is . . ."

Molly liked The Legend. Her four Oscar wins were well deserved. Despite her mythic status, she remained gracious and kind. Not that she had any other choice. Kindness and grace were what people had come to expect of her. It was merely good fortune that the instincts required for the role came naturally. Molly was more than happy—thrilled, in fact—to hear The Legend speak of her life. It wasn't arrogance or conceit passing through the earpiece. It was the truth, and the truth didn't bother Molly. No, what bothered Molly was the tone of postmenopausal confidence that certain accomplished women over sixty possess. They haven't forgotten the decades of fear and doubt—the sympathy remains—but they have adopted that most annoying of masculine traits, that tic which seems to pronounce, ad nauseam, and merely through a hollow word or a twist of the mouth, "What's the big fuss?"

"Have fun," The Legend said. "Enjoy it. Forget about the competition. It's just an honor to be nominated."

On her couch in her medium-sized living room, Molly Bit recounted all of this for her mother. Together, they looked out at the pool. It was yellow from the house lights. As the wind picked up, the japonica newly planted around the yard's edge twitched extravagantly. The silence was good, but then Molly felt the need to ruin it.

"How's my father?" she asked.

"I wish you wouldn't do that," Sarah said.

"Do what?"

"You know what. What is that? *'My father.'*"

A long moment passed in which they sat there in the telepathic silence of family life. Doing prep for *Certain Values*, she'd spent a week living with the girls who'd played her daughters. During their next to last dinner, she'd refused to speak to them. Her mother used to do this. Normally, it would last an evening. The longest stretch was four days. John had come home one night and pulled the screen door off its hinge. He'd kicked the kitchen table over. He'd put his fist through the bathroom wall right into Molly's bedroom. When the police arrived, Molly stood on the porch with her mother and watched her father being cuffed out on the lawn. She'd gone to school that week—everybody's favorite girl—but at home it was nothing but quiet, nothing but the loneliness of watching, until her mother put out her cigarette on a Friday night after McDonald's and said, "I guess I'll drop the charges."

With the *Certain Values* girls, Molly felt bad about the exercise—she remembered how awful it was—but she needed to see what would happen. The little one cried. The older one forked her peas into the shape of a lopsided star, went into the kitchen, came back with a pint of salty caramel ice cream, and ate the whole thing.

"Fine," Molly said. "How's Dad?"

"He's good," Sarah said. "I called him before I left."

"Do you think he'll watch?"

"Of course, he'll watch. He's your father."

"So because he has to," Molly said. It was a child's voice coming through her.

"Jeez."

"It's true," Molly said.

"It isn't."

"It is," Molly said. "I don't like that woman. What's her name?"

"You know her name," Sarah said. "Catherine."

"She's too young for him," Molly said.

"Ten years is . . ." Sarah started. "I'm glad he found someone. I'm glad he's sober. I'm happy for him."

"Is that your line now?" Molly asked. "Is that the line you're going with?"

They hadn't spoken about the role, how Molly had played her mother in a movie: the husband a drunk, the character a frayed nerve of stress, how every scene was about trying and failing and going at it again and how whenever the man showed up—he was all they wanted—he destroyed everything.

"You should go to Al-Anon," Sarah said. "I've found it helpful. You should deal with certain things."

"I've been," Molly said. "I've dealt."

"You've been?"

"No," Molly said. "Since when do we talk like this?"

"We talk like this," Sarah said. "Don't we? Sure we do."

"Not ever," Molly said.

The doorbell rang.

"Doorbell!"

"God, Mom."

"*What?*" Sarah asked.

"It's just more packages."

"Well, isn't your life terrible," Sarah said.

The last month hadn't exactly been a breeze, she'd have her mother know. The press junkets had been absurd, and fairly often embarrassing, at least inwardly, deep down inside Molly's stomach, where all her tension did its flexing. The car with her publicist inside would pick her up in the morning, and then it was the Standard, the W, or all afternoon at the Shutters in Santa Monica, room after room of print and web journalists and their pent up, adolescent rage. Like water balloons they hoped wouldn't burst, the first few questions were gentle—and then it was attack, attack, attack.

"You recently went through a very long, very public, and very nasty divorce. Who will you be bringing to the ceremony?"

"As a thirty-seven-year-old, how do you feel about the dearth of roles for older women in Hollywood?"

"How does it feel to be you? Do you like you? What do you think of you?"

But the gifts, the flowers, the jewelry: these things were nice. Most of them were sent to the agency first, collected there on some intern's desk, Molly imagined, and then couriered up to her in the hills.

She made sure to open all the letters. It had been two years since she'd received one, and never on Coldwater, but Molly remained afraid of the prospect. The detective said it wasn't anything to worry about, that whoever it was had most likely moved on, maybe died. All investigators could ever say for certain was that whoever was writing the letters did so from inside California. He made his own ink. He used a typewriter that couldn't be traced. That winter, just in case he'd switched envelopes, Molly opened all her letters wearing latex gloves. They were never from him. The rest of it—the orchids, the clothes, the lemon trees—she put in the dining room.

Usually, the agency sent an intern or an assistant over in a car, but sometimes they used a service. Molly went to the video screen to see which it was. There was no one there, no car in the exterior drive, nobody, and so she tapped the screen for the next camera angle. Molly saw a man in a hoodie at the street gate. It wasn't the best resolution, and at first she felt the pure fear—the mindless, spinal shock—but then the man flipped his hood out of his face and Molly saw he was black.

"Marcus?" she intercom'd.

"The one and only," her neighbor said.

She grabbed a cigarette out of a drawer and walked outside to the security panel. She tried four or five different code sequences before the gate opened. Marcus slipped in and started down the drive. His high-cut running shorts were way too short. They were also bright purple. She saw the box in his hands.

"Nice look," she said.

"I'm training for a role," he said. "The guy's an ex-SEAL. This was outside."

"Out there?"

"In the drainage ditch," Marcus said. "Maybe the intern had a hot date. Dumped it. Peeled off."

"Thoughtful." She lit her cigarette.

"Please," Marcus said, completing the distance. "Give me a drag."

He took an ex-smoker's pull. She watched all the old motions and memories come back to him. Marcus was handsome, and his wife was beautiful, and both of their sons were gorgeous.

She took the box from him. It was the kind of thing you put a hat in. It weighed practically nothing, but it was awkward to hold. She set it on the ground.

"What do you think it is?" Molly asked.

"A vase?" Marcus said.

"A vase?" she asked him. "What makes you say that?"

"I'm saying maybe," Marcus said. "I'm saying it could be."

With her toe, Molly nudged the box forward over the asphalt granules. "It's not a vase," she said. "But thank you."

Marcus was on a TV show that Molly didn't watch. It was a sitcom where he played a smooth-operating ladies' man, and it aired on one of the newer cable networks. She couldn't even remember the network's acronym. When he wasn't filming, he did plays: Chicago, London, New York. He'd pack the whole family up and they'd be gone for months at a time. His film credits were small and numerous: The Drug Dealer, The Gang Member, The Cop. He'd won an Obie Award for a play he'd starred in called *The Rights of Man*.

"Shouldn't you be at some fancy dinner-drinks thing right now?" Marcus asked.

"My mother," she said, and rolled her head back toward the house. "She's in there."

Last year, Molly had spent several weeks before the start of *Certain Values* with Marcus and his family. She went grocery shopping with them. She watched TV. She hung out in their backyard. She had hoped to steal a few behaviors from Alice, get an insight or two, but instead she became interested in how totally in love with her family Alice was. Molly's character was a good woman, but never not pissed off. Not so with Alice. She moved about her day behaving as if she hadn't been robbed of anything. Not her freedom. Not her time. Not her identity. In fact, Alice genuinely liked their company. She enjoyed asking them if they were okay. Was everything all right? What was the matter? Did they want to talk about it? She annoyed the boys with her affection, and they adored her for it.

Marcus gave her back her cigarette.

"How you feelin'?" he asked her.

"I'm very nervous," she said.

"I bet. You want some advice?"

"No," she said. "Go ahead."

"Don't trip on the stairs."

Molly looked at him. She remembered they were true friends. She had spent the month of December in the Arabian desert and had lived in a tent half the size of a football end zone. At night, when she wasn't shooting, she would sit outside the main flap and look up at the universe and rehearse her lines. A man came by in the morning with fruit trucked in from Europe. Kiwis. Mangos. She'd met a prince with five wives. But looking at Marcus she was jealous of his life. Not jealous of its exact details, but of its feeling, of what it must have been like to walk inside his home every day. She didn't want a family, so much as the energy of one, like a room she could stroll in and out of whenever she wanted to, and maybe close the door on when it got to be too much. Molly guessed the real truth was that she wanted to go on acting. It was her whole life.

He had to be on his way.

"Alice is making us throw a party. They're gonna wanna leave gifts by your gate. Is that alright?"

"If I win, sure," Molly said. "I don't want consolation prizes."

She took the box with her back into the house and set it on a table by the door. Earlier, she'd left her phone there. She depressed the circle and saw three missed calls and a voicemail from The Prostitute.

"You'll never guess where I am, Mol. Not in a hundred million years. I'm in Boise, Idaho, which is surprisingly temperate! I think I might buy property here! That would be . . . oh, down-homey. Listen . . . the jet I was on crashed. Not really. But we did have to make an emergency landing. A goose flew into the turbine. That's what the pilot said. '*Sorry, ma'am, a goose flew into the turbine.*' I was half-asleep. I didn't believe him. We're waiting on another jet, or maybe just a regular plane. I would accept a hot air balloon ride at this point—" and then the voicemail cut out.

The Prostitute lived in New York and belonged "to the third generation of a hip avant-garde family," as the *Times* had awkwardly put it last Sunday, stressing The Prostitute's Village pedigree and turning what should have been a straight puff piece into an elegy—it was like they couldn't help themselves—for old Manhattan. The Prostitute's grandfather was a sculptor whose work had been included in four Whitney Biennials. Her grandmother was a performance artist and an off-Broadway legend. Her older brother died from a heroin overdose. And on and on. The photo that ran with the article was of The Prostitute under the arch in Washington Square. Was she smiling? Was she frowning? Was she having an orgasm?

She tapped Call Back.

"Where are you?" Molly asked, even though she knew.

"Boise," The Prostitute said, all the excitement of her voicemail gone.

"I don't know if you've heard," Molly said, "but you've been nominated for an Academy Award."

"Ha-ha-ha," The Prostitute said.

"The ceremony is tomorrow."

"Yes, I know. I'm starting to freak out over here."

"When's the plane coming?"

"It was supposed to be here by now. I'm supposed to be on a new plane, in mid-air, right now."

"Do you want me to accept on your behalf?"

"Shut up. I'll accept on *your* behalf."

"I'm not going to win," Molly said, but she didn't really mean this.

"I'm not either," The Prostitute said (ditto, Molly knew). "That psycho's going to win. She'll be all surprised about it too! *'Little ole me?'* "

In the late '90s, Molly and The Prostitute had starred together in a horror movie called *Funhouse*. Last year, Molly had purchased a VHS copy of it on eBay for one hundred and sixty dollars and sent it to The Prostitute on her birthday.

"I had some people over the other night and we watched it," The Prostitute said. "It holds up. I mean, it's horror, so it's, you know, whatever, but we were good. It was a sort of pre-Oscar thing I was having. 'Before They Were Nominees' was the theme."

Molly asked who was there.

"Everybody," The Prostitute said. "Why don't you move to New York?"

It would have made sense. She wasn't really an LA person anymore. All the New York people were moving to LA, so why shouldn't she move to New York? When they were still married, during that time when they'd tried to make a go of it, Molly had suggested the idea to Andrew, and he'd been terrified. His career was going so well. What about the next project? The one after that? What kept them together in part was the way they were tapped into the industry: a deal would happen, and the tremor of it, the ripple, would set off an alarm inside one or the other of them. They were at the center of everything. Why would they leave that? Andrew asked. Because she was unhappy, Molly wanted to say. Because the stories of the other women had broken something in her. Not her heart, but her pride, a thing she had leaned on for years.

"You should move to New York, and you should get on Twitter," The Prostitute said. "Your social media is a disaster. Do you know how much money you could save? Who does your Facebook? It's a mess."

"I don't know," Molly said. "Somebody."

"I wonder how many times I'll tell this plane story tomorrow night?" The Prostitute asked.

"A thousand," Molly said.

Molly wouldn't tell a story. Her mother on her arm, they would do the slow walk down the world's longest red carpet, stopping here and there in the shadows of buildings and various press corps, the nervous, spastic energy of TV and internet correspondents forcing her to cross-step one way, and cross-back back, and twirl. "And who is this?" they'd ask. "My mother," she'd say. "Hi, Mom!" And if it wasn't so exciting and wonderful and addictive in its thrill, anyone would throw up from how ridiculous it was. They would vomit up all that went unspoken. And what about it? What could Molly say? This is my mother? I'm playing her? I found out her trauma was mine? I shook for two days after the movie wrapped? How uncomfortable does that make you feel?

Film was the secret art, Molly knew, the repressed medium, and all the celebrity bullshit kept it that way, hidden in plain sight. To be who she was, to act, to be free, all she had to do was lie most of the time.

"Oh my goodness, me-oh-my-oh," The Prostitute said. "*Ze plane.*"

Molly heard it. The jet was like an asteroid in the distance. It was supersonic.

"I love you, Molly Bit," The Prostitute said.

"I love you too," Molly said, and ended the call.

She needed another cigarette. Clutched under her arm, she took the box back outside. The evening cold had come. She was in the high desert again. She went into the garden, sat on the low edge of the broken fountain, and lit her cigarette. Using her keys, she cut through the tape on the box. It was difficult. She had to saw into the tape, and some of the cardboard along the flap ripped.

"What's that?" came her mother's voice.

She slid the box around to her right and kept on smoking. She had been having a moment. Her mother didn't need to be there for everything.

Sarah set herself down next to Molly. Always thin, she was beginning to gain weight in her hips; her jeans bunched up on either side of her. She shifted her knees a little so as to get comfortable, and then, once she was done moving, she sighed deeply, subatomically even, as if acknowledging that, yes, it had been she, she had been the one to give birth to the world.

"It's one cigarette," Molly said.

"It's not that," Sarah said. "I've made my peace with that. It's your life. Go ahead and kill yourself. Don't let me stop you."

"What then?"

"Nothing."

She exhaled again.

"*What?*"

"It's just that you made such a good mother," Sarah said. "Look how good. Oscar good."

Hardly anyone understood what it was she did for a living, not even the people who celebrated her for it—not even those who made money off her. It was good luck the girls who'd played her daughters hadn't been professionals. They were now, of course, and would be forever—you couldn't go back—but before the movie, they'd been found in a national search. Molly was nervous beforehand, worried to work with children, but the fact that they had no idea what they were doing had worked in her favor. On the first day of shooting, she explained to them what a mark was and how it was okay to ask questions if they were unsure about anything—if they wondered "why?" or "how?" or "what about?" The movie was a little master class in acting. Unlike most adults, the kids still understood make-believe and how it wasn't much different than real life.

At the wrap party, the seven-year old asked her, "Are we Method?"

The girl's shiny blond hair was parted to the side with a green barrette. The movie husband walked around with the five-year-old on his shoulders.

"In a way," Molly said. She told the girl they were the kind of actors who mapped their performances. They knew the why, but not the how until they'd done it. They did their research. They dreamt inside the brains of their characters. They knew every last little thing.

"But do you want to know a secret?" Molly asked.

The girl did. She really did.

"If you're Method all the time, if you're always in character—it's selfish," Molly whispered. "It's for boys."

The girl understood what Molly meant. She nodded.

"My brother never lets me call time-out when we play."

"Boys are the worst," Molly said. "Time-outs are important."

Remembering this, she took a drag off her cigarette and looked at her mother.

"It's a movie," Molly said.

"Acting's not just acting."

"What is it, then?"

"I don't know," Sarah said, "but I know it's not just that."

"It's not off the table," Molly said.

"It would be nice to have a grandchild, is all I'm saying."

"You have step-grandchildren."

"Not the same thing," Sarah said.

"Can we not?" Molly asked. "Tomorrow's the biggest day of my life."

"No offense, sweetie," her mother said, "but every tomorrow has been the biggest tomorrow of your life since you were born."

Why a baby? Molly wondered. It was absurd. The children of the famous were born into someone else's daydream and spent the rest of their lives trying to wake up from it.

"This whole town is creepy," Sarah said. "The privacy here. I find it creepy. Did I ever tell you that?"

"That you find me creepy?"

"Not you. I didn't say you. Your privacy. I find your privacy creepy."

"What choice do I have?" Molly asked.

"None. That's true," Sarah said. "But that's how you like it. That's what everybody here wants—to be so famous that their privacy is a really big deal. They want everybody in the world to want them so badly that they finally have a good enough reason to say, *'Leave me alone!'* I used to think it was *E! News*'s fault or whatever but it's not. It's the actors' faults. You're all so strange and creepy and weird. *'Look at me! Stop! Don't look at me! I need you! Get away from me!'* It's bizarre."

Molly pushed the box lightly with her hand. She assumed it was from her dad. It would be exactly like him to send a gift through the "proper" channels. John was her father, but he'd always let it be known that he was himself first, all alone and unattached. If most people sent gifts through the agency, then he would too—he wasn't anyone special.

"You're saying I'm creepy again," Molly said.

"Am I?" Sarah asked. "So maybe I am." She finished her wine in one long gulp and stood up, a little wobbly.

She looked at her mother standing there. Why did everyone have it out for actors still? You didn't need to be an actor to be famous anymore, she thought. You didn't need to do anything. Everybody knew that. The way the century was going, actors would soon be extinct, replaced by holograms, or next-generation CGI, or maybe only regular people with cameras pointed at them. Movies were bound to die, like plays, like books, like anything. And what then? What would happen to the people who played the people? What would happen when everybody, finally everybody, was famous?

Her mother walked back toward the house. Halfway there, she stopped and spun around.

"You know how I felt watching your movie?" Sarah asked. "You know how it made me feel?"

"How?" Molly asked.

"Tough," Sarah said. "I felt tough for the first time in my life. Good job."

It was the nicest thing her mother had ever said to her. Sarah went back inside the house. Molly finished her cigarette. It had been a good one, one of those that made all of the others, and the end result, worthwhile. Sitting by the fountain, she dragged the box closer to her. She opened the flaps and found it was filled with light-pink tissue paper, layer after layer of it. Finally, there was an end. The box was empty, there was nothing inside, she thought, but then Molly unfolded two sheets of paper apart and shook them, and the letter fell out. She recognized it instantly, the stalker's letter—it was like an old idea, or the same recurring nightmare—and she couldn't bring herself to touch it.

DEATH

IN MEMORIAM

JUNE 2014

7

ABIGAIL WANTED A MOMENT. IT WAS WHAT THE DRY-ERASE board was for. She wrote down certain terms and questions— *Establishing Shot, Jump Cut To: Interior, How does time work?*—zinged around the classroom like a lightning storm for fifty minutes, and then, when it was all said and done, stood with her back to their departures, erasing everything. Up-and-down, side-to-side, little circles: a mindlessness conspired. Years passed this way. Forget time signatures, she'd told them. Show a newspaper with the date for godsake, or a website, or a phone. No need for an interstitial *Eight Months Later.* It was a gimmick, anyway. It meant that part's over, but a certain shadow will remain. This was what she felt as she erased. It was almost charming. She erased the professor and became herself again. Abigail's panicked energy released. Her dead mother, the teacher, watched her. It was a silence of *I told you so, look how well you've done*, and *sober, honey!* Her dead mother brought along her dead father, and her dead father, her dead brother. All of her dead people watched her. All of her dead people, except for Molly Bit. It was too soon after Molly's murder, only eight months, and there was no getting used to that.

"Professor Kupchik?" said a voice behind her.

It was the summer program, or what the college called the Institute for Interactive Thinking and Advanced Learning. Every summer, the institute made three million dollars' profit, out of which Abigail saw $1,311.13 after taxes. Unless one was a small child or indigent, this wasn't very much. Still, it supplemented her visiting professor's salary during the regular school year. And what was she going to do about it? Complain? And say what? They paid her to talk.

"Abigail's fine," Abigail said. "Call me Abigail."

She set the eraser on its rail and spun around. It was Christine Gallagher, one of the older students, perhaps sixty, a close-to-timid-but-not-quite woman who'd come out of a marriage, or a long illness, or some life event as equally bone-draining with an old revived dream to write a screenplay in her hand. She had a terrific bob.

"Sorry," Christine said. "*Abigail*. It won't happen again."

"It's okay."

Minus a few, rare exceptions, Abigail liked all of her undergraduates. With the summer students, her reactions were more like those she experienced in civilian life. Some students she liked. Some students she didn't. Some students she didn't think about at all.

"I have a question," Christine said.

She held her spiral-bound notebook tight to her chest. There was her real life right there. This was going to be a thing, Abigail knew, and whatever the thing was going to be, she didn't have time for it. She needed to catch the train into the city. She had plans to meet up with Diane, catch the screening of *Trust*, and then there was the Q&A to cap off Molly's three-day memorial tribute.

"Of course," Abigail said. She couldn't help herself. "What is it?"

"Do you think I belong here?"

They were so heartfelt. You couldn't turn them away.

"Why did you come?" Abigail asked. "What were your reasons?"

Her husband had died. All of the time and all of the money belonged to her now. One thing led to another, and on a certain day Christine realized she'd been sitting at a computer writing scenes for the past two years.

"About your husband?" Abigail asked.

"God no," Christine said. "About these two people who work at an aquarium."

"That sounds good," Abigail said, and she meant it. The movie would practically film itself. She could see the manta rays undulating in their tanks. Their need for freedom.

"No one here likes the idea," Christine said. "They say I should write something more marketable. They say no one cares about aquariums. All I hear is superhero, vampire, werewolf."

"Zombie, witch, Navy SEAL," Abigail said. "I get it."

"So what do you think?" Christine asked.

After her brother overdosed, Abigail had her second moment of clarity in as many years. She couldn't stick around Minnesota, taking care of the dead and the dying. She would need an actual existence, because the very real, but simple joy of sobriety was no longer enough. She needed a job. And since there was only one thing in the world she was any good at or had any experience with, she called up an old friend who taught film, apologized to her about the time she'd made out with her dad, and asked for a favor.

Almost upon arrival, she met a man who was so nice to her, and so good in bed, and who was able to put up with her moods in such a way that she still had respect for him, that it took a year to realize she was in love. Tom asked, *why don't you write again? Just for you?* and she said, *I don't think I can.* But she tried it, and he was right. To hell with everybody, she thought. She wrote and wrote. She didn't like it. She threw it out. She did it again. She tossed it. And once more. And in the end, from the time she started the script until she got the call for the greenlight, it took seven and a half years. There weren't any werewolves, vampires, or superheroes in her movie either, and she didn't know if it would get distributed or if anyone would care about it if it did, but she'd done the thing. She'd put her life back together. And it was good, and her movie was too.

She said all of this to Christine Gallagher, who, it turned out, she liked.

"So that's what I think," Abigail said. She mentioned they could get coffee the next day, but she had a train to catch.

"The tribute?" Christine asked.

"Right."

"It's terrible. It's horrible. She was a friend of yours, wasn't she?"

"We were friends," Abigail said. "A long time ago."

It was an hour-and-a-half ride coasting along the Hudson, little bridges and goats in the yard, three blue suits in her car drinking beer out of paper bags. At 125th Street, she remembered a man she used to love. The train went down under the earth into Grand Central. She took the 4 uptown to Eighty-Sixth Street and ascended the stairs into the last good day of summer.

Diane's wife's parents were rich-rich. A lot of their money was tied up with the construction of an island near Nassau—but still. Near Eighty-Fourth, Abigail took the elevator all the way up to the penthouse. When the doors opened, she was in the living room. It was the size of her entire apartment. She walked past two tan couches low to the floor and stepped up into the gallery between a pair of black marble statues, one a man, the other a woman, both of them on their knees, either praying or screaming. Diane was out on the patio, her back to the park. When they saw each other, they leaned fast into a hug. Without saying a word, both women held on for a minute, until Diane, the executrix, laugh-cried into Abigail's hair, "She was so bad with money. Just so, so bad. She was like a rapper or something."

Diane had been in New York for two weeks, setting up the tribute. Most of her time was spent on the phone, she said, and then in the afternoon she'd go down to the theater, or to a meeting with the director of programming. It was fifteen films in three days, the Q&A, plus a short documentary.

"It's a rough cut," Diane said, "but it's beautiful. I've watched it about ten times. They found this old TV footage of her when she was a girl. She's sledding."

Years before, Abigail had written letter after letter; none of them had been addressed to Molly. Generally, she was decent at amends. To everyone else, she could find her apology. With Molly, it was more difficult. Abigail knew the truth: it was her own fault. No person interested in their health, sanity, or career would have committed to her movie, but her understanding of this would not split off from how she felt. The pain of certain breaks kept. Petty hurt creeped into the letters she composed to Molly in her head. There were stacks of them—but now the pettiness was gone, replaced with guilt. Wherever Abigail went, she took the letters along. She flipped through them as Tom raged all over again about his problems at work, or on the drive to Poughkeepsie for some research that went nowhere. All those blank moments when people believed they knew her position—thought she was right there, or would be soon—but she was somewhere else.

A hawk flew by at eye level. Down in the park, a squirrel posed for a tourist's photograph.

"I received an email yesterday," Diane said.

"Weird phrase."

"I'm supposed to give a deposition."

The trial of Roger Michael Vincent hadn't been a trial at all. It was juryless—his guilty plea worked out in a deal with the district attorney. The state of California had wanted the case dealt with as quickly as possible. The industry too. Molly's murder was something Hollywood didn't want to think about too deeply. Everyone needed her death to be simple, explicable, a chance thing in the world, like a car accident or a drug overdose. They'd put Vincent in a maximum-security prison, but there were rumors of transfer. The psych evals were troubling, the internet said. He didn't speak.

His mother was a different story. She wanted the attention. She'd filed a lawsuit against the estate seeking compensation for mental anguish. She claimed the excessive media coverage of Molly's murder by her son had resulted in depression. *Depression by celebrity*, her lawyers were calling it.

"It's inhuman," Diane said. "He stabbed her. He broke into her home."

She knew the terrifying details. She had learned of the murder as she stood in line at the Student Union. News broke in across the flatscreens. "Sweetheart," an Aramark worker had said. "Sweetheart, *hello*—your coffee."

"It'll never happen."

"But still," Diane said. "What kind of a person?"

"All sorts," Abigail said, nodding at the park. "Everybody down there is messed up."

They could go downtown, Abigail knew, and see mugs, T-shirts, posters with Molly's face on them. There was a wax replica of Molly at Madame Tussauds. Fanned out on collapsible tables in China-town were bootleg DVDs of her early stuff, *Starcatcher* and *Funhouse*. There was a mural of Molly inside a Greenpoint warehouse where they'd shot a major scene in *The Last Century*. To get a look, you had to pay the owner twenty bucks.

"Can I confess something?" Abigail asked. "Can I be honest?

Otherwise, I'm going to walk around with this thing, and it will feed on my silence and eat me alive."

"Sure," Diane said.

"I don't want to go to dinner."

"Me either," Diane said. "Nobody wants to go to these things. Anyone who says any different is lying."

"So do we have to?" Abigail asked. "Do we have to go?"

"Of course, we do," Diane said. "Yes. We have to go. Has it been that long?"

"I haven't been to one of these dinners since the '90s."

"So you burned some bridges. Who hasn't?"

"Bridges?" Abigail asked. "Whole villages will be smoldering in there."

"Oh, please," Diane said. "Just follow my lead. All you have to do is eat, talk, and shake hands. I'm bringing antibacterial."

They had time and so cut across the park to the West Side. How it worked was, the film (*Trust*, in this case) was screened for the regular people; while that was going on, the important people ate dinner; after dinner was finished, the important people went across the street to the theater for the Q&A with the regular people; then the important people plus the regular people who'd paid for the extra ticket recrossed the street to the restaurant for the reception. Certain people, like Diane, could be both important and regular. Abigail was positive she was neither.

It was a long table in a special backroom of the restaurant with fifty or so guests. The movie stars were at the other end. As usual, most of them looked weird in person, sort of out of proportion, like they'd been sucked through a vacuum tube or run through a trash compactor.

Two production partners Abigail knew from the internet, from

TheWrap.com and the news blasts she got from *Variety*, approached. She knew each man's name, what movies they'd made, and their current deals. She had heard, and even spread, gossip about them. About her, they knew absolutely nothing.

"When are we doing lunch?" the blonde one asked Diane.

"When am I gonna see you?" the other one asked, staring at his phone. "What's this I hear about you producing? I love that. What's the project? Whose is it? What is it?"

In the restaurant, Diane explained Abigail's screenplay to the money men. Words like *grief, hope,* and *public assistance program* obliterated their attention. They drifted over in their own minds toward other, more reliable projects, where stars were attached and the formulas were sound. This was one end of the whole bullshit deal: the great guffawing boardroom side of huge tits and ass. Of high-wire explosions. Of dreams are the crushed bones beneath our feet. It was terrible. Box office. But the other end was maybe worse. Abigail had a friend, an always broke experimental filmmaker who'd shown at the Whitney once three decades ago, and who, upon her Facebooking the news that her movie could possibly exist, had promptly direct-messaged her that she was a Hollywood whore. The truth was, she'd have that arthouse fundamentalist know, she wasn't serving his god, or any, or the cash cow in the sky these two bros worshipped at either. She was serving people, human beings, if they were still around, and weren't all hooked on heroin or streaming Netflix. But to get to the people, you needed distribution. You needed an infrastructure beyond enough folding chairs, a projector, and a wall. Diane would take the movie only so far. After that, Abigail would need more money. The one guy, the not-blond one, occasionally got all philanthropic and took movies like hers on. Abigail's instinct would always be to burn her life to the ground: to say, "You don't like it? Fuck off." But she couldn't do that anymore. It wasn't about her. It was about the women in the theater she would never know.

When Diane was finished describing the movie, she made introductions. The men shook Abigail's hand. It could have been her own paranoia at work, the feeling that she didn't belong there, or anywhere, but she felt treated with a certain amount of skepticism, as if she were the pure product of someone else's imagination, rather than her own.

"Great," the one said.

"Looking forward to it," went the other.

Then they were gone.

She ordered the vegetable lasagna. Salads arrived. She took a bite of a pale radish freckled appropriately in gorgonzola. Leonard Roth walked in.

The last time she had spoken to him was during a therapy session in which he'd been a red throw pillow. In that setting even, her hate had been too much. After two minutes, she'd whipped him across the room into a Maxwell House tin of chewed-on pencils that rocketed off her therapist's desk into the wall. In the dining room, he came at her quick. She had only enough time to fast-forward through their history a half dozen reps before he was above her.

"Abigail," he said.

"Leonard."

"Diane."

"Hi, Leonard."

"I'm sitting down between you two," he told them. Using his pointer finger, he made a come-here motion, minus the eye contact. A waiter brought a chair.

"Look at this," Leonard said, nodding at a movie star. "That doesn't make any sense. Molly hated his guts. Am I wrong? Am I remembering?"

"You're right," Diane said. "She hated him."

"I knew it," Leonard said. "I thought so." He turned to Abigail. "I hear you're not doing drugs anymore."

She saw his age on him. As with everyone, it started around the eyes. Some men aged well, it suited them, but not Leonard. He looked tired, sad, and fat. She remembered him from before. When they were something close to almost friends, Abigail had liked Leonard's sister far more. Emily was a quasi-monster too, petty and vindictive, but she'd handled Leonard like the little brother he was. In meetings she'd had with the two of them, Abigail could feel Leonard's attention chasing Emily around the room. He would hope for a touch, a word, a confirmation. Maybe in private he'd managed to capture one or the other, but never that Abigail saw. Still, when he'd ruined her, and Abigail had called Emily to beg her way back in, the coldness in Emily's voice ("How is this my problem?") had put an end to everything.

"Just crack," Abigail said. "I only smoke crack now."

"Crack?"

"It's prescription," she said. "So it's cool."

"Where are you?" he asked. "Where are you living?"

"Upstate."

"But where?"

She was surprised to find all of her molecules were intact, that the conversation hadn't disassembled her body. She took a second bite of radish. She said the name of the town.

"I have a house near there."

"I know," she said. "Your helicopter flies over."

"It is loud," he said. "I'll give you that. Don't you go crazy up there? I make it three days—then I have to get back."

"No," she said. "I don't. It's where I live."

In Abigail's daydreams, hallucinations, homicidal fantasies, what-ever one might call them, she would always be screaming at him by this point, destroying him with a monologue so exact it had accounted for all possible rebuttals, alternate versions of the truth, and misin-formed realities. She was a consummate rehearser of scenarios. Long car rides. Hot showers. Dead eyes out the window drinking coffee. Coursing through her was a pure streak of vengeance like a fault line. She was ready for him. That prescription-for-crack retort had been stored up for years. She'd used it on other people, but it was Leon-ard's. She was prepared for anything. Then he screwed her over again.

"I miss her," he said. "I keep remembering the weirdest shit. I'll be walking down the street, or talking to someone on the phone—*bang*."

"Like what?" Diane asked.

"Like I went to see her in Virginia once," he said. "Years ago. I'd forgotten all about it. She'd found this woman who'd been in the CIA, called this woman up, told her about *Tribes*, how it was Cold War and all of that, and got invited down. It was in the middle of nowhere. This woman was ancient. She knew Hoover. Molly lived in a shack. That old biddy walked her through the whole thing, trained her like it was 1959. She ran like eight miles every morning. Read declassified manuals. Target practice."

"I remember that," Diane said. "She was there for six weeks."

Diane's wife, Susan, came into the room. Abigail saw her before Diane or Leonard did. Susan gave her a smile, pretty and crooked, and then she touched Diane's shoulder.

"What's this?" Leonard asked. "Reinforcements?"

"Finish your story," Diane said. She grabbed Susan's hand and held onto it.

"What story?"

"You went to see her. She was living in a shack."

"She was living in a shack," Roth said. "For six weeks. I watched her skin a deer. That's the story."

If you were tired, you slept. If you were hungry, you ate. If you were cold, you bought a sweater, or made a scarf, or something. To these three mantras, Abigail had long ago added a fourth. It went like this: if you wanted to get the hell out of there, you got the hell out of there.

She stood up and gave Susan a hug.

"Take my seat," she said. "I need a little air."

The restaurant was packed now. She had to navigate her way through the crowd. She went around four cranky-faced girls in bright-colored dresses and a man whose cheekbones had the sharp angularity of a Siamese cat. The producers from before stood at the bar. The philanthropist tipped his drink at her. Abigail went to say hello, started with her hand, but then the men resumed their conversation, and she at once regretted and hated the part of herself that, even after all these years, had the habit of shrinking.

Outside, it was almost night. New York was the color of rum. It took her three elaborate minutes of going from one traffic island to another in order to cross the street. Every car ripping by was operated by a stressed-out maniac. Once she was on the correct side of Broadway, she walked a half block north, and went up the stairs to the Walter Reade. Her old student, Kimball, was working the ticket booth.

"Bonjour," he said, for some stupid reason he least of all understood. "I put a sign on your seat."

She grabbed a program off the info desk. The cover was a black-and-white publicity still. Molly's hand was up against her cheek. A vein in her wrist stood out. The photographer had asked her to do sad and knowing, and she'd done it. It was like a premonition, Abigail thought, but it was also cheap because of that. She pulled open the heavy door, and slipped into *Trust*.

It was the scene in the movie where Molly playing Abigail leaves the funeral reception. The wife knows all about her. Feeling young, stupid, and used, she catches the train back into the city. The camera watches her looking out the window for a while. She cries a little. She gets it together. She heads to the bathroom, goes inside, and loses it again. When she gets back to her apartment, her dead lover's teenage son is waiting for her out on the stoop. He's seventeen years old.

                      MOLLY
Do you drink coffee yet?

                       SON
Sometimes.

                      MOLLY
Do you know who I am? Do you know my name?

                       SON
You're her.

                      MOLLY
Who's that?

                       SON
The other woman.

>   MOLLY
>
>   Gross.

The two of them go upstairs to her apartment. She makes coffee. He wants to hear the story of how she met his father.

>   MOLLY
>   Where does anybody meet anybody?

>   SON
>   I don't know.

>   MOLLY
>   In a bar. We met in a bar. I was there with
>   some friends. He said hello. It was like
>   something you can't help. I thought he was
>   sweet, and sexy, and kind of a jerk. I tore a
>   napkin apart the whole time we were talking.
>   I loved him right away. It took maybe thirty
>   seconds.

The son continues to visit her. They get to know each other. The seasons change. It's fall. It's winter. It's spring. They talk about the father. They make him into someone they can know. One day the son leans in for a kiss, and she smacks him hard across the face.

Claiming it was preparation, she'd taken Molly to Robert's house once. They'd sat in the rental car across the street until the wife came outside and chased their wildly reversing car out of the cul-de-sac. They were young, and sometimes cruel, and they laughed about it, but on the way back into the city, Abigail had told Molly that she felt guilty. Maybe it was wrong to make the movie.

"Only if you do it poorly," Molly had said. "Only if it isn't human."

Abigail had seen *Trust* a hundred times. She couldn't take it again. She sat there for another ten minutes and then went back outside, where Kimball was arguing with a man twice his age through the window of the ticket booth.

"I'm sorry," Kimball said. "I don't know what to tell you."

"I'm on the list," the man said. He wore an oversized red and black cardigan to hide his stomach. His face was adorned with an unwise hipster porn 'stache. "I know I'm on the list. Last name: Os. First name: Eric. Eric Os."

"You aren't here," Kimball said. He waved good-bye to Abigail as she walked toward the exit. "I can't see you. How many times do I have to say it?"

There was a memorial at the corner of Sixty-Fifth and Broadway. A dozen poster board photographs of Molly were propped up or set flat on the ground. Lit tealights and larger, lopsided candles were down between them. It was hard to identify the flowers through their cellophane arrangements. The teddy bears, as usual, looked brutalized, as if they'd been rescued from a garbage dump. For how many thousands of years had this been going on? A person is murdered or dies unexpectedly, a person who had been revered as a god, and in the aftermath of that death—the fire, the objects, the tribute. Honor after the fact was no more than a gesture toward superstition, or (if Abigail was feeling generous) an instinct for the afterlife, so that somehow the most cynical New Yorker, the most "Oh, yeah? Show me. Prove it," was down on her knee, communing with the dead.

Like any decent, less-than-well-adjusted person, Abigail ran on guilt and shame, and the suspicion that something terrible was about to happen. Retroactively, the blame for any actual tragedies belonged to her, along with an almost limitless anger at how unfair this dynamic was—as if she herself hadn't created it. In this way, in a way that made no sense unless viewed through the warped prism of human nature, Molly's death was Abigail's fault. She hated Molly for making her feel this way (for being murdered to begin with), and this too resulted in guilt and shame. To top it all off, she understood these feelings were ridiculous as well as perfectly natural, but she couldn't stop having them. Abigail asked herself: had her feelings and thoughts always been one and the same, or were they only now achieving a maddening unity and clarity thanks to therapy and middle age? Probably. But never mind. And never mind drinking. Not drinking was super easy now. It was thinking itself that continued to present a thinking problem.

"This looks like a sacrifice," she said to a redheaded woman setting a box of chocolates on the ground. "I don't like this one little Molly Bit."

She was in the middle of New York City. The cars and the people and the textures of the buildings were always morphing into one great sonic and physical energy. She looked at the candles and flowers and teddy bears.

"Oh, professor!" said a man's voice behind her.

She turned around. It was goddamn Leonard Roth. She saw him, and Diane, and Susan, and fifteen midlevel executives. Behind them were the movie stars, each beautiful and desperate, each ready and willing, waiting in a line.

VISITORS

JULY 2014

8

THE PHONE CALL LUKE HUTTON RECEIVED THAT MORNING came from a reporter at *Star* magazine, which was this piece of trash weekly his mother read as she lay dying. From her bed, she would ask him if there was anything in it about Molly, and since at some point his mother had stopped wearing her glasses, he'd have to flip through the issue. He did so carefully, slowly, because his mother listened for the sound of the pages turning. There was always at least one item, if only a picture, and Luke would either read the article aloud or describe Molly's outfit. His mother found his powers of description disappointing. His inability hurt her. He didn't know much about women's fashion or how you were supposed to describe a haircut, except to say if it was short, long, or kind of in between. "It's a red dress," he might have said. "It's not *not* tight. Her hair's sort of up in this thing. She doesn't look thrilled."

When the phone rang, he was in the truck, driving to John Bit's. Luke mostly screened his calls, hoping to avoid debt collectors and his ex-wife's lawyer, who'd been harassing him all week about the alimony. And yet today had the potential to be different. He answered his phone for several reasons. He was first of all lonely for the sound of another person's voice. Second, if John was serious—if he wanted Luke to pack up Molly's house in California and put it all in storage—he could tell this to Ashley's lawyer, who would inform Ashley, who would find it infuriating. She'd always felt he'd kept a secret flame going for Molly. It was an idea that Luke found both demeaning and backward, since Ashley was the one with the obsession.

His mind-set was this: his ex-wife should leave it alone. Molly was dead. It had happened. There was nothing to do. Just shut up. Stop it. Why mention it at all?

"*Hello!*" he shouted.

"Is this Lucas Hutton?" a woman's voice—British—asked.

"That's me," he said. "Who's this?"

"Bronwen Davidson," she said.

He stopped at the red light where Main and Elm met, across the street from the movie theater and its small concrete rotunda. As part of its "Not in Our Village" anti-heroin campaign, the town had set up speakers in the trees. *AM Gold* blasted for fifteen hours a day through the moth-eaten leaves downtown. Nate Braun, a guy Luke had gone to high school with, stood in front of the theater with his shirt off. His defined abs were greased with sweat. A tattoo of a lion's head growled across his chest.

"I'm with *Star* magazine," Bronwen said.

"Never heard of it."

"We're a news organization."

"News?"

"Correct," she said.

Across the street, he watched Nate flex. This seemed to be the manner in which Nate would spend his entire morning. Without realizing it, Luke felt jealous, not only of Nate's body, but of the life it seemed to represent: carefree, wild, stupid. Someone had shot him in the ass last year over an unpaid debt.

Once, in eighth grade, changing after gym, Nate had surprised Luke. "You're gonna wanna see this," Nate had said. Standing in only his boxers, Nate hoisted Luke up, and then they'd crab-walked across the top of the lockers to a crack in the wall while the other boys watched them, holding their breath. Nate closed one eye and stared through the crack. After a very long moment, he slid over to make room for Luke. He gestured with an upturned hand. Squinting, Luke peered into the girls' locker room, and saw a naked Molly Bit—one terrific flash of her—before Nate shoved him ("Don't hog her. I saw her first") and that was it.

Luke's engine revved as he pulled forward. Nate took this as a greeting. He stuck his hand in the air.

"How can I help you?" Luke asked the reporter.

"I was hoping to speak to you about Roger Michael Vincent," she said.

He should have pulled through the light and gone straight up the hill, but instead he turned left and cut into the bank parking lot. There was a ten-foot-long giant plastic triceratops that he hardly noticed dumped near the back door of the movie theater. He parked at a diagonal across two empty spots.

"What's your name again?" he asked.

"Bronwen Davidson. From *Star* magazine," she repeated. "Is this Lucas Hutton? The Lucas Hutton who knew Molly Bit?"

"Depends," he said.

"So you know the name? Roger Vincent?"

"Who doesn't?" he said. "What about him?"

"I was hoping I could get a quote from you."

"On what?" he asked.

"Him."

He finally processed the triceratops. Nine years ago, the movie theater had burned to the ground. A teenage pyromaniac had started a fire in his bathtub in one of the apartments above. A door had opened. The fire had jumped. The whole block went up. For a year and a half they took donations on the rebuild, but it wasn't looking good—not until an anonymous donor had sent in the rest. It hadn't been difficult for everyone to figure out who it was.

For those first few days after Molly's murder, he'd put a Google alert on his phone. He'd assumed it was the ex-husband. Everybody knew it was always that guy. Then they cleared Andrew Kessler, and Luke waited. Once or twice a minute his phone would buzz or ding. The news blasts and updates were constant. *TMZ* got to everything first. A television host showed a diagram of a generic body and said Molly had been stabbed here, and here, and here, and here . . . Luke found himself clicking on websites he hadn't known existed. Before Molly's murder, he'd never encountered a Tumblr blog. Other pages were littered with YouTube clips, one after the other, sometimes the same one five times, where the comment person wrote, *Sorreee, too sad for words, OMG, HAD to repost this again. #RIPMB #Loveyouforever #diedtoosoon #greatestofalltime*. He found a page that gave a complete history of Molly's life starting with her probable moment of conception. There was a Google Maps image of her father's house. There was a picture of the waterfall downtown. At a certain point, Luke stared at his own senior yearbook photo. The caption read: *Lucas David Hutton. High School BF. Talk about a lucky guy.*

"What about him?" Luke said into the phone. He couldn't breathe right. He stepped out of the hot truck onto the hotter asphalt. He unbuttoned his collared shirt. Earlier, getting dressed, it had seemed like the thing to do. It would come off as respectful, wouldn't it?

"Mr. Vincent was attacked," she said. "He was stabbed. Did you know that?"

Nate Braun, from twenty yards away, seemed to sense what was going on. If he had any business at all, it was the business of making things worse. He walked over the way he walked, like a one-man-parade, arms and legs jangling loose, his chin way up and his chest puffed out.

"That's good," Luke said. "I'm glad someone stabbed him. Is he dead?"

"Is that a quote?"

From the curb, Nate shouted, "What up, Hut!" He wore his hot-pink Oakleys. His hand was on his nuts. "Somebody got a problem with you? Fuck those motherfuckers! I'll get my gun!"

Luke put his hand up to Nate, and Nate understood.

"Okay!" he shouted. "I'm here! I got you!" Nate pointed to his right. "You see this fucking dinosaur? They found it in storage! *Jurassic Park!*"

"Mr. Hutton?" Bronwen asked. "Are you there? What is that? Is everything fine? Are you safe?"

"I asked you if he's dead," Luke said. "Answer me."

In that moment, he shooed away, as if it were an invisible fly, a certain truth about himself—which was, of course, that Ashley was right, and he was obsessed with Molly. He could never admit this to himself, not in a hundred million years, because doing so would have been far too embarrassing and would have required serious excavation of the therapeutic kind. Luke didn't go in for language, or for using his words, because language was for faggots, he'd actually once said to a college professor during her office hours, and he wasn't going to sit around all day long talking bullshit on his mom and dad. As a result of this, when Luke tried to shape the hows and whys of his hurt and disappointment into words, the frustration proved enormous, so that the only space he found comfort in was his own anger, the level and intensity of which never failed to correspond to how much shame he felt.

"He's alive, as far as we know," Bronwen said. "We were hoping to get a quote from someone who knew her and who isn't a part of the industry. You said you were glad."

"Of course I did."

"Can I quote you as saying that? Can it read, 'I'm glad Roger Michael Vincent was stabbed'? Would that be okay? It would really help the story."

"I don't understand why you're calling me."

"As I've said—"

"But why *me*? Why are you calling *me*? I didn't know him. I didn't know her, really, anymore. What do I have to do with anything? Did you talk to my wife?"

He heard a furious typing on the other end of the phone.

"I have not. I don't know your wife, nor have I ever spoken to her. Should I? Would that be a better person to talk to?"

All that last year, Ashley would find him in the dark of their living room. After a certain point, he stopped pretending it was porn. Sure, he was searching on his iPhone. It was a tragedy. Why shouldn't he be interested? No—he hadn't checked on her before this. He didn't think about her. Why would she ask him that? What was her problem?

"Do not call her," he said. "Don't you dare fucking do that."

"Why would your wife have me call you, Mr. Hutton?"

"Ex-wife. I don't know. It's something she might do."

"Did she know Molly too? Were they friends?"

"No."

"Was that difficult for her? Knowing you had dated Molly? Was that difficult for you?"

Of course Luke had searched for Molly Bit before her murder. Molly had lingered out among his edges—not as a vision, or as a memory, but as a feeling he wouldn't acknowledge. But now his obsession, mainstreamed into the fabric of his life, was out of his control, and as a consequence of this he was more than a little crazy from trying to act normal all the time.

"Get fucked," he said to Bronwen and hung up.

He got back in the truck, slamming the door behind him. He actually thought about—he took the time to consider—punching the dashboard or the windshield. But then he remembered John Bit. He could not show up with a broken hand, and so he sat there pulling and pushing on the steering wheel until his arms, shoulders, and his entire body got into it more and more, and the whole chassis rocked.

Five minutes later, he walked over to the triceratops. It wasn't something he encountered every single day. It was life-sized, made out of a low-density plastic that wobbled in the summer breeze. The skin was a grayish blue, its eyes were rheumy and sad, and some other, superior predator had torn several of its ribs out. It had been placed against a loading door. Next to its horns were three potted ferns. Staring down at it, he thought he might cry. It was ridiculous. The thing wasn't real. It was extinct.

"He's checkin' it out," Nate Braun said, walking over to Luke. "He's givin' it a look."

"That's true."

"I remember this shit. I snuck in three different times," Nate said. "Did you know that kids don't go to the movies anymore? I met this high school girl the other night. She said she hadn't been to the movies since she was seven. It's all Netflix now. That's where the action is."

"High school?" Luke asked him.

"Yessir," Nate said. He smirked and raised an eyebrow above his sunglass frames. Not since childhood had Luke seen Nate indoors. He was always out on the street. He lived with his mother, Luke guessed. Aside from his chest and arms, which belonged to a twenty-five-year-old athlete, he looked his age, which was forty. He had a number of prominent, missing teeth. The rumor was the guy who'd shot him was a reject from the Crips, somebody's dumb-ass cousin they'd sent up from Hartford or New York to profit off the country market. Nate used to buy his drugs from the guy. No longer.

"I'm like Matthew McConaughey," he said. "You know what I'm talking about."

He was connected to Nate through the peephole. It was the single moment of any substance they had ever shared. All throughout high school, Nate had lorded it over him. "I saw your girlfriend's tits before you did," he'd whisper to Luke in between classes. And later, after Molly was famous (and half the world had seen her naked), Nate would still remind anyone who'd listen, "I scoped her out when she was prime." After her death, Nate seemed to have stopped saying this.

Or maybe it was a grace period, Luke thought.

Or maybe it was only him.

"What was that about?" Nate asked. "You were gonna murder somebody."

"Forget it."

Nate took a few steps back and then he ran at the triceratops as fast as he could and kicked it in the head.

"Shouldn't you be at work?" he asked.

"I got let go," Luke said. "First man in. First man out. You know how it goes."

"I hear that," Nate said. "This place is cursed."

"I guess so."

"You bet your ass it is," Nate said. He raised his arms out at a perfectly lovely town full of empty storefronts and a quiet madman in a

Boston Red Sox jersey pushing a shopping cart across the street. "Tell me different," he said. "Look at this shit and tell me it's improving."

"I'm moving down south," Luke said. "I'm starting over."

"Where to?" Nate asked.

"Texas maybe," Luke said. "Florida. Dave's in Tennessee. He says there's work down there."

"That's a real statement," Nate said. "That says so much. I've been hearing that from a lot of people lately. I know exactly what it means."

"What does it mean?"

"It means you go down to paradise," Nate said. "Meanwhile, I'm up here, living with the monkeys."

Molly's house was out on Skitchewaug Trail. Luke drove up East Hill, past the funeral home, and the closed-for-good-elementary-school, and the campground that was all third-growth pine and dark as a freezer. From the top of the valley, he cruised back down. On his right, across the tree line, he saw the foothills of the Green Mountain range. As it always had for him, the road curved left under an awning of maple trees. The Humane Society was still out here on a little knoll. He took the sharp right you had to be on the lookout for, down another hill, drove by the dairy farm where the Holsteins lay in mud, and then went up another short rise that veered, once again, right. He only knew one other family who lived out here, the Wallers. Luke's father used to work random jobs on their farm. Fall cleanup. Tractor maintenance. The like. Their youngest daughter, Jilly, was what everyone called slow. When his mother died, Jilly had sent him a card that read, "I'm so sorry about your mother. First your dad then your mom. You are the only person left alive and that's good. Good luck selling the house you grew up in."

It was the only card he'd kept.

His phone started ringing again. This time he looked at the ID, and saw it was Ashley. He hit the side button to shut it up. A minute later, he played the message.

"Listen," she said. "I saw John Bit at Shaw's. He told me about—about whatever it is you're going to do, Luke. It's the dumbest idea I've ever heard in my entire life. It's just plain stupid. He's an old man. He thinks that because he's had an idea, it should happen. Don't go out there. Do. Not. Go. I'm saying this because I care about you. Not *us*. But *you*. And also—*fucking asshole*—stop calling me drunk at two in the morning. The next time I see you, I'm playing you the messages. They're deranged. You sound totally deranged."

Luke didn't want to know what he'd said. He had no interest in hearing the messages. Whatever it was, it wasn't the truth, because he could not remember it (he had not experienced it), which made it not quite real, and what wasn't real, or not quite real (because he hadn't lived through it) did not exist.

He was thirty feet from the mailbox when he saw a car reversing across John Bit's lawn. It was a navy blue BMW with New York plates. It was going far too fast. The back end cut sharply to the left. Luke knew what was going to happen before it did, and so it did not register as a surprise exactly when the car's rear bumper smashed into a tree stump, and its brake light erupted into a fountain of glass.

John Bit had built the entire house himself. It was one story. A large faded swatch of blue insulation showed from where the clapboards had either fallen off or blown away in the wind. It leaned very slightly to the right. In the field behind the house, Luke saw a woman. She was running as fast as she could back toward the house and what he assumed was the car. She had short blond hair that bounced. In her hands, she held a camera with a telephoto lens.

"We're sorry!" she screamed. "We're sorry! We loved her!"

A man stepped out of the car. He had greasy black hair down to his ears and he wore a very tight pair of jeans.

"Run!" he shouted at the woman.

"I'm running!" she screamed back. "Shut the fuck up!"

At the far end of the field, way back behind the running, screaming woman, Luke saw John. He seemed to be following the woman's path through the high grass. He moved at a slow, deliberate pace. By its grip, he held a chainsaw. It was very much on.

"We just wanted to see where she grew up!" the man yelled over the small motor sound. "We didn't know you were home! We didn't mean to snoop!"

"Get in!" the woman screamed.

Luke watched the woman run around the side of the house, slide past the stump, and all but dive into the passenger seat of the BMW. The man was already in. He threw the car in gear and peeled out across John's lawn, dirt and grass and pine needles spraying out behind the tires. The car squealed out of the drive, swerved to avoid Luke's truck idling there, and accelerated gone.

As Luke pulled in, he heard the chainsaw switch off. He stepped out of the truck and watched Molly's father approach the house. John came around the same way the woman had, and set his chainsaw down on top of the tree stump. He took off a pair of gardening gloves and some protective goggles. He set those down too. For a moment, he stood there with his hands on his hips. His face looked a lot like Molly's face, except it was destroyed by wrinkles, and his eyes were a different color than hers. His eyes were a very light blue, like a pair of pilot lights on a gas stove.

He walked over to Luke and shook his hand.

"I was cutting brush," he said. "They snuck up on me."

"Sorry I'm late," Luke said.

"All of the sudden they were there. The kill switch was stuck. I looked worse than I was."

"I got talking to Nate Braun."

"He's an idiot," John said.

"He's alright."

"No, he's not," John said. "I ran into Ashley. She refused to understand."

"It doesn't matter," Luke said.

They watched the BMW come back down the road. A tinny, hip-hop reverb shook its chassis. The passenger side window rolled down. The woman stuck her entire arm out and gave them the middle finger.

"Charming," John said. "Come inside, Luke. We need to actually talk."

INTERROGATION

AUGUST 2014

9

MARCUS WAS STUCK IN TRAFFIC ON BEVERLY. HE HAD HIS WIFE on the Bluetooth.

"Where are you now?" Alice asked.

"He's headed toward Coldwater."

"I don't understand what you're doing. What are you doing? Why don't you come home?"

"I'm following him."

"Why?" Alice asked.

He didn't know why exactly. At first it was to see if he should call the cops on the guy, or maybe pull up alongside him at a stoplight and ask if he hadn't changed his mind? Did he want that ride now? "Hey, idiot," he'd imagined saying. "You're gonna kill somebody. Get in the car." This dude, this Luke (that was his name—he'd forgotten), had dropped his keys twice outside the restaurant and when Marcus had asked him how he was feeling, Luke had said, "I'm fine, bro. Be chill. Take it easy."

"How's the kid?" Marcus asked Alice.

"Tyler, you mean? Our firstborn son?" She was still mad about it. "He's upset."

"Tell him—"

"You tell him," she said. "I'm not the messenger girl here."

At the intersection where Beverly and Coldwater and Rodeo and Canon and another road he couldn't remember the name of opened wide into one another, he watched Luke's rental car half-stop and roll on through—and then he saw a CHP cruiser. It was parked under a looming palm tree out in front of a house that, if you broke it down, was ten years' TV work. He let a Mercedes go, and then a Cayenne Sport, and then he went too. Until he hit the bend, he kept it at twenty-five. He checked the rearview going up the mountain and saw the cop wasn't there.

"He turned onto Carolyn."

"*Jesus.*" Her voice cut out and returned. "—so maybe he's staying there."

"He's not staying there, Alice."

"He could be."

"Who would stay there? It's not a place to stay. He told me he had a hotel."

"Where?" Alice asked. "The Beverly?"

"The DoubleTree."

"Oh," she said.

His wife had always been a little classist, even when they were poor.

"People stay there," Marcus said. "That's a place where people stay."

"I've stayed at those places," Alice said.

"*When?*" he asked her.

At first, everything had been fine at the restaurant. He'd showed up with Molly's keys and knew the guy right off, saw him at the bar with shit on his boots. They shook hands. It felt cordial. Hunky-dory. Honky-tonk. He thought he might as well eat. Molly's father had said the guy was down on his luck, but that was half of everybody. Fish tacos it was. Luke ordered another beer and a shot of Bushmills.

"What about the hotel behind the prison that time?" Alice asked him.

"That was twenty years ago," Marcus said. They'd been driving across the country and had almost run out of gas in the middle of nowhere Colorado. He remembered waiting in the car while she went to see if they had a vacancy. "We didn't even see the prison until the next day. I forgot about that."

"You make me out to be some kind of diva," Alice said. "How could you forget that? I think you should get checked out."

"You get checked out," he said.

But then this guy, this Luke, had gotten drunk. He'd started talking about Vincent.

"They transferred him."

"Where to?" Marcus asked.

"Sensitive Persons Unit," Luke said. "Same prison, different wing. He doesn't speak. He moves. He eats. He looks. But he doesn't speak."

"How do you know all this?"

"I hear things."

"From who?"

"The internet," Luke said. "You live next door? I could have met you there."

"We moved," Marcus said.

"Makes sense," Luke said. "Someone tried to stab him with a toothbrush. You gotta wonder: how do you fuck that up? How do you not keep on stabbing until the job's done? You *stab-stab-stab-stab-stab-stab-stab-stab*. You check to see if he's breathing. If he's breathing, you stab some more. It's simple. Somebody quit on that job is what. And you can't ever quit. Not ever. You can't just give up because something's difficult. That's the whole problem with this country. That's it right there. We gotta stop it with these fucking handouts. That's the first thing."

On the flatscreen above the bar, the news ran a story about a kid who'd been shot to death outside St. Louis. They'd left the kid's body out there all day long rotting in the street. They'd thrown a tarp over him. They'd let the heat of the sun bake his corpse. His family came. His neighbors cried and screamed and pointed at the body. They'd left him there. Marcus sat next to this guy and watched it.

"So wait," Luke said, as if the sound of his voice was capable of changing the subject. "You're on TV?"

"Got canceled," Marcus said. "It was a good run. It went six seasons. My kids won't starve."

Luke wanted to see a picture of his family. He scrolled one over on his phone.

"That's your wife?"

"Yup."

"That lady right there?"

"Her name's Alice."

"We're here," Marcus said.

Maybe he wanted to see it for himself was why. Their old road was narrow, like all the roads off the canyon. Luke parked his car at an angle outside the fence. Marcus pulled over beside an embankment and switched off his headlights. He rolled his window down. He missed the cool air and the darkness of the hills. Silver Lake was bullshit. It was old hipsters.

"What's he doing?" Alice asked him. "Can he see you?"

"He can't see me. He's just standing there. He's doing the code."

Whatever it was, the rental car was a piece of shit. The headlamps were plastered with dead bugs. Luke stood there in the yellow light and tapped the panel.

"He's wasted," Marcus said.

"What's he doing?" Alice asked again.

"He can't figure out the damn code. He keeps trying different combinations."

From where he sat in his car, Marcus could see his old gate too. The place had been astonishingly easy to sell. There was a market for everything. Sooner or later, the new owner would turn to a bored dinner party guest and say, "She was murdered upstairs. You wanna see?"

It had been hard on all of them. Eric, who was seven, didn't speak for three days. Finally, Marcus had lifted him out of his bed one grim night (the boy would wake up in a cold sweat, like a faucet had been turned on inside of him) and had him sleep with them. Marcus turned over the next morning and looked at his son. He asked him how he was.

"Hungry," Eric had said. "What do we have for breakfast stuff?"

Ty was thirteen. He had fallen back into his own kind of silence. Everything was, "Yeah, ma." "Alright, ma." "Everything's good." He'd go to his bedroom, close the door, and post memes. The night before, scrolling through Instagram, Marcus had asked him what a particular acronym of his had meant.

"That Hoe Over There," Ty had informed him.

"What about now?" Alice asked.

Molly's gate slid open on its electric runner. Marcus watched him get back in the car.

"He's driving down to the house."

"Come back home."

"I just wanna see what he's doing."

"He's probably going to sleep."

"He's not going to sleep, Alice. If you had talked to this guy, you would know he wasn't going to sleep," Marcus said. "He did the gate wrong. It's still open."

"Come home," Alice said. He heard something rhythmic in her

voice. She was worried, but she liked it. One of the reasons their marriage was successful was because he was never boring. He was a lot of things, but he was never boring.

"This isn't a detective movie, Marcus."

"I'm aware of that," he said. "Our banter's too good."

He took her off the Bluetooth and put her back to regular.

"Please don't get out of the car."

"Too late," he said.

The show was called *The Heights*. It was supposed to have been a two-episode run for his character—the charming, handsome lawyer next door—but the ratings had shot up, especially in the all-important Atlanta metro region, and by the second season he was a regular. At least once an episode (more often twice) his character, Gerard, would either say or be greeted with the tagline, "Oh, hey now." A gorgeous woman would enter Gerard's room, or he'd catch a girl who'd fallen from a ladder, and either he or another character would say, "Oh, hey now," one syllable stressed more than the others in order to convey that scene's particular information. The line had become famous, and Marcus along with it. For the first year and a half of his Gerard-ness, every time he and Alice heard or saw the line, they would make the slot machine motion. They added on to the house. Alice began to audition again. More important, Marcus looked forward to a life in which he no longer had to play Gangbanger number 3, 7, or 22. Stereotype and pigeonhole aside, it was also boring. A man could only scowl in so many ways.

From the edge of her driveway, he could see the addition Gerard had paid for. Ty's room more or less looked out onto Molly's property. There were trees in the way, but what teenage boy wouldn't crane his neck for a better view? But Ty hadn't seen anything. He'd slept through it.

Marcus watched Luke open the front door and enter the house. He walked down the steep driveway. He'd taken a class on modern architecture at Villanova, but he couldn't remember anything from it. The house looked like a series of shrinking boxes stacked on top of one another. There were a lot of windows. The fountain out front was off. If one of the neighbors called the cops, he'd get down on the ground spread-eagle and scream, "My show's syndicated!"

"Where are you?" she asked him.

"*Whisper,*" he whispered.

"*Where are you?*"

The exterior floodlights came on, and Marcus ran behind the fountain.

"*I'm hiding.*"

"*Is he after you?*"

"*No,*" he said. "*He's not after me. He doesn't know I'm here. He's in his own world.*"

"*Can you see him?*"

He could see him. Luke was standing in one of the living rooms. He looked at one part of the living room, then quarter-turned and looked at the next part. He kept doing this.

"*This motherfucker has lost his goddamn mind.*"

"*How long do you plan on watching him for?*"

"*I don't know. Until he does something.*"

"*Does what?*"

"*Something,*" he said.

It wasn't the answer Alice was looking for.

"*You need to talk to your son,*" she said. "I'm serious." And then she hung up on him.

He thought about texting her "*What do you know about it, white lady?*" but decided not to.

It was inevitable that "Oh, hey now" would catch on as a phrase at the boys' school. Both of his sons were popular. Ty described it as "No big deal, Dad." Friends addressed them with it in the halls and the cafeteria. "It's nothing," Ty had said, but it sounded like something to Marcus.

It was a majority-white private school, and Marcus felt that anytime a white person took a black person's saying, a black person's gesture, a black person's story, and made it their own, it was ninety-nine times out of a hundred racist, and even that hundredth time, that "exception," had a stink about it, a questionability that sat uneasy with him. The white writers, and they were mostly white on *The Heights*, had every so often carted out a message script. When Marcus became an executive producer during the third season he'd gone into the writers' room and told them they should tread softly. The last thing Marcus wanted was to perform in an episode solely to make someone else's—some white person's—point. He wasn't a lesson. He wasn't a point to be made. Gerard was a character. He was a person.

Before Molly's murder, Ty had told him not to worry. He'd suggested the line was tossed around within the proper boundaries of inflection. They were his friends. He busted on them too. It was a joke, right? Wasn't it? Wasn't it supposed to be funny?

Marcus didn't know if he found it funny. And what he definitely hadn't found funny was when a camp counselor had called him earlier that day to let him know Ty had punched another camper in the face. And not just any camper, but Xander Rice, who'd been Ty's best friend since they were five.

The first thing Alice had said to Marcus when they'd met at the athletic compound was, "I told you something like this would happen. You need to talk to him. You don't talk! He punched Xander!

Xander!" And Marcus had said, "Well, hold on. Maybe Xan had it coming," which it turned out Xander had.

The two of them, Ty and Xander, and the rest of their little eighth-grade friend group had, like usual, lined up like orphans in the lunch line. It was an open secret among the parents that puberty had hit Xander hard, and that almost overnight he'd changed from a sweet-tempered, goddamn wonderful kid into what was pretty much unanimously understood to be an arrogant, conceited little asshole. The only exception to this New Xander Rule was Ty. When he was with Ty, Xander felt bonded to someone who "knew the real him" (this was Xander's mother, Patricia, talking to Alice outside of yoga) and he could relax a little and not say things like, "Nice face, bitch." But today the exact opposite chemical reaction had occurred. In front of Ty in the lunch line, Xander had suddenly spun around and said, "Oh, *hey* now! Oh, *hey-hey-hey* now!" letting it out like the last minstrel act on vaudeville, snapping his fingers in a *Z* formation, and Ty had banged him one right on the nose, the blood instant and everywhere.

Marcus watched Luke go to a small end table, pick up a vase, and smash it on the floor. Then he watched as Luke tried to pull a picture from off the wall, but the picture wouldn't come down. Luke walked out of the living room and Marcus lost him for a second, and when Luke came back into view Marcus saw he had a knife in his hand. Luke took the knife blade and wedged it in between the frame and the wall and jerked the blade back and forth until he'd made enough space for his fingers to slide in. It took effort, but finally the picture came down. It landed with a crash at his feet and then Luke picked it up off the floor and threw it like a Frisbee across the room. Luke turned around slowly. He raised the knife high over his head and then stabbed it hard into the wall. It went in easily, all the way to the handle. Marcus watched Luke stare at it there. It was like something he didn't quite recognize. After a second, he went upstairs.

Marcus didn't drink much. He'd always been paranoid of potential excess. Like anybody's family, it ran in his. As a boy, he'd once looked out the window of his aunt's apartment and seen his uncle chase her down the block with a brick in his hand.

He walked to the back of the house where the pool was. He was less worried about being seen or heard, least of all by Luke, and it was unlikely the neighbors knew what was going on either. They hadn't seen or heard anything the night she'd been killed—why would they now?

Hiding in the overgrown poolside greenery, he thought about his son. He was furious Ty had been kicked out of the day camp, but he couldn't very well say this, considering Xander had been given the same exact punishment (mostly, Marcus thought, because the administrator hated Xander), and also because Ty had in fact broken his nose. Ty had ridden with Alice back to the house, and when Marcus pulled in behind them, the two of them were hugging in the driveway. When Ty saw Marcus's car, he wiped his eyes, said something to his mother, and walked inside.

"Say something," Alice had said.

"Can I get inside the house first?"

Marcus waited for him in the kitchen. Ty was always coming into the kitchen. He ate twice as much as anyone in the house. He was 5'11" and weighed one hundred and twenty-five pounds.

He sulked on through.

"Hey, Apollo." It was maybe the wrong note.

"Funny," Ty said. He opened the refrigerator door and stuck his head inside.

Marcus and Alice weren't in town the night Molly was killed.

They were in New York. Marcus had a press junket at the Standard. Ty was very much home.

A maid had found Molly's body. An hour later, two detectives cut through the bushes, knocked on Marcus's door, and encountered his son. As the nanny tried to console Eric, the detectives spoke to Ty for two and a half hours.

What was it like living next door to a movie star? they'd asked. She was pretty hot, right? Did he ever take a peek? Sometimes? Who wouldn't? Is this a photo of your mom over here? You into white girls? You like your dad that way? What's wrong with black women? Black women are beautiful too. But maybe they're too sassy for you guys? Do they break your balls too much? A little too strong for you? Where were you last night? We're just talking. We're just having a conversation. Let's start again. You're tall for your age, son . . .

Marcus had filed a complaint. As if he had done something wrong, he'd apologized to his son. He'd talked. He'd talked and talked. But even Marcus's voice, with all that feeling, with all that feeling they paid him to give, could not give his son's feeling back to him.

Months later, they were in the kitchen.

"You hit that boy hard," Marcus said.

When Ty came out from behind the refrigerator door, Marcus looked at him and saw that he was crying. It wasn't a full-on cry. It wasn't what he had been doing with his mother, but it was there in his eyes. He had two apples, a plate of honey ham, and a piece of string cheese in his hands.

"Whatever, Dad."

Ty closed the refrigerator door and began to walk out of the kitchen. Marcus had been sitting on a stool beside the enormous butcher block. He stood up. He'd been trying to say something.

"What did you say?"

"I said, *whatever.*"

They were both enraged. Marcus felt it. It was a frightened thing between them. He stepped in front of his son.

"*Who are you talkin' to like that?*" It felt as if his mouth was all teeth. He was still from Philly. That was him.

"*You.*" Ty took a step left to go around. Before Marcus realized what he was doing, he had reached up and grabbed his son's shirt. He wasn't holding it tight, he was only trying to keep him close, but then Ty pulled, and Marcus tightened and pulled, and then they both pulled hard, and all at once the fabric of the T-shirt ripped along the neckline and then down the front—*zip*—both of them leaning the way they wanted to go. Marcus had only wanted things to be calm, quiet, to have them sit down together and talk, or so he believed, but then suddenly he was thumping into the butcher block with the entirety of the white T-shirt hanging limp in his hands. Ty staggered back, naked now from the waist up in the kitchen. They stood there, breathing hard, and looked at each other. The plate of ham had fallen to the floor. Ty ran out. Alice ran in.

"What happened in here?" she'd asked him.

"Nothing," Marcus had said.

At Molly's, he walked around the pool to the edge of the yard. He was in darkness. He stood between a Japanese elm and some faintly sweet japonica. The realtor had left all the shades open. He watched Luke get halfway up the stairs, walk back down into the living room, and pull the knife out of the wall. He took it back upstairs with him, walking with his head down. Marcus looked back over his shoulder at the canyon, at the half-hidden bungalows and the larger, illuminated compounds with tennis courts. He saw the houses in the foothills, and then Hollywood, and then downtown and the rest of the greater city: everyone with their lights on because it was night, and that's what these people, all nineteen million of them, did.

He watched as Luke stepped into her bedroom. Marcus's phone rang on vibrate and he took it out of his pocket. He admired the illuminated picture of his oldest son. They each said hello.

"Mom made me call."

"I figured," Marcus said. "What's going on over there?"

"Xan and his parents are downstairs," Ty said. "They say they aren't pressing charges."

"Charges?" Marcus asked. He sometimes could not believe the planet he was on. "You talk to him yet? Xan?"

"No."

"You want to?"

"I don't know. I'm supposed to go down there. Where are you?"

"Had a meeting," Marcus said. Then he corrected himself. "I had to meet a guy who knew Molly. I had to give him her keys."

Luke was standing over her bed. He had the knife in his hand. He bent over and ran his hand over the mattress. Marcus watched his lips move.

"Was he a friend of hers?" Ty asked.

"They grew up together," Marcus said. "Listen, Ty. I'm sorry."

"I'm sorry too."

"It's been a bad year."

"Totally," Ty said.

"Things'll get better. Everything'll be fine."

"Okay," Ty said. "You always say that."

"Always say what?" he asked.

Marcus watched as Luke took the knife and stabbed it into the bed. He did this with care at first, coming down slowly, as if he were a detective interested in reenactment, but then the motion took hold of him.

"What was he like? Her friend?" Ty asked.

"You know," Marcus said. "A guy."

"Did he talk about her?"

He watched Luke stab down with all his force. He did this again and again and again. A lamp fell off the bedside table.

"He talked about her. He said a few things."

"Is he nice?"

Marcus heard the blade crack against the springs of the mattress. Goose down filled the air. A shout came through the windowpane.

"You want the truth?" Marcus asked his son.

"Yeah."

"No," Marcus said.

AFTERLIFE

BIOPIC

2015

10

ABIGAIL MERGED ONTO THE 5, WHICH WAS JUST LIKE THE 405, bumper-to-bumper, and then she took State Highway 14 East, a road she had been on maybe two or three times before in her life. Tom punished her by playing Pearl Jam, a band he loved, and she hated, although mostly for dramatic effect. It was a fun, meaningless thing to argue about. She honestly didn't care what he listened to. Taking a quick look down, she thumbed out of the navigation on her iPhone and checked the weather. It was ninety degrees outside with thirty percent humidity. She could feel the distance between them and the ocean. They were entering the agricultural zone—its yellow-brown edges. High-tension wires drooped over outpost communities. The spines of the desert flora hackled up in the sand like the arched backs of starving dogs.

"You should have told me," Tom said.

"I did tell you," she said. "I told you last night. And I told you months ago that it might happen."

"I thought you were kidding. I thought it was one of your Abigail jokes."

"What's an 'Abigail joke'?" she asked.

"It's a joke that's more fucked-up than funny," Tom said. "Or something that at first seems like a joke, but in the end it's not, because it's horrifying."

"Is that a thing?" she asked. "Like with our friends?"

"Absolutely. With my family too."

She looked at him. He had a great head of hair. It was dark and wavy and full. It was *90210* hair—but he was forty-five.

"I can live with that," she said.

They went over a rise. When the road flattened again they were surrounded on all sides by neat rows of almond trees.

"What is this about?" Tom asked. "Do I need to tell you that you're crazy? That you remain unhinged? That you're still the terrible infant? What other compliments can I give you? What else do you need to hear?"

"That I make bad decisions," Abigail said.

"You do."

"That I'm selfish."

"You're selfish."

"Tell me I don't think about anyone but myself."

"I wouldn't go that far," Tom said. "That's obviously not the case. You think about her."

She did. She thought about Molly, and she dreamt about Molly. It happened four or five nights a week. On the nights she didn't dream about Molly, or when she woke up unable to remember, Abigail missed her. The dreams were unremarkable. They were conversations about nothing. Sometimes they sat in a room. Other times, they walked down a dirt road that Abigail guessed was her idea of a dirt road. It was her stock dirt road. Strange dream shit went down. A bush turned into a giant syringe. Molly became Abigail's mother. Who else would she become? She never told Tom—it would hurt his feelings—but when Abigail woke up in the morning having remembered these transformations, it was often the best part of her day.

"I want to see him," Abigail said. "I want to see Vincent. I want to look at him."

"This doesn't make sense to me," Tom said. "I think it's a bad idea."

"It doesn't have to make sense to you," Abigail said. "It doesn't make sense to me. And it is a bad idea. Of course it's a bad idea. I'm still gonna do it."

They pulled into one of those lonely, damned towns straight out of *Hud* or *Badlands*. There was no sense in even looking at it. Abigail parked her rented Prius in one of the angled spots.

"I need to use the bathroom," Tom said. "I'm gonna pee in that McDonald's."

She turned her head to see what he was talking about—and there it was: a gleaming McDonald's in a lot that had probably once been occupied by an older brown McDonald's recently demolished to make room for the new one. This was definitely the case. The hurricane fence used during construction was still up.

"Can you even get in there?" she asked.

He placed his hand out before him on the spot where the air bag would deploy if necessary. He closed his eyes. Tom was kind. He asked her how she was feeling thirty-five times a day. All the same, there remained in him the usual homicidal rage that had to be acknowledged and contended with in order that he should be able to give and receive love.

"Easy does it," he said to himself.

Five seconds later, she was alone. In total disregard of climate change, she cranked the AC. The actual engine burned on. The cool manufactured air was dynamite. Everyone was awful in their own way. She reached for her phone because her phone was drugs. Three texts from Davros, who she could not wait to be rid of. *Have you left yet?* he'd asked. And then, an hour later, *How's it going?* Finally, almost now, *Call me when you can.*

Was it wrong of her to say she would write the Molly Bit bio-pic when she had no intention of ever doing so and found the very idea distasteful? Yes. Was it unprofessional? Most assuredly. Did she have a problem doing this? Apparently not. She considered it a kind of intervention, a way of slowing down what would sooner or later be—the movie version of Molly—inevitable. It also gave her grief a focus. It was a form of revenge. It was a lot of things.

She put him on speaker.

"Davros."

"The screenwriter!" he said, excited, as always. "I've been texting."

"We're on our way to the prison."

"We?"

"Me and my husband."

"You're married?"

"As of last week," Abigail said. "His insurance is incredible. It was too good to pass up."

Both *Film Comment* and *Variety* had announced she was some-body again. *Echo Chamber* (fifteen years after the first draft had been written—and with an entirely different plot) had done better than anyone could have predicted. Not *Spiderman* good, not *Lord of the Rings* good, but the film had turned a profit, and was positively re-viewed. It wasn't just boomers with nothing better to do on a Sunday afternoon who'd seen it either. The Brooklyn kids had caught on. It made a strange sense to Abigail. Even if zombies were played out, millennials still had within them the urge and capacity to admire those who had come back from the dead. She'd met Davros and his producing partner, Neal, at a BAM event. They were determined to make a *Molly Bit*. It wasn't that Abigail disliked them, only that she found them capable of doing harm. They had money. They were big on ideas.

"We're so pleased we could make this happen for you," Davros said.

They'd paid for her airfare, her rental, and her hotel. Neal's step-father had a connection in the California state legislature. The warden had taken some time. On the other end of the phone, Davros was silent. He was waiting for a thank you.

"Thank you," she said.

"You're entirely welcome."

He was from Argentina. His mother had been born in Buenos Aires. His father was Russian. He'd never in his whole life had an actual job.

"This visit is important," Davros said. "You'll get a sense of Vincent. Who is this guy? He comes out of nowhere. We know nothing about him."

This wasn't entirely true. There were court and employment records, long reads, timelines, but, because of Roger Vincent's silence, the world wanted more.

"Right," Abigail said.

"We know the end of the movie already," Davros said. "We know Molly dies. That's the end. It has to be. You can't escape the confines of a traditional narrative story arc in a life like Molly Bit's. The story is built in. It precedes her by about five thousand years."

"I mean—" Abigail said.

"But if you go back and forth in time so it's *Molly, Roger, Molly, Roger, Molly*, then you get what you need."

"You call him Roger?" she asked. "You use his first name?"

"We've been thinking about him a lot lately," Davros said. "Right now, he's all we're thinking about."

Abigail had a tendency to sympathize too much with others. In its own corrupted way, it was why she was so judgmental. She identified with people to the point where she was embarrassed on their behalf when they made a fool of themselves, or spoke out of turn, or did the wrong thing—whatever that meant. She felt what should have been the other's anguish as if it were her own and then resented them for it. It was something she was working on. At the same time, this problem of hers as she understood it also provided her with a distinct advantage in life. She knew damn well when someone—Davros, in this case—hadn't bothered to consider her, or her murdered friend, at all. Even though she was lying to him and had insinuated that it was her exact cup of tea that she meet Vincent so as to fill out his character, Davros had never once asked how she might feel about the encounter. He had never suggested it might be too painful, too much, or, as Tom had put it, a bad idea. More than anything else, this was why she was going to ruin everything and make it so that no one from the industry—at least not for a while—could go back again. She was sick of ideas. She missed a time that never was, when everyone owned up to their broken heart.

"Have you given any thought to our last conversation?" Davros asked.

"A little."

"Both Neal and I feel it's important that we see it," he said. "It's one of the criteria that we're demanding from potential directors. Their interpretation of it will be their own, of course, and it must be executed with care. But the death scene is essential. We need to see him stab her."

The McDonald's was in fact open. There was no PlayPlace. Tom was in a silver booth designed for someone with a giant caboose. One look at him and she knew his back hurt.

"Do you want some Aleve?" she asked him.

"No," he said. "I just need to stretch."

She took the seat across from him. He got up and started doing his weird, subtle hip thrusts.

"That's it, baby," Abigail said. "Nice and slow."

"Stop."

"Don't be mad."

"I'm not mad," Tom said, wincing. "I've been in here, sipping the hottest coffee known to God, going over everything."

"I should have told you sooner," she said.

He sat down again and rubbed the back of her hand three times with his thumb.

"My mom had a friend who was murdered," he said. "In college. I'd forgotten all about it."

"So did my mother," she said. "She was older."

"It was the boyfriend."

"Same deal."

"Then he killed himself."

"*Uh-huh*," Abigail said.

"They buried them side-by-side in a cupid grave," Tom said. "They thought someone else had broken in and killed them both. It took a year for the police to put it together."

"Then what did they do?" she asked him.

"They dug her the hell out."

It was another hour and twenty minutes before they saw the prison. From the road, there was no possible way to comprehend how enormous it was. Abigail knew its actual size because of a Google image search. She'd put her finger on her computer the night before and counted twenty large buildings in what looked to be an octagon that had at some point broken apart into a more chaotic shape. These were the lock-ups. They were grayish-black. Small yellow buildings were scattered across the outer expanse. Wide paths connected everything. A giant fence was a giant fence was a giant fence.

But that was on the computer. Real life was different. If they had been two other people, they would have been quiet, but they weren't two other people. They were them.

"Turn this garbage off," she said.

"Roll your window down," Tom said.

"I'm rolling," Abigail said. "What do you call this?"

The entrance post wasn't special. It was old school, or simply old. The white paint, the linoleum, the shingles on the roof: everything was peeling. There was a man inside with an assault rifle.

"Identification," he said.

Abigail could only see the correction officer's chest and nothing of his face. He didn't bend down to make the experience any easier for her. She was forced to lean out the window and look up at him. He had the round German head of someone she'd gone to high school with and couldn't remember the name of. The Ray-Bans on top of his skull looked like a tiara. He had pretty blue eyes and a sunburn.

"That's me," she said, handing over their IDs. "And that's him." She felt Tom do a little hunch-and-wave move behind her.

"Hold on," the officer said.

Outside the Prius, the sun was murder. California was a bad idea. White people shouldn't live out in the desert. They got heatstroke. Its vastness mocked the tidy confines of their tragedies.

"He's not on the list."

"Right," Abigail said. "We spoke to someone—"

"*Told you*," Tom whispered.

"And they said he would be able to get a visitors pass—"

"No."

"And wait," she said.

Her head was still out of the window. He wasn't stooping for anybody. At least not her.

"I don't know who you spoke to," he said, "but that information is bad. You're on the list—okay. He's not—no way."

"You'll have to go back to that diner and drop me off," Tom said.

"If you drive out of here," the officer said, "you can't come back. You'll have to file the paperwork again."

"That took a month," Abigail said. "It took three months of planning—then another month."

"Well," the officer said, leaning down finally. Abigail happened to be the kind of woman who liked the smell of Copenhagen. "I don't know what to tell you. This isn't a La Quinta."

She took in the sight of the long road. The prison was a flat castle. They made tires in there, she'd read, and finely crafted tables using nothing but nontoxic glue.

"What if he gets out of the car?" she asked the corrections officer.

"Seriously?" Tom asked.

"Can we do that?" She turned to Tom. "I'm sorry."

"That diner was five miles ago."

"He can do that," the officer said. "He'll have to climb out the back. If he goes out the front, he'll have crossed the line, and I'll have to detain him."

Both she and Tom raised themselves up in their seats and looked down at the road. There it was. The blue line. One couldn't cross it.

Tom unbuckled his seatbelt and started climbing. "You know what's so challenging about our relationship?" he asked. His ass was in her face. "It's not that I'm a man, and you're a woman. It's that I'm a person, and you're another, different person."

She watched him flop down onto the pleather. He righted himself.

"Head rush," Tom said. "I love you." Grabbing his Nalgene, he opened the door and got out of the car. In a moment, he stuck his head back in. "Text me," he said. "Please be careful."

Abigail thought there would be more checkpoints to drive through, but there weren't. She parked in the teal FOR VISITORS zone. She was pretty sure that what she saw in the distance were the foothills of the Sierra Nevadas, but it could have been any mountain range, because Abigail didn't care about that kind of stuff. Tom told stories about how he and his family had gone to every single national park when he was a kid, and it sounded terrible. She understood the value, but it was like, come on, really? Every one? They'd lost and found Tom's sister on three separate occasions. The family still teased her about it. Whenever they did, Abigail saw the rage in Tom's sister's face.

It seems like a joke at first, she thought, but then it's not, because it's horrifying. The Prius beeped. Her hair was up in a wild pony. She walked—already sweating—through the lot. The visitors' building was a common warehouse. As she checked her purse, she heard and felt the rubber of her Converse stick to the tar.

It was only women and children inside. The blue plastic bucket seats reminded Abigail of certain emergency rooms she'd passed through once upon a time. She could tell she was a bougie sight because no one bothered to look at her. Not the black women. Not the Latino women. Not the white women. Not the Asian women.

Not even the kids. She checked in with the corrections officer behind the melted, bulletproof glass. It was hard to discern a face
back there.

"You've got a red star next to your name," the man said. "So sit
tight. If they open the door, stay put. Don't go followin' with everybody."

It wasn't as if Abigail had conversations with Molly in her head.
She saved those for her mother. Her dead mother had free rein to
say anything—positive or negative, insult or praise. Abigail still refused to discuss things with her father. He would try to talk, and
she'd think, "*Shut the fuck up, man.*" Sometimes she'd tell her dead
mother to tell her dead father to mind his own business. It was pretty
much crazy. Molly spoke to Abigail, when she did, in words and
phrases. It wasn't a dialogue. "*This is insane,*" was all Molly said, as
Abigail sat there in the appearance of silence, and thought about
how everyone—all the living ones, at least—spoke to their dead.

At the check-in, she'd had to give up her phone. She was seated,
staring at her actual hands for the first time in fifteen years, when
a middle-aged white man appeared. There was something of the
1970s about him. Or the '20s. His wrinkled gray face and suit were
ominous. His moustache screamed economic collapse.

"You would have to be Abigail Kupchik," he said.

"I would?"

He looked around the waiting room.

"Yep," he said. "I'm Associate Warden William Claflin."

They'd emailed. It had been strange to type without the aid of
exclamation points, without the necessary courtesy of enthusiastic
punctuation. She was so used to it. Everyone was. Even Leonard
Roth had direct-messaged her CONGRATULATIONS!!!! when

Echo Chamber came out. But Claflin wasn't an emoji man. One did not winky-face a warden.

He shook her hand, sat down on her left, and sighed.

"Today's my last day," he said.

"I'm sorry?" Abigail asked.

"I'm retiring," Claflin said. "This is it. There's an ice cream cake in the coffee room with my name on it." He was staring out into the air in front of his face. His moustache roiled as he spoke. "I don't feel anything yet. It's like nothing. That's how it is with me. A week will go by, a month, ten years . . . and then one day it's, '*Oh, wow.*'"

He turned and took her in with his sad eyes.

"Did you know that you're the only person Vincent's ever agreed to see?" he asked. "So many requests, and yours was the only one he's ever granted. Not even his own mother."

She followed him across the waiting room. They pushed through a set of double doors that he'd key-carded to open and went down a long outdoor hallway that was in fact a cage. On her left was an empty basketball court in the shadow of a three-story lock-up. The lock-up was made out of cinder blocks wedded together in a rush of concrete and spray-foam insulation. She could not believe the arms—the arms were everywhere; hundreds after hundreds; skinny; muscled; deformed; some without hands; some stumps; others fine, or nearly; most of them tattooed. The arms hung out between the bars of the cell windows either all alone, or in pairs, or in threes, or in fours. They swayed back and forth. They reached out and touched the exterior wall. They did nothing at all. Somebody coughed. Then another. Then one more.

They stopped at a door that was still inside the cage. The warden pointed at the lock-up.

"It's a hundred and twenty-five degrees in there," he said.

"That's inhuman," Abigail said. "How can they stand it?"

"They can't," he said. "You hear that?"

She heard nothing.

"No."

"Exactly. Best not to move. Best not to speak. Hell is wasted energy," he said. "Can I tell you something? I think you'll understand."

She already knew what he was going to say. It happened to her all the time. She knew it was her penance. She knew why they came. God had plenty of imagination, but He rehashed the same plots over and over and over again. He sent forth Abigail's own kind to her in droves, as if out of Egypt, or the Betty Ford Clinic.

"I might've had a drink or two today," the warden said. "A nip."

"Whoop-dee-doo," Abigail said. "How many people tried to see him?"

"Hundreds," he said. "At least thirty-five kill-fan women. All the media requests. Not to mention your group. How many screenwriters does it take to write a movie?"

"How many put in requests?" she asked him. "How many from the production company?"

"Twelve," he said. "You didn't know?"

"Nope," she said. "Those little fuckers."

"You can't trust anybody," the warden said. "But you're the winner. You knew her."

Somebody somewhere buzzed them through the door. On the right side of the cage was a small dirt yard in front of a two-story cement building without any windows. A stooped black man who was about three hundred years old stood in the yard all alone with a green rake in his hand. His convict blues bagged around him. He stared at her. She waved. He didn't wave back.

The cage ended at what appeared to be a white trailer with a high-security door welded onto it. Again, an anonymous finger buzzed them in. She was disappointed by the bulletproof Plexiglas that divided the interior in half. She had hoped it wouldn't be there, that somehow her televised understanding of the procedural would be proven wrong, but nowadays real was fake, or vice versa. In the trailer she felt the cold gurgle of the AC unit coming from the wall. The carpet underfoot was nice and dark like an HBO limited series. The light above was a new sort of fluorescent—less horrible, less invasive, longer lasting. She took a seat on one of the gray metal chairs the warden pointed to and looked at the conversation holes drilled into the Plexiglas that was somebody's job.

"Hollywood," the warden said. "Tinseltown. The Big Easy."

"That's New Orleans."

"Sure it is," he said. "Here's how this happens. I will be sitting in that chair next to you. You will be sitting where you're sitting. Two officers will bring in the inmate. You will read from the preapproved questions list only. Do not deviate. Don't improv. No little skits."

On her side of the Plexiglas was a short table with a manila folder on it. She opened the folder and looked at her questions. She doubted very much the warden had bothered to look at them, but maybe he had, and anyway it didn't matter. Who knew what would happen? She wanted out of there. It was a bad idea. They didn't get any worse. There was something wrong with her. She didn't make good decisions. She was selfish. She didn't think about anyone but herself. The makings of a panic attack were speeding through her brain. Her life was cracking through. She heard the clink and swish of ankle chains. The keypad beeped. A guard said, "Watch your step."

It was like a joke:

Two drunks sit in a trailer. The door opens. A murderer walks in.

Or:

Knock-knock.

Who's there?

A murderer.

A murderer who?

PRODUCTIONS

1981-2013

11

His last apartment was near the Robertson exit on the 10. The building was out of the way but cheap. A white and blue metal sign bolted to a lamppost out on Robertson said *La Cienega Heights*. At night he went walking in the fancy neighborhood up on the hill. Sometimes he ran there. Not often. He could tell by the short grass and the polished cars it was Jews. There were a lot of them in LA. He didn't know any Jews back in Massachusetts. He worked with the young ones when he did production. The guys were funny. They made a lot of jokes. The girls were pretty with faces like you'd see on old coins dug up out of the earth. You had to watch out for them, though. They had bad attitudes. They were always talking about the news. Roger didn't care for that, but still there were times. He would go home, run a cold bath, and sit in it for an hour. He kept himself honest that way.

He was from Turners. The bridge over the falls had been under construction for his entire life. It was one lane. You had to wait on the light. The bridge was green and spanned the half mile over the river so that when he rode his bike into town it was like coming back home to an island. Any bike he'd ever had he'd stolen. Every March he'd go halfway across the bridge in the middle of the night and throw his old one in the river. The waterfall was so loud his brain wouldn't work.

•

When he was eight, his mother was supposed to buy him a bike for his birthday, but then her old boyfriend came over. The next day he took the bus south to the town with the girls' college. Bunch-a dykes, his mother liked to say. The kids left their bikes out in the yard down there. He walked in the neighborhood for an hour, saw the Mongoose up against a porch, and took it. He biked for a while. At some point he caught the bus to the hospital. His mother liked to say she was barely older than he was. She told him the government didn't care about white people anymore. She drank. All the nurses remembered him. They said, "Hi, sweetie. Whatcha got there? *Oh, wow!*" They let him bring the bike inside. It was her own room, but the curtain was up. She was talking to the new boyfriend. He was there when the old boyfriend punched her in the face, but he didn't do anything about it.

"Course there's somethin' wrong with him. You think I don't know that? You think *I'm* retarded?"

Four times a day they walked him over to the other classroom. The aides were always women. He looked up at them. After fifth grade they said he didn't have to hold their hands anymore. It wasn't necessary. How *was* he today? It was whispers in the big classroom. Soft talk. The aides were tired from all their kindness. They were the sorts of ladies who never got haircuts. It was long braids for them, like Indians. Roger watched a wheelchair kid who looked twenty-seven get fed white gunk through a tube. The ladies had to shake the bag. They had to flick it with their fingers. Roger had to sound everything out. An aide told Roger her son was hooked too, but not on phonics. Her boyfriend had a motorcycle, she said. Did Roger like motorcycles? Did he think they were cool? Numbers made him want to kill somebody. The angry kid, Kevin, would lose his temper and then they'd have to put

him in the area. Hadn't they talked about this? Use the straps! the ladies screamed. The straps! The wheelchair kids would start to moan.
They liked it. They were blind. It gave their ears something to do. If
they banged their heads around enough it was like a roller coaster.
Roger would watch. He'd sit there. He'd flip the pages of a book. An
oversized laminate on the wall told him to IMAGINE THE POS-
SIBILITIES! It was a picture of Mars. Maybe Jupiter. Outer space.

Years later he drove to California. He took his time. He kept off
the interstate. His favorite town was in Indiana. It was only the one
street. From the Citgo, he could see the library, the police station,
the elementary school, the grocery store. Everything was made out
of brick. He saw a cornfield that went all the way to the horizon, it
looked like. The wind blew the stalks around like the hair on a cater-
pillar. The middle of the country was a bright green thing. He slept
in his car the whole way.

He kept the Mongoose for longer than the other bikes. He intuitively
grasped sentimental value. He connected memory with pain. Certain objects were more distinct than others. Certain glances. Certain
views. A space between two sets of trees that looked out onto the
river. He'd stand there for an hour. Feel. Pedal.

The movies were in Greenfield. The next town over. At twelve,
thirteen, fourteen, he'd go there three times a week. They'd let him
sweep. They'd let him take out the trash. The theater was right there
on Main Street and nothing about that struck Roger as old-fashioned.
He was among the last of that tribe who had populated the earth
for a century. He took it for granted the marquee should power on
at dusk. Green bulbs. Red bulbs. Gold ones. Titles announced with
drooping and sometimes backward letters. It was called the Garden.

He liked most everything. Not the boring art ones, but everything else. He liked the trailers. He loved the *flip-flap-flap* of the catching reel. The smell of the burn at the edges. How the volume had to settle, then rise, get used to the room. The beam of light. Dumb comedies. The dumber the better. Cartoons. Dramas. Thrillers. Action. Romance. Horror. The dark box inside of night.

It was about his mother with the other kids. Him too. But his mother first. It was endless. It was years. He kept his head down. The long hallway. The empty athletic field, but for the lump of them in the corner shouting hey! How's your mom? Your mom good? She still suck dick? She still like that? We got money—can she come by later? What'cha think? Can you work it out? White trash asshole. Hey retard. Yo retard. Dick-slexic motherfucker. Hey fuckhead. Why you lookin' at your feet all time? Your brain down there? That ain't your brain, dummy. Should kill you.

His life was boring, repetitive, gray, human. It was like a movie he would have walked out on.

He slept in his car. When he woke up, he drove. He kept his money hid inside the spare's well. He drove through Chicago. He'd never seen a real city before. He went at a slant across the country. One night he walked through a cavernous parking lot of idling semis, the diesel heat surrounding him, brake lines decompressing air into his legs. When he got to the diner, he shifted back around and took in the parking lot. He raised up his chin and admired the stars. Here was Oklahoma. The panhandle. Heat index of a hundred and one.

He did first grade twice. Eighth grade twice. He dropped out just before graduation and started full-time at the movie theater. He saved.

His mother had a baby. He didn't know what to call it. He didn't know how to hold the thing.

The kids he'd grown up with and been around his whole life came into the theater. He did concessions. They acted like they'd never seen him before. He was like that. He was like someone you could sit next to for eight years and then forget he even existed. A lot of the guys from high school spoke ghetto talk now. They'd come in with their girlfriends, who were still redneck country girls, but harder, and say, "Gimme some a dem jew-jew bees. Make that two. Gimme one a dem tall johns to drink."

He didn't tell his mother about the computer. He kept it hidden in his closet in a brown paper bag. He could look them up now, and not only the famous ones, but the other ones whose names he didn't know, like from the horror movies. Those ones were always new. They came out of nowhere. He'd sit in the theater after the credits were over and write down their actual names. This was hard. It meant that he had to keep notes during. He had lists he'd made in the dark like: *bad friend number one, impaled sister, decapitated girl in bikini, Emily?* Certain words he could spell. They'd been blasted into him. He would sound shit out. He'd go home with the list. He'd ask Jeeves. It was difficult finding out what other movies they were in, but he could do it.

"Because her daddy's black, Roger. That's half of why I kept her. Maybe she'll turn out pretty. Where's the rent?"

He bought a car the same color as the Mongoose. Electric blue. It had a spoiler. His second try he passed the driving test. "Con-gra-ju-la-tions," the tester said. He'd had a stroke or something. His mouth hung. People were Massholes now. It was a bumper sticker. He'd go into the convenience store on Fifth Street, down from where he lived with his mother and the baby, and there would be a fat woman in the store screaming at the guy. The fat woman's shorts said HONEY. Others butts said BOOTY, LUCKY, MEOW, HOT, TUFF. His mother borrowed the car and totaled it. Everything was a thing. Tons of heroin around.

They searched his car at the dam. Dogs sniffed around his tires. From the top, he looked down the spiraling road at the cars braking. The sky was red with mountains. Mars. Jupiter. He took the elevator down into the loud hammer of water and steel. It was a group tour. At a certain point they ducked their heads and entered a well-lit tunnel deep under the earth. Later, he drove through the desert. He saw whole towns on the edge. Grass was a plant you could grow.

Everything was closed on the eleventh. Roger understood what was going on. He was always a part of what was large, all-consuming, out of his control. He grew up on *Today*. He sat on the edge of his bed and stared into the screen. He called up. His boss told him don't be crazy. They were closed too. Maybe tomorrow. Maybe the day after. Who knew? A war was going on.

The way he knew time had stopped was when he stuck his thumb out and a car pulled over. He went to the Garden. He'd had that key forever. If a movie didn't do that well, a distributor might forget about it. There were reels and reels.

After his mother had wrecked the Hyundai, she was in the hospital for two weeks. He watched the baby. He didn't know what to do with it. It wasn't exactly his sister. A neighbor lady came over and cleaned her up. Don't lay her out on the floor like that, the lady said. If she's cryin', she's hungry. You got to use the wipes. Like that, but gentle. *Gentle*. It was awhile back. He'd missed a lot of work. A lot of movies.

He watched *Funhouse* all alone on a Tuesday.

There was a carnival at the edge of the woods. A Ferris wheel rotated against the moon. *Aaaaaaah!* teens screamed. Three high school girls who looked around twenty-five bought tickets at the booth. A slutty blonde with tits. A brunette too sassy for her own good. The third one had dirty blond hair and eyes that weren't exactly green.

If it hadn't been for the third girl, he would have stopped the reel. She was the only good thing about that whole movie. He liked her face. He liked her neck. He liked her legs. He liked her breasts as they pushed against her white T-shirt. He stared at her with his mouth open as she ran through the woods, the condiment station, the turnstile. She killed the clown by throwing him off the Ferris wheel. By the end of the movie, she was covered in blood. She had a limp. She was beautiful. But for her, everyone was dead. Everyone.

He overhead a guy at work say, "Just google it." He didn't know what the guy was talking about. He had to look it up on his computer. Years went by like that.

hellomagazine.com hollywoodrag.com okmagazine.com eonline .com thenationalenquirer.com justjared.com starmagazine.com gossipcop.com radar.com thehollywoodgossip.com celebitchy.com

•

He'd never kissed a woman on the lips before.

thesuperficial.com laineygossip.com celebgossip.com popbytes.com tabloidcolumn.com intouchweekly.com toofab.com people.com gossipcenter.com egotastic.com showbiz411.com

She was from an hour north. Not even.

celebritypuke.com

He did the last leg. There was a presidential debate on the car radio. The president was the decider. The other guy was married to the ketchup lady. He sounded like his mouth was full of mouth. Roger sat in traffic for so long he had to piss in a Lemon Iced Tea Snapple bottle. Everything was numbers. What was a Cahuenga? For two weeks he lived in a hotel downtown. The street looked like an old dirty wok. Machines turned entire city blocks into holes. There were what sounded like explosions all day long. Men and women with plastic bags shoved down inside their shirt collars and in their socks and up their sleeves tumbled across the street. They pushed shopping carts and dragged wagons stacked six feet high with flat cardboard boxes from one corner to another. Trash blew into them and stayed there. They waited for the bus but didn't take it. They made beds out of actual mattresses and slept under bridges between enormous cement dividers so that if they fell out on either side a car would run them over.

"California?" his mother asked him. "What are you gonna do out there? You're gonna end up homeless."

•

He tore a stapled flyer off a telephone pole that said BE A MOTION PICTURE EXTRA! MAKE $100/DAY!*. The girl on the phone told him she was quitting. She was going back to Nebraska.

"This thing's a scam," she said. "You have to pay money to get work, and then there's no work. You really wanna do something like this? Be an extra?"

He thought he did.

"Let me give you another number. This one's real. This one pays you."

Only one of the star maps had her house listed, but it was an old address in West Hollywood from when she was younger. It wasn't even the nice part. There were blacks.

The oversized trailer in the valley was next to a junkyard. The old man took his picture eight times and wrote down his measurements. He told him he wasn't so big. He wasn't so small. He was average, the old man said, but he had a sort of look about him.

His phone would ring at four in the morning.

"We've got a call for a John Cusack movie in Tarzana. Restaurant scene."

"There's a Faith Hill music video downtown. It's mostly crowd stuff. Pays cash."

"A pilot about a kid who can talk to horses."

"*Six Feet Under*."

He worked eighteen, nineteen, twenty days in a row. He mostly sat around. A lot of the other extras looked sick. They looked tired and thin. Nothing too bad, but some disease that kept them from doing real work. When the PAs told them they could eat, everybody ate as much food as they could. He did TV shows down at this hospital that wasn't a real hospital anymore. All of the equipment was still there. He sat down in a chair in the waiting room all day and pretended to talk with this Chinese lady who couldn't speak English. The AD told them to mouth the words "apples and pears," or "green peas makes me sick." He did a party scene for a black comic's movie in Laguna Beach. The comic was dressed up as a big old fat lady. They shot the whole thing in a restaurant called the Crab Shack. The other extras said the comic was having a nervous breakdown. He couldn't take it anymore. They shaved Roger's head once and dressed him in a white robe, and then he and four hundred other people prayed in a gymnasium at a God to be later created in post.

Men in vans. Men who smoked cigarettes. Men with great heads of hair but with gutted faces like dried, cracked ravines. Men walking down the side of the highway in camo pants with army duffels strapped to their backs. Men in old trucks that were never rusted but with telephone numbers painted on their sides and under those numbers the words HAUL AWAY or TRASH GUY. The busses were full of Mexican women holding brooms and plastic bags. None of the women seemed to have cars. The men waited in trucks at the bottom of the canyon roads and then the women came walking down the roads at five o'clock in the afternoon. The women spoke to one another in Mexican as they went down the hill and then they got in the trucks driven by the men and they were gone.

He bought a phone that flipped. It had a keyboard. It sent him news updates he didn't want. He bought a typewriter in Culver City. He was dumb, his mother used to say, but he knew how to be invisible.

•

The popcorn machine broke at the hospital. One of the actors liked the movie popcorn with the butter substitute. It was in his contract. You couldn't read *US* magazine on set and you couldn't eat the popcorn unless somebody offered it to you. The popcorn belonged to the actor.

"Anybody know how?" a pretty Mexican asked.

Roger was eating a Danish under the canopy by the craft trailer. He put his hand in the air like a child. They took him inside the trailer where they kept the machine. He pulled a small pin out one half-inch. It worked. The bucket dumped.

The manager said his name was High-May. He asked Roger if he wanted a job.

"It's union," High-May said. "Good benefits, but no dental. This isn't SAG."

You didn't have to go to the movies anymore, but he did. It wasn't fair to steal her off the internet. People would talk about her at work. She was blowing up, they'd say. She was exploding. She was an ad exec. She was the ex-girlfriend of a drug dealer. She'd gone on a rampage in that one. She'd delivered.

Every morning before work he retyped the letter. It was three hundred and eighty letters before he found her address. The website told him she was selling. It was up for sale. He drove around Coldwater for a year. One day Roger saw her assistant go by him in her BMW. The assistant was a dyke, but she wasn't. He followed her. The assistant went to the place in Malibu. She came back down the 1. She went to the mansion the new husband was building. She drove to the old place on Coldwater. In the end, it took him four hours. A year and four hours. He sent the letters to every address but for Coldwater. He wanted her to have one place that was hers.

He was with High-May on the Warner Brothers lot. The big one on the other side of Barham. The other lot was yellow. It was TV. Horror was the woods. You could shoot it anywhere.

"You're quiet, man," High-May said.

They were setting up the breakfast table. The lot was a valley carved up into parking lots and small ranches with actual horses sometimes and soundstages and a racetrack. He liked the smog. He didn't really care. High-May told Roger he had a daughter he didn't see much.

"I used to work in porn," High-May said. "Boom work. A little post when I could get it. You meet the girls. Some of them aren't even dumb. Most are. That thing's a meat grinder. This is much better. Way more civilized. Once you're in, you're in. I can get a job anywhere. Like that."

A year later they were doing the same job at the same place for the same amount of money. Roger and High-May hopped in the golf cart. Macaroni needed getting over. A line of a few hundred men in Civil War uniforms jogged into a soundstage. A pale girl in a red blouse and a black miniskirt walked across the street in front them. The girl carried a big orange binder. She was someone, Roger guessed. She gave them a stare, because you never knew, but it was only them.

"Fuck these people," High-May said. "All these people are in the future. That's where they live. They think they're somebody else already—some hotshot. Fuck them."

•

Time didn't matter. A year went by. Another. More. He lived in his head.

High-May knew a guy. Roger took the bus to Vancouver. "Mumbles takes the bus!" High-May shouted. He was two days early. He rented a cheap room in a motel downtown. That was what men did, he thought. They rented cheap rooms.

He walked around downtown Vancouver. He tried to remember that he should call her an actor—that it was sexist to call her an actress. It was hard for him to care. He preferred the word *actress*. It was a prettier word. It looked like a dress to him. He saw an old movie poster on a building in what he guessed was the cool part of town. Half her face was torn off. The temperature on a digital bank clock was one digit shy of her birth year. He was drawn to numbers now, to strangers, to less obvious forms of coincidence. One afternoon he sat down on a bus stop bench. A girl who looked like her crossed the street and Roger almost passed out.

It was depressing. She wasn't scheduled to arrive for another two weeks. The crew shot B roll and the scenes she wasn't in.

That bitch put it in her contract, Roger heard the director say. She was a real pain in the ass that way, he said. It didn't matter how nice they were supposed to be or how professional. They were all the same. Hard to deal with. Particular. They acted like they were the whole goddamn movie. My four-year-old can act natural.

"This coffee's cold," he said to Roger. "Can I have some hot fucking coffee? What is this? Am I on set here or what? Where am I? What the hell is wrong with you?"

Roger went to the director's trailer that night and unplugged his refrigeration line. The next night he stuck a wad of gum in the AC plug. The third night he took a dump on his front step and threw a brick through his window.

It was all anybody could talk about. It was like they weren't making a movie.

A detective came around. He had a moustache. His voice sounded like it was coming out of his forehead.

"I'm speaking to the entire production the same way," the detective said. The eight of them had been gathered around the food trailer. "I'm speaking to you like I'm speaking to the actors or to the technical crew. We don't cast blame here in Vancouver. I don't care where you're from."

Roger watched the detective smile at all the Chinese people he worked with.

"So if you're worried about that, don't be," the detective said.

Four of his coworkers didn't show up for work the next day. Roger didn't understand.

"Immigration," his manager said.

That afternoon the detective interviewed him.

"You're American. Why are you here?"

He tried to explain himself.

"That doesn't make any sense to me," the detective said. "Did you have an argument with the gentleman?"

He didn't move at all—not even his face or his eyelids.

"Sure you did," the detective said.

He hadn't even seen her.

There were several routes to get there, but he liked the long way best. Lower Laurel Canyon to Upper Laurel Canyon—across onto

Mulholland—and then over onto Coldwater. He drove it every few days. Four or five times a week if he felt the need. He never once understood she was his discipline. She made him better. His internet browser history grew more diverse.

It poured in LA. He drove up the night the rain let up and parked his car on a side street. He parked illegally under a private security sign. He put the laminated orange piece of paper that read LA COUNTY CENSUS on his dash. Holding a clipboard, he walked a half mile until he came to a construction site. He ate a sandwich under some scaffolding as the sun went down.

He changed into his all-black clothing and took out the pocket shears. He left his backpack behind some drywall at the construction site. When it was dark enough he hiked along the ridge where the plants had it out for humans. If he came across a plant that would have cut him up, he took out the pocket shears. Her house was only a quarter of a mile away, but it took him an hour and a half. Standing outside the back fence, he was impressed with himself. He wasn't bleeding. He didn't feel any pain.

Roger found the control box on a post beside the tree. He used a tiny Phillips head. The switches were labeled. A company never knew who they would send. POWER SOURCE D (CAMERAS). POWER SOURCE B (EXT. LIGHT/SECURITY). The rain shorted wiring out all the time. He wore gloves and clacked the switches down. He climbed over the fence and after twenty minutes, he found a window on the first floor he could lift up. He slid through like an overgrown fat snake into the kitchen. He stood up and looked at the gleaming counter. The maid had left the key out.

•

"How many copies should I make?" the locksmith on Ventura asked.

Comic-Con. The People's Choice Awards. The Venice Film Festival. The Tribeca Film Festival. United Amnesty International Gala Event. SXSW.

He bought an iPhone. The internet was as near to an exact science as he would ever know.

Her bedroom was bigger than his entire apartment. She didn't have a dresser. All of her clothing was in the walk-in closet organized by color and up on hangers. Her underwear was laid out on shelves, splayed out like cards in a deck. Same with her bras. It seemed like if she wore a thong even once, she didn't wash it, she threw it in the trash. She had a few hundred dresses. Two hundred and seven. It would have taken all night to count the shirts and the pants. He opened the safe because it wasn't locked and anyway the code was written down on a Post-it note stuck to the front. She owned pearl necklaces. Gold necklaces. Silver necklaces. Diamond necklaces. Necklaces he didn't know the types of—pale green stones and blue ones and reds like actual fire. Bracelets. Rings. She had all sorts of hoop earrings she never wore and that Roger wished aloud to himself in her walk-in she would.

If he went once, he went a dozen times.

He pulled off her comforter, stripped the top and bottom sheets, and then yanked the cases off her pillows. He washed and dried it all in the upstairs washer/dryer and then remade her bed.

•

Western Europe and Southeastern Asia Promotional Tour. Turks and Caicos. Shanghai. Breast Cancer Fight for a Cure Foundation. The New York Film Festival.

He sat in every chair in the screening room. He rubbed his hands on her eating utensils. He stopped keeping himself honest and masturbated in front of the life-size cutout.

In every room he would lie down on the floor and pretend he was dead. She was old enough to keep photographs of people she knew in shoeboxes. He saw pictures of certain film people when they were young. She had books with pictures of art in them that cost a couple hundred dollars brand new. Old paperbacks on acting. On directing. There was a closet with five neat piles of film scripts. Each of the piles went up to his chest. She owned three thousand DVDs.

He took a bottle of shampoo home with him. He found her vibrator. He clicked it on and put it up against his cheek. His mouth and teeth and whole head shook. He smelled it, but it didn't smell like anything. She must wash it, he thought. It's not like she would be dirty.

"New York?" High-May asked him. "New York? You never told me about Vancouver."

He'd never been there. There was no one around to ask him how this was possible. He'd never flown either. He began to think of his life in terms of adventure. He checked into the Howard Johnson near the airport. The union had set it up. Nobody mentioned Vancouver. There were rules in place to protect his privacy. Taking a cab into

Manhattan for the first time in his life, he felt like he was going to have a heart attack. It was so much city—and booming loud—and all of it was worming in and out of itself.

He called his mother. His mother wasn't home.

"Who is this?"

She was a teenager now.

Brooklyn. He saw a flash of her. Roger was inside the food truck. He was getting the woks ready for the stir-fry station. He looked out the open rectangle. At first there was no one. A brick wall. He couldn't perceive depth. Then she passed from left to right like the words on a page. A bunch of feeling like light pulsed out of her. When he recognized her, she started to flicker. Then she was gone.

The crew was all white ladies. He missed the Mexicans. All the white ladies did was complain. They smoked 100s. They wouldn't shut up. "Where you from, honey? You're the silent type, aren't you? I love that. All the men in this city do is talk, talk, talk. That's all they do. All day and all night. Talk, talk, talk. Who cares? Not me."

He did what they told him. He was the wok guy. He was the prep guy. It didn't matter where they set up. People came over.

"They shootin' a movie? Who's in it?"

He told them.

"No shit."

He was the driver too. The ladies told him how to get where. Greenpoint, they said. Central Park North. Ludlow and Rivington. Fucking Harlem. Take the FDR. Take the BQE. Wherever they went, he saw the usual machines. The usual flatbeds. The usual pallets of chairs no one ever sat on. The tints. The metallic poles. The soundboards with a hundred different plugs. They would put down wires like speed bumps in the middle of the street. Their hips were walkie-talkies.

The idea was to meet her. To stop with this version. He was sick of this version. He wanted it to be over. He wanted his real life to begin now. He wanted the life he had inside himself.

The assistant would come get her food for her. The assistant, or the assistant's assistant. She was busy. She was the director, the whole thing. He understood. He could wait one more day. Maybe another. But how many? When? He already knew how it would be. It would be easy. "Hello." "Hello." He only needed it to happen.

The ladies told him Grand Central one night—or morning. A two-thirty call time. Skeleton crew. There was just no way for them. He didn't have a family. He didn't live there. They didn't have to go on explaining the differences, but they did.

He parked the food truck on Forty-Fifth Street. He turned the griddle on low. He put the veggies in the silver tubs. He filled the oil bottle. He double-checked for eggs, tortillas.

He walked down to Forty-Second. He looked west down its length. The road was a wave the cars went up and down. He thought there was a law against honking? He saw the heat in the glow of the brake lights and how there wasn't much of a difference here between the day and night. All of the buildings were clean and black. When he went into the station he thought he'd done something wrong. It looked like a church. The silence surprised and embarrassed him. He felt like he shouldn't be there. The sound of his boots came back to him from the ceiling. He walked down a slope into the center of the station. He looked up. The ceiling wasn't quite green. It wasn't quite blue. It was a painting of outer space. Of the gods. The possibilities.

An hour later they called him on the walkie. She wanted a burrito.

He made it extra careful. He didn't wrap it too tight. He pulled back the foil at the top so she wouldn't have to. He locked up the food truck and went back into the station. He saw her against the far wall. She was staring at the ceiling. She raised her hands up. She made them into a square. She looked through it.

When he got to within three feet of her, a man put his hand on Roger's chest.

"Whoa, whoa," the man said. He was a young guy. The first AD. He had gel in his hair. "That's far enough."

Roger stood there.

"*What?*" the AD asked. "It's done. Go back to the truck. I've got it from here."

Roger stared at her. She was right there. She was still looking up at the ceiling. He loved her throat.

He did as he was told. Roger walked away. Five steps later, he turned around.

"I don't know where they get these people," he heard the AD say to her. "Did you see that guy? Fucking Igor? Jesus Christ."

Back in LA he didn't leave the house. He stopped going to work. He stayed in his apartment. A month passed. He saw the world more clearly. Life was a story. It went A B C. 1 2 3. Beginning middle end.

"Where the hell are you?" High-May asked. Every few days he would leave a voicemail. Roger had never considered him a friend.

"I've got a job for you. It's PA work, but it pays. Are you alive? Call me."

It was called *How Clean Are You?* and the hosts were two old British ladies. People lived like animals—they were disgusting—and the ladies would go into their houses and make them feel bad. A crew from Compton did the cleaning, but the ladies acted like they were the ones. "Ta-da!" they'd say. It was all product placement. Lysol. Spic and Span. Joy. Clorox with Bleach. Swiffer WetJets. Yankee Candle.

He'd never worked production before. High-May said it would take awhile to get him back in the craft rotation. "You disappeared, man." The work was the kind of thing any idiot could do. If some asshole needed coffee, he went and got the coffee. They'd send him out on a run, and he'd be gone for hours, drive around and around. As long as the coffee was hot, and the trucks were loaded and unloaded, nobody cared what he did.

He went to Starbucks one morning, picked up the coffee, and drove into the hills. The road was off Mulholland. Diamond Terrace. He waited for everyone to get there. It was 5:45 a.m. A little house behind a garden gate. The producer came. She needed Roger to start cleaning up. The owner was a woman, the producer said, a real piece of work. The producer didn't know the whole story. She didn't get it. Roger walked into the house, and he understood right away. The woman was tiny and her hair was dyed purple and she was on drugs. Her little dog was dyed purple too. What wasn't the whole story? What wasn't there to get? The producer and the woman went outside and smoked a cigarette. The woman wanted to renegotiate. Times were tough.

It reminded him of his mother's house. All the rooms were full of stuff. Nobody could use the shower because of all the wire hangers in it. The living room floor was covered in paper towels stained with blood. There was dog shit everywhere. You couldn't see the bed in the bedroom because it was overflowing with paper bags stuffed with clothes. He cleaned out the downstairs bathtub wearing yellow gloves. He picked up a syringe with blood in the gauge. He set the syringe down on the toilet seat. He pawed through the wet stuff in the bathtub some more and found a pregnancy test. It was positive. He set that down on the toilet seat next to the syringe. A pretty girl he worked with arrived and saw the test and the syringe. "This is totally fucked," she said. "I went to Oberlin."

The Compton crew showed up. They got it like Roger did. It was the first time he'd talked to any of them.

"Somebody needs to get fired over this shit," the crew leader said. "There's no motherfucking way my people are going in there."

"AIDS. Hepatitis," a woman said. "You went in there?"

Roger told her that he had.

"That's crazy." She took Roger's hands into her own. She looked at his right hand first, then his left hand. She smelled like something he wanted to call coconut. "You're good."

"This is some bullshit," the crew leader said to Roger and the woman. "Nobody checked this shit out. How do you come out here and not see?" He looked at Roger like they were friends. Like they were the same. "I mean, really, how do you work in reality and you don't understand reality?"

The producer told Roger to go get cigarettes down on Hollywood Boulevard. If the woman didn't get her cigarettes, they weren't allowed to film in her house anymore. She was threatening to back out. There was a special shop that sold her particular brand. She would only smoke those cigarettes. Get going, the producer said. What are you waiting for?

Roger couldn't find the place. He parked his car and walked up and down Hollywood. First one side, and then the other. He looked at the stars under his feet. He didn't know half of them. Who was Veronica Lake? Who was William Powell? Who was Gloria Swanson? He found the smoke shop. He bought the cigarettes and drove back up to the house on Diamond Terrace. It turned out they were the wrong brand, but it didn't matter. He'd been gone for hours. The situation had changed, the producer said. The Compton crew was gone. A HazMat team was going at it. The producer had given the woman two hundred dollars. A man in a Datsun had arrived soon after.

They waited. It was after dark. Finally, the Datsun pulled up. They pointed the camera at the woman, and the British ladies walked her through the house.

"Look at this, dear! Look how much better! Think of the filth! The filth! You were living like an animal, dear. We've changed your life. It wasn't too difficult. A few hours' work is all. A little elbow grease! Some gumption! Isn't that what you Americans call it? Hold on to me, dear. You're falling over, I think. Open your eyes! Look at this floor! You could eat off this floor! You could live a life, if you'd only try! Wash a dish! Keep it tidy! Up by your bootstraps, dear, right? What do you say? Have we cleaned you up? 'How Clean Are You?' "

"So clean," the woman said, her eyes half closed, her head nodding. "Thank you. Thank you so much. You're all wonderful. All of you."

•

This was the end. Everything would make sense. It would all come together. Her body. His. That was the story. Girl meets boy. Boy meets girl. He wanted her. What wasn't there to get?

Roger had skimmed a book on acting once. He'd stolen it from her library. He'd understood very little of it, but he remembered one thing. The book said an actor could play a character, but he could never be the character. To be the character would be insane. It wouldn't be reality. You were always you no matter what. If you remembered this, you'd be able to react without thinking. You would be there. Not you, the character, but you, the actor. You could surprise yourself. Every scene, no matter how many times you performed it, would be new. You wouldn't be thinking. You'd be doing. Thinking was the problem. You only had to be.

He didn't bother thinking about the rain. He didn't bother to bring the placard along. He parked where he always parked. He wouldn't need the car anymore. LA could have it. It would be one more car on the side of the road.

He held the knife in his right hand. He walked through the plants at the pace he wanted to. Not fast. Not slow. He let the cacti and the sharper edges of the larger plants cut into him and he bled. It didn't matter. He didn't need to be invisible. He could make a sound. The door could creak. The floor. The steps. The blinds could tick against each other.

He didn't want her to survive. That would be too bad. She shouldn't have to walk with a cane her whole life, or be in a wheelchair, or on oxygen with the machine going. She shouldn't be disfigured.

That wouldn't be right. She should die. She should be all bloody. She should scream. He wanted to hear the sound of metal tearing through muscle. The *ftt ftt ftt*. He wanted to feel it.

His mind was gone. There weren't any lights on in the house. Only the moon outside. Flat light on the windows. Security spot. He passed through the hall using sense memory. He saw her sleeping in her bed. Her face was to him. Her right arm dangled off the edge.

React, the book had told him. Do what comes natural.

"Molly," he said.

THE NOVEL

2013-1993

12

THE RAIN MACHINE WAS NOT RAINING. IT WAS A MACK TRUCK with special hydraulic feet welded to the frame. An eighteen-foot-tall steel mast was positioned in the middle of the bed. Hoses of all sizes and lengths were attached to the mast, and water leaked from the hoses down onto the roof of the truck, rivering off into the already flooded street. The machine cost five thousand dollars a day to rent, and all it had done so far was produce deep belching sounds that echoed off the factories there in Greenpoint, and put the shoot, which was already behind schedule, even further behind schedule. It was near to nine p.m. in August of 2013, and Molly Bit stood in the Brooklyn street wearing a Hydrogen Productions baseball cap and green rain boots. She held a bullhorn in her left hand. She looked down at the spotlights reflected in the water around her boots, and then at the moon reflected there too, a blue one, and good luck supposedly, and then back up at the rain machine. Fifty some-odd people, including production assistants, gaffers, grips, best boys, light techs, four police officers assigned by the city, her first AD, her DP, her two young leads—all her people—stood around waiting for her to tell them what to do. The sky was bright and starless.

"I'm asking myself if it has to rain," she said to the prop master.

"That's a question," Tony said. "That's something you could ask."

He was a short, almost-sixty-year-old Teamster with a Tom Selleck moustache. She'd known him for fifteen years and adored him in the way she adored men who were around her father's age but who weren't her father.

"What do you think?"

"I think it's your show," Tony said. He wiped water from off his cheek. "If you say, 'No rain,' then no rain."

"Then no rain."

"But just so you know, it'll take me and my guys two and a half hours to clear the street."

"Do it."

"All right!" Tony shouted. He didn't need the bullhorn. Everybody heard him. "Grab the brooms! Grab the buckets! Get that goddamn thing outta here! No rain!"

Everything was money. More to the point, everything was her money. Hydrogen was the only partner she'd been able to secure. They had a small stake in *The Last Century*, enough that they could place their name before the title, but the majority of the twenty-three million had come from Molly's "production company," which was nothing more than a second mortgage on her house stamped with the name of the road she'd grown up on, Skitchewaug Trail. No one had been interested in the idea of her directing—although they wouldn't come right out and say that. Instead, they lied.

"Love, love, love."

"Of course. I was thinking that. I was going to say that."

"Perfect."

All the second and third meetings were to pitch alternative ideas.

"*The Last Century*—is that it?—it's always on the table as far as we're concerned. But we'd also like to talk about this remake of *Xanadu*. It's family friendly. We've got young leads, but we really need someone established to hold it all together. You'd be playing the Gene Kelly role, but you wouldn't have to dance or sing, and of course you'd be a woman."

"She's one of the leaders of the mutant rebellion. A figure the others look up to. A kind of sexy matriarch. She shoots lasers out of her forehead."

"Picture this: Your daughter is mute. Your plane crashes in the Alaskan wilderness. There's a number of bears. How do you survive?"

"I'm old now?" she'd asked Diane one day. "Is that it?"

They were getting hers and hers massages in her living room. Molly's masseuse said he had a light sensitivity. He kept his eyes closed the whole time.

"You're thirty-nine," Diane said. "*Right there. Oh. Wow.*"

"You're forty," Molly said.

"I can be as old as I want to be," Diane told her. "We're not talking about me. Why don't you take one of the deals they're offering you? Do the mutant one. Make it contingent upon *The Last Century*."

"*Because I'm thirty-nine,*" she said. "I don't think it's ridiculous for a grown woman to decline mutation. I don't want to sit in a makeup chair for six hours a day having scales applied to my tits."

Molly felt a tap on her shoulder and flipped over onto her back. She had slices of kiwi taped over her eyes. Her neck was slathered in honey.

"But what about the money?" Diane asked.

"I don't care about the money," Molly said. "I just want it."

"*God.*"

"I know what you're thinking—I'm spoiled, I'm rotten, and maybe that's true. But this movie is my child. This is what I want to put out into the world. Not some goofy-looking thing that cries all the time. I want to direct."

"But what if you *did* want to have a baby?"

"I'm not in the mood for this."

"I mean it," Diane said. "Imagine if you wanted to have a baby."

"I don't. But I'm imagining."

"Don't get mad at me here. Just listen to me."

"All ears," she said.

"Did these guys sign something?" Diane asked. "Did you guys sign something?"

"Yes," one of the men said. "We did."

"You're not married," Diane said. "You're not dating anyone. Nobody's on the horizon. But all of the sudden you want to have a baby. What do you do?"

"I just have the baby. I get a donor. I adopt or whatever. I just do it."

"So just do the movie," Diane said. "What's the difference? You're sort of rich. Kind of. Sometimes."

In Brooklyn, she bull-horned her men over.

"No rain?" Tomasz asked. "I had conceived of rain."

"You'll have to conceive of it differently," Molly said.

She and her DP had gotten along well at first. Tomasz Eggles was Hungarian. Years ago, they'd met for dinner while Molly was promoting a film in Pest. Tomasz had walked her through the old quarter, pointing out buildings where his family used to live, gesturing at a square that had once held public executions. She admired his work. He had a way of framing shots in such a manner so as to make them seem elegiac. He understood how the past lived in the present, the way it clung to shadows. What better eye to see *The Last Century* with? They'd kept up an email correspondence over the subsequent years. Theirs had been a warm, professional exchange, but when Tomasz arrived, he'd been irritated with his accommodations. He had not traveled all the way to New York to stay in Brooklyn, he said.

Only the day before he'd accused her of micromanaging him, of not allowing him to do his job. This may have been true.

One of Molly's fears was that people would think Tomasz was her ghost director, and so, when he framed a shot in his usual style—tight, contained, the actors had to hit their marks exactly just so—she would sometimes ask him to pull back, to give her the dark hallway to the left, some emptiness. He always agreed—he nodded his head in the old bloc Communist style—but first he bitched.

"This is not at all what I had envisioned," he said. Tomasz was sixty. His gray skin reminded her of a leaky faucet. "There is no hope for the machine?"

"None."

"We cannot readjust the hoses?"

"It's not the hoses," she said. "It's something with the motor."

"Motor?"

It was incredible, the times he chose incomprehension.

"What is this?" he asked. "Motor?"

"You know what a motor is, Tomasz," Molly said. "Don't fuck with me right now."

"I'll let everyone know," Ray Odette chirped in.

Her first AD was a man-boy in the last throes of his fake humility. In a matter of years it would either be real or he would have succeeded enough to stick it to everyone who'd ever crossed him. These types were cute at first, Molly thought, sort of like baby wolves, but then there comes that morning when you wake up and your throat's been torn out. Ray's uncle was a producer named Vincent Odette. She had a passing friendship with Vince. They'd had a single decent conversation at the Golden Globes a decade ago and had been trying to rekindle it ever since. "You should try my nephew," he'd said to her at an Alzheimer's benefit. "He'll work for cheap. He wants out of commercial."

"What about the talent?" Ray asked her. His brain was stuck in Nike, Chanel, Velveeta Mac & Cheese.

"I'll talk to the actors," Molly said.

"Actors, right," Ray said. "Sorry."

Her leads, Ashley Peele and Dom Kirkwieler, were smoking by the makeup tent. They were both twenty-two. Ashley had grown up Hollywood. At age nine she'd begun starring in *The Warriors of Time* series based upon the YA books of the same name. The series was about a group of human-alien-hybrid children tasked with . . . Molly had never seen it. She liked the way the girl carried herself. Like the character she was playing, Ashley was without apology. At the audition, Molly had put a table close to the door where the actors came in. She placed it so that when the girls entered the room, the door would hit the table. Five, six, seven girls walked in, banged the table, and apologized. When it was Ashley's turn, the strength she'd used to open the door knocked the table to the floor. She gently closed the door behind her, turned to Molly and Ray Odette, and said, "That's a terrible place for that."

Dom Kirkwieler had been in one other movie before this, a low-budget mumble-core directed by his brother. He was untrained, in over his head, and everyone he met on set intimidated him. He was perfect.

Molly sloshed through the water in the road, hopped up onto the sidewalk and over to them.

"Would you call this a no-rain delay?" Ashley asked.

She was lovely and knew it. Her shoulder-length blond hair was all angles and messy, something the stylist had called "late-late punk." For the months leading up to the shoot, Ashley had studied the early 1990s, its music and fads. She'd decided her character would probably have a secret soft spot for the era's more mainstream music. "Outwardly, she'd be all Sonic Youth and Nirvana," Ashley had said to Molly over the phone, "but come on, really? In the shower? Who's going to sing 'Rape Me' in the shower?

"'All I can say is that my life is pretty plain,'" Ashley sang, in perfect pitch. "'You don't like my point of view, you think that I'm insane.'"

"He was a babe," Molly said. "That was sad."

At Molly's urging, both Ashley and Dom had handed over their cell phones to their assistants. She'd wanted them to experience actual downtime in the same way their characters would have. She wanted them to understand true boredom, true solitude. One unfortunate side effect of this character note was that both Ashley and Dom had begun to smoke an incredible number of cigarettes. Molly had a feeling the sound guys were to blame for this. It was always the sound guys. The sound guys were always up to something.

Molly herself would have killed for a smoke, but no. No. No.

"How are you, Molly Bit?" Dom asked. He always said her whole name. Everybody loved him. He still looked awkward maneuvering the cigarette to and away from his lips. Molly was glad for that. She liked the green of him, his sweetness.

"It's going to be a late night," Molly said. "This will push us back, and then there's Grand Central. That's gonna be more complicated."

"No sleep 'til Brooklyn," Ashley said.

"No sleep 'til we're back in Brooklyn, yes. But you feel good?"

Ashley gave her the hang-loose sign.

"I feel great," Dom said. The cherry of his cigarette had a lopsided burn going on. The smoke blew into his eyes. Molly knew it must have stung. "I feel awesome."

She spent the next few minutes telling them how wonderful they were. The importance of this could never be underestimated. When an actor spoke of how incredible it was to work with a director, it was because that particular director had told them they were God's great gift to performance. To speak, to say, "Terrific . . . " with the subtle direction wedded in, was also exhausting. It too had the added effect of putting Molly's own career into strange relief. How much of her life was the result of a man or woman blowing smoke up her ass so they could move on to more important things—like where was Tony and his crew? Like why wasn't anyone brooming the water down the sewer drain? Like come on. Like what the fuck?

The film adaptation of Greg Watson's novel, *The Last Century*, had proved a challenge to shoot. Her old college friend had published a weird first book. It had taken him forever to write, and it wasn't even that long. Hardly anyone had read it. The plot followed a young, confused writer (played by Dom) and his sister (Ashley), a performance artist. Most of the book took place in New York, but then it jumped around to LA and San Francisco and even Boston. The first thing she'd done when she'd hired Greg to adapt it was to have him cut all that out.

"But I mean—" he'd said over the phone.

"Cut it," she'd told him. "It's strange enough as it is. I love it. I love the creepy atmospherics, the dialogue, all of it. We don't need the time jump. Let's keep the focus on when they were young. Trust me, New York is enough."

Molly was hungry. She thought to text Diane, but then she remembered Diane was off with Susan, who would—sooner or later—take Diane away for good. For the thousandth time, Molly reminded herself she needed to be calm about it when it happened. She needed to be happy for Diane. She couldn't act like a selfish bitch. She liked Susan. She did.

Molly stood in the middle of the street and looked around for the craft truck. Everyone was either doing their job or pretending to do their job. Instructions had been handed down via Ray. Crew members were deliberately avoiding her in case she might want them to do something.

The truck was down the block, in the direction of McCarren Park. Walking, she felt the water splash around her boots. The sound of a pump started. The draining, sucking sound began to echo off the buildings in Greenpoint, which in the script wasn't actually Greenpoint, but Williamsburg in the early '90s. Times had changed. One thing looked like the other now. Or if it didn't, it would.

A few extras wearing oversized MC Hammer–style parachute pants stood by a table stocked with vegetables and deli meat. They stepped aside for her. Each of the extras offered Molly a kind, closed-mouth smile. She tossed it back at them. *There you are. Here I am.* Over the last several years she'd grown worse at performing this gesture. She didn't trust people. She didn't care if the letters weren't being sent anymore. When it came to fans, strangers, normal people, she had to work at producing kindness and a sense of human feeling.

Up in the craft truck window, an older white woman leaned with her elbow on the counter. She typed into her phone. Her face held the familiar glow.

"Hi," Molly said.

"Hey there, honey," the woman said. A real New Yorker didn't blink at her. They were all actors. "How's the movie comin'?"

"Pretty good. Pretty good." She was tired. What was she supposed to say? Something memorable?

"We're all rooting for you over here," the woman said. "What'll it be?"

What she really wanted was a cheeseburger, but she ordered an egg white omelet with mushrooms and green peppers. Molly stepped back and looked at the apartment building behind the food truck. It was one of the few apartments on the street. In one of the top windows, she saw a shirtless man smoking a cigarette. He waved at her. She waved back. A purple cloud roamed across the moon as one long strip of weather.

"Here, honey," the woman said. She handed over the Styrofoam box. Molly admired her arms. The muscle definition was almost upsetting.

"You know, I wish you'd a come on another night. We gotta kid working with us. He's a big fan, this kid. Works hard. Real nice kid."

"I'll be around," Molly said. "I can't go anywhere."

Molly thanked the woman and walked back toward set. She hooked a quick left down a side street. All of the trailers—the tech, the personal, the Porta-Potties, the otherwise—were parked on the right. She went up the steps of her own trailer. Placed upright against her door was a thick red and black FedEx envelope. She grabbed it and brought it into the trailer with her. Even though Molly wanted to be cool about it, act like no big deal, whatever, she zip-ripped the-whatever-it-was-called and pulled from out of the envelope the script for—she could not believe Abby had kept the title—*Echo Chamber*.

She began to read it immediately.

In June, she had gone to see Greg Watson. She'd been in New York to do a location scout and took a car two hours north to Kingston. She only had the afternoon. Greg's house was nearby, close to the river. It was his mother's father's place—it was something like that. Greg's mother moved about the house in a long, flowing dress the color of a lilac. His wife had on a pair of very chic overalls. His father wore a Hawaiian shirt. "He lost a bet," Greg explained. The five of them ate lunch on the porch overlooking the Hudson and slapped mosquitoes against their arms.

"The kid's napping," Greg said. "If you're into that sort of thing, we can go in and stare at him later."

None of them could believe the movie was actually happening. Greg's mother was a painter. His father was a writer too. They seemed to expect the whole deal was going to fall apart. Disaster felt inevitable.

"Nothing's going to happen," Molly said. "I've put the money up. Everyone will show because they want to get paid."

"But what about the other backers?" Greg's mother asked.

"Hydrogen owes me."

"How many theaters do you think?" Greg's father asked. "What do you think it will gross?"

For some reason, writers always thought they were film business experts. It was both annoying and hurt her pride. They had it pretty much figured out. It wasn't NASA.

"A few hundred theaters, I imagine," Molly said. "The gross? I don't know. I have to make it first. You can never tell anyway."

Greg's wife reached her hand out and touched Molly on the shoulder. She had a cool, calm way. "You'll do great," she said. "I know it."

"I hope so," Molly said. She was terrified.

After lunch, Greg drove Molly back into town. Her car and driver followed them. Kingston felt familiar. It was as though her hometown in Vermont had been zapped with a ray gun, some superhero bullshit that magnified and multiplied zombie buildings and deserted factories. But the downtown was from another time, the eighteenth century. It had been refurbished with weekend-getaway cash. Kingston was close enough to New York that the locals going about their business on a Saturday pretended they didn't care about her. In the hipster coffee shop Greg had chosen, at a table in the back, forty-somethings who'd grown up with her face beamed into their lives peeked over with a look that said, "How do you like that?"

They drank their coffee for all of two seconds.

"Gimme a cigarette," Greg said.

"Secret smoker."

"Until I die."

There was an alley out back. Graffitied on the cement wall opposite them was a neon green sentence that read *September 10th was a hoax*. Molly bummed Greg a cigarette and then she told him he looked exactly as he had in college.

"Please," he said.

"You do."

"Flatter me," he said. "Go ahead. I love it. I'll be forty this weekend. That's why we're up here. A birthday getaway. I'm getting old."

She didn't want to hear about getting old or talk about getting older. Driving down from the house, Molly had felt young—or, if not young, at least happy not to be discussing age, time, or what to do about these things, as if anything could be. Southern California tried to rob you of your deep interiority. LA did. Hollywood. It was impossible not to lose at least some of it, for shallow thoughts and conversations to cast a spell that sealed a layer off. For six months she'd been contemplating an ass lift. Her dermatologist had told her about a new procedure that lasered ten years away. There was no possible way her teeth could be any whiter; if they were any whiter, they wouldn't be teeth. All of this considering took time. All of her focus. All of her ambition. All of her success.

"I'm really into kindness now," Greg said. He exhaled a locomotive plume. "I meet so many assholes. If someone is courteous to me, or just not a dick, I want to buy them lunch."

"Everyone I meet is nice to me," Molly said.

"Sounds great."

"It's not. It's annoying. It's like they think there's something wrong with me. *'Hel-lo. How are you to-day?'*"

"If I could do it all over again, I'd be a movie star," Greg said. "Not being a movie star was the single greatest mistake I ever made in my entire life."

"There's still time."

"I don't think so," he said. "I think that ship has sailed."

The back door to another restaurant slammed open. An over-stuffed black garbage bag sailed out, and landed in a puddle. The door closed again.

"*Molly Bit*," Greg said. It was as if he'd only just then seen her standing there.

"What?"

"Thank you."

"You're welcome," she said.

Back out on the street, beside her rented black car, she told him of course he could visit the set. "But it'll be totally weird for you," she said. "It'll be like when a parent goes to see their kid at college. Nothing will make sense. No one will know your name."

"Enticing," he said.

"Give me a hug good-bye."

It was a nice little town car. The driver was Russian. He had a handgun in the glove box. The PDF paperwork attached to an email said he was licensed and trained to use it. At a stoplight in the middle of downtown, Molly put her phone in her lap and stared through the windshield. She watched the people use the crosswalk—and saw how one of those people, her arm around the waist of a man who in turn had his arm draped across her shoulder, was Abigail Kupchik.

The surprise was like getting slapped in the face. "Oh," Molly said. She watched Abigail tip her head back and laugh. It was physical enough that Molly could almost hear it. She wore a black crewneck T-shirt with someone's giant white face on it. She carried a beat-up jean jacket under her arm. Abigail's hand was in the man's back pocket. Molly watched her and the man continue across the street. When they reached the corner, they waited on the other crosswalk. Sitting there, being that close, Molly almost tapped on her window. If she had done it, one hard knuckle, Abigail would have seen her. The driver would have pulled over. They would have spoken. And Molly would have said—what exactly? I'm sorry about your mother? I've been keeping tabs on you? Your skin looks amazing? Instead, her car drove through the light. Abigail was ten feet away. They were side-by-side for a moment, separated by the glass. Molly watched Abigail laugh again. She was completely unaware and totally sober, Molly saw, as the car pulled away.

For a whole week, the shoot montage'd through a heat wave. Shirtless men, their backs and shoulders covered in hair, schlepped air conditioners down the street. Comparisons to hell, sweaters, and clothes dryers were made. Local news outlets kept a running tally of how many old people had died. The five boroughs smelled of straight-up piss. It was one hundred and eight degrees outside.

"I get strange rashes," Diane said to Molly. The trailer hummed like an icebox. "Out of nowhere, I'll feel dizzy. For two weeks every October my breathing is labored. When I go to the doctor, they always say the same thing. There's nothing wrong with me. I'm healthy as a horse. I'm telling you, it's the weather."

"Of course it's the weather," Molly said. "Hundreds of millions of people are going to die. Groups of men are going to kill other groups of men over water. Angry, starving hordes will flood in from—who knows where? Everybody knows that. It's definitely going to happen. But did you read the script?"

It was the last day, the last scene, the last everything. Molly needed answers to all her questions like yesterday.

"I read it," Diane said.

"And?"

"It's amazing."

"Right?"

"It's incredible."

"I know!"

"I'm not sure what you want me to do with it."

"Produce it," Molly said. "What else?"

The professional boundary between them—always porous—had completely broken down.

"I'm not sure if I want to produce."

"Come on, Diane," Molly said. "What else are you going to do?"

"Stop bossing me."

"I am your boss," Molly said.

Diane tapped her phone. She checked the time.

"For six more hours," she said. "And, anyway, you can't boss me about this. You can't tell me how to spend my money. It's my money."

"Initially," Molly said. "Pony up the lousy thousand dollars or whatever. I'll pay you back. I'll cut you a check right this second. Then, once the ball gets rolling, once I'm done with *The Last Century*, I'll come on board."

"Why not come on board now?" Diane asked. "Why don't you 'pony up'?"

"Because I don't want her to know yet," Molly said. "If she knows it's me, she might . . . I don't know how'll she react. She might refuse. No one else will make this movie."

"Why not?"

"Because nobody has any idea what they're doing. They all say they do, but they don't. All day long it's *blah, blah, blah, I think this, I understand market trends,* but then they go home at night, and they're lying in bed, and it hits them—they're frauds. Everybody is. Me. You. The whole planet. It's really ridiculous."

"As soon as I call her, she'll know it's you who's calling."

"But there'll be psychological distance," Molly said. "She'll be gratified enough to slip into the space that exists between me and you. First, we'll get her up and running. Next, we'll get her in deep— as far as preproduction. Last, we'll close the distance. *'Ooops. Molly Bit's here. I guess I'm making a movie with Molly Bit.'*"

"Why are you doing this?"

"Because I want to be in this movie," Molly said. "And because I owe her."

"But you're not even friends."

"I've given that some thought," Molly said. "What we are, really, are two people who don't see each other, and who never talk. That doesn't mean we aren't friends."

The rain approached. Where had it been when they'd needed it? It was two weeks late. The crew watched the storm bank move in over Manhattan. Movies had ruined them. There were so many apocalypses to choose from that it took a moment for the awe to settle in. When the updraft pulled the heat out of their lungs, when they could breathe again, and feel the cool, wet air on their skin, they knew they were alive. The sky turned dark. They each felt magnetized. The compasses in their minds went berserk.

One minute later, outside Molly's trailer, the rain beat the hell out of everything.

"We can push it back until tomorrow," Ray said.

"No," Molly said. "We can't. Tomorrow is forty-five thousand dollars I don't have. See those guys out there." The two of them looked through her window at eight exhausted crew members. The men stood in the warehouse entranceway, bullshitting. "We go one minute over, and they're on the phone with their union rep."

"Fucking unions," Ray said.

"What are you talking about?" Molly asked. "I'm union. You're union. We're all union."

"But it's just one day," Ray said. "We could call Leonard. We could see if he would pay—"

"No way," Molly said. "I love Leonard, but fuck that guy."

"Then how?"

"Is there lightning?" she asked him. "I don't think so."

"What?"

"Thunder?" Molly asked. "I'm not hearing any."

"Huh?"

"Let's go ahead and do it."

Tony said she was out of her mind. They were underneath her umbrella. The rain was pouring down onto the vinyl above their heads. The air had cleared to the point where she could smell the bread from a nearby factory.

"Move the scene inside," Tony said. "This isn't a sprinkle we're talking about here. It's a monsoon."

"Inside ruins the mood," Molly said. "It's an outdoor scene. We need what little light there is."

"What about the lenses?" Ray asked.

"We've got hoods," Molly said. "We've got backups. We'll figure it out."

"The rain will kill the sound," Ray said. "We can't control it. This isn't the machine."

"I'll fix it all in post," she said. "I'll have the actors yell."

"Yell?"

"*Like this!*" Molly said.

The crew wrapped the camera up in water-tight plastic. They built an open-air tent for it to live under. The sky hailed for a minute. Everyone looked at her, hoping she had changed her mind. Ice on metal *tink*ed. It splattered in the road.

"This is happening!" Molly yelled. She stuck her hand out through her long poncho sleeve and waited until the ice turned back to rain. "There! I did that!"

The squashed, wet faces of the men and women all around her said the exact same thing: what a bitch, what a crazy person. She didn't care what they said. Her whole life had been about getting people to like her, but not anymore. The rain fell harder. It wasn't a problem, she told Ray. It was a master shot. They would use the best take. Never mind the wind, she said. They'd do the sound over again. The poor stand-ins were over there without any cover. They were soaking wet. She spoke to Ashley and Dom underneath the warehouse awning.

"Of course I'm crazy," Molly said to them. "We're all crazy here. You're crazy. I'm crazy. Everybody's crazy. You don't do this if you're not crazy. I love you."

Ray had set up a little tent for her. She could watch the monitor and stay dry, he explained. She said no. If her actors and her crew were out in the rain, then she was out in the rain. She was with them.

They all stopped hating her then. The whole crew came around. They thought she was fantastic all of the sudden. Molly Bit was a story they would tell.

They were there that day, they would one day say. You wouldn't believe the rain. It came down like rainforest weather. The street began to flood from newspapers and plastic bags clogging the sewer drains. The PAs had to clear the drains by hand so the wiring wouldn't short—so no one would be electrocuted. The boom guys knew they were pointless, but they held their mics up anyway. The actors screamed their lines over the sound of the rain. Ashley and Dom would do a take, run under the warehouse awning for a fresh shirt and a hair-dry, and run back out. The wind blew off the river with the power of a hurricane. Styrofoam cups and water bottles and leaves cycloned through the air. The crowd behind the police barricade, and the crew, and later on plenty of others who weren't even there at all (who had heard it from a friend, or who had read about it on the internet, or watched the documentary, or seen her films more times than they could count), would say how Molly Bit, that legend—how could they have known?—had stood there in the wind and rain and shouted "Action!" with her voice that triumphed over everything.

Or so the story goes.

ACKNOWLEDGMENTS

ENDLESS GRATITUDE AND THANKS TO MY EDITOR, MARYSUE Rucci, whose talent, honesty, and belief made all the difference.

Thanks to the entire team at Simon & Schuster, especially Zack Knoll.

A profound thanks to my agent, PJ Mark, for his guidance, terrific insight, and support. Thanks as well to Ian Bonaparte, and everyone at Janklow & Nesbit.

Thanks to: Ethan Hon, Jen Zaborowski, Josh Shaffer, Eli Kooris, Ish Goldstein, Geoff Hilsabeck, Johanna Winant, Chris Ward, JoAnna Novak, Thomas Cook, Michele Christle, Emily Hunt; 39 West Street: Sara Majka, Ben Estes, Mark Leidner, Arda Collins; Peter Gizzi, Ingrid Becker, Ian Morgan, Erdim Yilmaz, Jason England, Jane Gregory, Adam Wilson, Matt Maggio, Matt Parker, Annie DeWitt, Anya Yurchyshyn, Christina Rumpf, Julia Burgdorff, Rachel B. Glaser, my colleagues and students at Western New England University, and my brother Keith Bevacqua.

Thanks to my parents, Mario and Cynthia, in memory.

Most importantly, thanks to my wife, Hannah Brooks-Motl, for her love, brilliance, and crucial suggestions throughout the writing of this book. *Molly Bit* and my life are better because of you.

ABOUT THE AUTHOR

DAN BEVACQUA was born in New Jersey and grew up in Vermont. He earned his MFA from Columbia University's School of the Arts. His short stories have been published in *The Literary Review*, *Electric Literature*, and *The Best American Mystery Stories*. He lives in western Massachusetts. This is his first novel.